Readers love
Shira Anthony

First Comes Marriage

"Yes, It's fabulous and romantic and perfect."

—Joyfully Jay

"The author did a good job of dragging me into the story, keeping me engaged, and of course hoping for the always present HEA."

—Two Chicks Obsessed

Running with the Wind

"This novel has action, adventure, magic, heart and emotion. The characters are complex and believable…"

—Prism Book Alliance

"I loved how Shira practically paints a picture of the scenery with words. The sights and smells and tastes are so real."

—MM Good Book Reviews

A Solitary Man (with Aisling Mancy)

"WOW. I have to pause and breathe because this story was so unbelievably moving."

—The Blogger Girls

"I devoured this book… I loved the characters, and the majority of the story."

—GGR Reviews

By SHIRA ANTHONY

The Dream of a Thousand Nights
First Comes Marriage
With Aisling Mancy: A Solitary Man
Take Two
With Venona Keyes: The Trust

BLOOD
Blood and Rain
Blood and Ghosts

BLUE NOTES
The Melody Thief
Aria
With Venona Keyes: Prelude
Encore
Symphony in Blue
Blue Notes
Dissonance

MERMAN OF EA
Stealing the Wind
Into the Wind
Running With the Wind

With EM Lynley
A DELECTABLE NOVEL
Lighting the Way Home

Published by DREAMSPINNER PRESS
www.dreamspinnerpress.com

TAKE TWO

SHIRA ANTHONY

Published by
DREAMSPINNER PRESS

5032 Capital Circle SW, Suite 2, PMB# 279, Tallahassee, FL 32305-7886 USA
www.dreamspinnerpress.com

This is a work of fiction. Names, characters, places, and incidents either are the product of author imagination or are used fictitiously, and any resemblance to actual persons, living or dead, business establishments, events, or locales is entirely coincidental.

Take Two
© 2016 Shira Anthony.

Cover Art
© 2018 Paul Richmond.
http://www.paulrichmondstudio
Cover content is for illustrative purposes only and any person depicted on the cover is a model.

ISBN: 978-1-63477-384-3
Digital ISBN: 978-1-63477-385-0
Library of Congress Control Number: 2016904991
Published September 2016
v. 1.2

Printed in the United States of America
∞
This paper meets the requirements of
ANSI/NISO Z39.48-1992 (Permanence of Paper).

For Bob, the captain of my heart.

Acknowledgments

Special thanks to Kim Fielding, Tali Spencer, and Venona Keyes for their help with this manuscript.

CHAPTER ONE

WESLEY COOLIDGE gazed out the window as the plane banked to the left and began to descend through the thick clouds. The first half of the flight from LaGuardia had been relatively smooth, but now the plane shuddered and bounced. Wesley gripped the armrests and closed his eyes, forcing himself to breathe through the stab of panic to his gut.

The shot of bourbon had helped his nerves—there were advantages to flying first class—but when Wesley had asked for another, the flight attendant patted him on the arm and retrieved his empty cup. "I'm sorry, Professor Coolidge," he said. "There isn't time for me to get you another. We've already started our descent and we need to ready the cabin for landing."

Across the aisle, the little kid who'd been running the flight attendant ragged shoved a finger up his nose.

"Reese. Stop that," the woman next to the boy—his mother, Wesley guessed—admonished as she pulled his hand away from his face and went back to reading her magazine.

Wesley caught the kid's eye. The kid stuck his finger back up his nostril and smirked.

The plane bounced again as they continued to descend. Wesley glanced out the window and tried to stem the rising tide of his panic. *You're not going to die today.* He *couldn't* die today. His life had finally started to fall into place. He'd just found out a week before that he'd finally made full professor, which, along with prestige, meant a significant bump in his salary over what he'd been earning as a tenured associate professor. He'd also started seeing Carl Stephens four months before. Carl was hot *and* smart, an academic just like Wesley, a postdoc with a bright future in global health. After Wesley's last relationship, Carl was a perfect fit.

Wesley had recently moved into a new apartment on the Upper West Side—his own place he'd paid for with his own money. He'd been short-listed for a huge grant from the Restus Foundation that would fund his research for the next five years and maybe longer, and he had every reason to believe he'd be selected for one of the three awards. He had everything to live for.

Breathe. In and out. In and out. The sense of panic abated a bit. Wesley had never liked flying, although he flew often enough that landings like this one rarely bothered him. Today, the unease that had dogged him for the last few weeks caught up with him, and he felt himself slipping into old habits.

"Bad news," Carl had said when he'd called from Guatemala ten days before. "Robert's going to come down to oversee the project here in Quetzaltenango. He'll be staying in the apartment."

So much for the summer plans Wesley and Carl had made together and the adorable apartment they'd rented when they'd flown to Guatemala only weeks before. Having the primary investigator on a grant oversee a postdoc's research wasn't unheard of. But staying with Carl?

"I thought he and his wife were taking one of those riverboat cruises through France." Wesley hoped he didn't sound like he was whining.

"They cancelled the cruise."

"I'm sure he and his wife will be able to find a place of their own," Wesley pointed out. Of course. That would solve the problem.

"His wife isn't coming. Her mother needed surgery."

"We could book a room at a nearby hotel. Then Robert would have a place to stay and——"

"He insisted we stay together," Carl said, "and I didn't know what to tell him. We'll be reviewing data on the delivery of medical equipment to area hospitals, and Robert expects me to be available at the apartment."

Carl wasn't exactly in a position to argue with the man who paid his salary, let alone the preeminent expert in developing world medical technology. But with this news, Wesley's plans of enjoying his first summer off from teaching in six years had gone up in flames. Summer classes had started the week before, so it had been too late to scramble and add something to the schedule. Instead, he'd resigned himself to spending the summer in the city and working on long-overdue revisions to his textbook.

Until, that is, he received the call from Worldview Studios.

"Professor Coolidge?" Marnie Mason, the studio liaison, said when she finally caught up with him in his office after they'd traded half-a-dozen voice mail messages.

"That's me."

"Good. I'm so glad we finally connected."

Wesley wasn't as glad, but he wouldn't be rude. He'd done some work for the studios before he and Sam had separated, but he'd pretty much avoided it since. "Sorry I've been so difficult to catch up with," he excused blandly. "Summer's a bit slow in my neck of the woods, and I've been out of the office."

"That's perfect," she said with far more enthusiasm than he expected, "because we'd like you to consult on a picture this summer."

"I don't do much consulting these days," he began. "But I might be able to recommend—"

"We lost our historical guy, and you're the only other person who specializes in pirates in the Carolinas. We've heard great things about you. Van Brenner gushed about your work on *Into the Sunset* and *Swashbuckler*."

"I suggest you contact Marv Hatfield," he said, happy to finally get a word in edgewise. These Hollywood people were a pain in the ass to deal with, and he didn't particularly want to be reminded of that part of his past—not so perfect—life. And the man he'd finally gotten over. "He's got plenty of expertise in—"

"But Professor," she said, desperation creeping into her voice, "Professor Hatfield *was* our expert."

"Oh." Marvin had been dying for a gig like this. In fact, for years he'd been after Wesley to put him in touch with the studios. Why had he pulled out of the project?

"We'll pay all your expenses," she said before he could ask the question.

"I really don't think—"

"You'll have your own place on the beach with a housekeeper and whatever else you'll need."

"I don't come cheap for last-minute gigs," he said. Maybe if he priced himself out of the deal, she'd move on.

"Name your price."

"Ten grand," he tossed out, sure she'd reject it.

"Ten grand a week it is," she answered without hesitation.

He'd meant ten grand for the entire gig. But by the time he'd scraped his jaw off the well-worn linoleum floor, she'd offered him a ten-thousand-dollar bonus if he could make it to North Carolina by the weekend, and he'd accepted.

Now, as the bumps smoothed out and the lights of the airport winked below, he wondered if he'd made a mistake in relenting so quickly. Hollywood could fuck itself, for all he cared about movies and the stars who sold their souls to headline in them. Then again, six weeks in North

Carolina and $70,000 to show for it would go a long way toward shoring up his retirement account.

"Ladies and gentlemen," the flight attendant said over the PA, "please make sure your seat belts are fastened and tray tables are in the upright and locked position. We'll be landing shortly. Thank you for choosing American Airlines, and welcome to Wilmington."

With the vague thought it might be premature to welcome them when the plane still hadn't returned to terra firma, Wesley popped the earbuds to his phone in and cranked up the volume on the guided meditation he'd downloaded before leaving New York.

"Close your eyes and imagine you're sitting in a forest...."

CHAPTER TWO

WESLEY DIDN'T need the placard that read Professor Coolidge to spot Marnie at the baggage claim. The white-blonde hair in frizzy pigtails, dark lipstick, leggings, black hoodie, and fuchsia Nike running shoes all screamed "production assistant." Wesley couldn't fathom how someone who spent so much time with actors could have so little fashion sense. Not that Sam, big star that he was, had much more of it, but at least he had people who dressed him in pretty things.

Sam had always loved to tease Wesley about how academics were supposed to be sloppy and unshaven. Wesley just laughed and told him that *some* gay men had to fit the stereotype, or what use would it be? Wesley kept his beard and mustache neatly trimmed, wore his hair perfectly mussed, and took pride in the fact that he still washed and ironed his own shirts. Sam hadn't complained. In fact, he'd appreciated the care Wesley took with his appearance, even though he was more a T-shirt and jeans kind of guy.

"Good to meet you, Professor." Marnie's overly cheerful voice brought Wesley back to the here and now. "Easy flight?"

"It was fine, thanks." He shook her outstretched hand. She gathered up his bags over his vocal protests, and they made their way to the curb, where a stretch limo waited, door open.

"You'll be taking a boat over to Bald Head Island," she said as they pulled away from the airport. "Have you been there before?"

"Never. I spent some time on Ocracoke Island the last time I was in North Carolina. Nice place." He didn't add that his stay had been with Sam. She didn't need to know about that, and he wasn't in the mood to answer any questions.

"We scouted Ocracoke, but we got a better deal on Bald Head," she explained. "Besides, Bald Head is easier to film since there are no cars allowed on the island."

"Really?"

She nodded. "Golf carts and bicycles. No cars or trucks save the emergency vehicles. Do you play golf?"

"No."

"They rent kayaks, paddleboards, and sailboats," she continued, undaunted. "The complex we've rented has a pool. Your house is near the beach."

"Sounds wonderful." He meant it too. Other than a long weekend in the Hamptons, it had been two years since he'd seen the ocean.

"Shooting's already started. We put the battle scenes on hold after Professor Hatfield left."

"About that," Wesley asked casually. "Why did Marvin leave?"

Marnie shrugged. "I was still in LA when it happened. All I know is that it was abrupt, so we had to scramble to find someone else."

The limo stopped about five minutes later at a large waterfront marina. The driver opened the door, and Wesley and Marnie stepped outside.

"I didn't know there were ferries from Wilmington," Wesley said as he glanced around the docks.

"There aren't." Marnie pointed to a large powerboat on the T dock at the far end of the marina. "We figured this would be more comfortable."

Wesley couldn't argue. The seventy-foot-long Hatteras Express cruiser would have been comfortable for a transatlantic crossing with its huge salon, large staterooms, and bevy of watersport toys. Years ago he and Sam had dreamed about buying a boat like this.

Why couldn't he get Sam out of his mind? Maybe it was the Hollywood connection, or maybe it was being near the water. Either way, he needed to stop it. Life with Sam had been a roller coaster of emotion. Ancient history that Wesley didn't care to remember. Things were better now. Solid beneath Wesley's feet.

A slender young man met them at the top of the gangway, his curly blond locks tumbling over and nearly obscuring his bright green eyes. "Welcome aboard the *Neverland*," he said with a warm smile. "I'm Jeffrey Maris." The name sounded vaguely familiar, and Wesley guessed they'd spoken at some point about his travel plans. He was quite sure they'd never been introduced.

"Wesley Coolidge." Wesley offered his hand to Jeffrey, who shook it firmly and met Wesley's gaze.

Jeffrey took the luggage from Marnie. "Follow me, Professor." Despite the swish in his walk, the too-tight Hollister jeans, and the logo tee that screamed "twink," Jeffrey handled all three of Wesley's bags without breaking a sweat.

"We'll put you in the stateroom for the afternoon," Jeffrey said with obvious pride. "Captain's orders."

"Beautiful ship," Wesley said as they walked down the deck and into the enormous salon. Half the room was set up as what Wesley could only describe as a screening area, with a huge flat-screen TV and a half-dozen leather recliners that looked comfortable enough to sleep in. The other half was decorated with a comfortable sofa and love seat arranged around a small fireplace. Wesley had never seen a private boat with a separate dining room, but he caught a glimpse of a large table through one of the doorways. Entirely decadent but, Wesley supposed, not surprising given the Hollywood connection.

"Isn't she?" Jeffrey beamed. "Not like the square riggers the pirates sailed. I bet the salon on this boat is bigger than all the living space on the *Queen Anne's Revenge* put together."

"You'd be right." The old ships were a lot smaller than Hollywood portrayed them.

"I saw an exhibit about the wreck," Jeffrey added as they descended a set of stairs. "You know, the one they found near Beaufort Inlet?"

Wesley nodded. He'd followed the archeologists' work on the ship with interest. "Are you interested in pirate history?"

Jeffrey shrugged. "I do my homework. Not that it's not interesting…."

"Jeffrey wants to be a producer," Marnie put in as Jeffrey set the luggage down outside one of the cabins.

"I said *someday*." Jeffrey put his hands on his hips and glared at her. "Nothing wrong with that, is there?"

"Nothing at all." Marnie smiled knowingly. "By the way," she added in a conspiratorial undertone, "word is that the producer's coming to check out the set this week."

Jeffrey's eyes lit up. "He… he's coming here? Cyrus?"

She caught Wesley's eye and winked. "Gotta run."

"But when is—?" Jeffrey began.

"Later." Marnie waved and left Wesley with Jeffrey. "I've got a few errands to run. I'll see you both on the island."

"Thank you," Wesley said.

"No problem!" She waved again and made her way back up the stairs.

Jeffrey gestured him through the doorway. Wesley had never seen a cabin as large. The king-size bed fit easily inside, and the flat-screen TV seemed bigger than the screens in some of the movie theaters at the multiplex near his apartment. The bathroom, with its tempered glass shower enclosure, sported two sinks, a closet, and drawers. The orchid on the dresser reminded Wesley of his own burgeoning collection.

A delicate *Dendrobium bellatulum,* with white petals and an orange center, it reminded him of one of the first orchids he'd received as a gift from his great-aunt. He'd eventually inherited her collection, and now the second bedroom in his apartment had barely enough room for a desk with all the plants he'd gathered over the years. Sam had always admired his ability to keep the delicate plants alive, and from time to time had added to Wesley's collection. Wesley hoped the house sitter would take good care of all the plants while he was gone.

What would it be like to live aboard a boat like this, orchids and all? Wesley pushed the errant thought away. This was work, for all its luxurious trappings, and the last thing he wanted was to get used to the luxury. He needed to get out of his too hot jeans and into clothing better equipped to handle the humidity outside the air-conditioned room, and focus on the job at hand. He settled on a pair of pressed khaki shorts and a white polo, then slipped into a pair of boat shoes.

He pulled *The Curious History of the Gentleman Pirate* from his carry-on and flipped through it. He'd read it several times, and it had added nothing new to the mystery that was the subject of the film, the pirate Stede Bonnet, but rereading it relaxed him and helped him focus on the job instead of the boat. He'd been considering writing his own history of the Carolina pirates, including the most infamous of all, Blackbeard. Maybe this movie would give him the inspiration he needed to finally get around to it.

As he glanced through the pages of the book, pausing over some of the engravings, his mind wandered to Carl and Guatemala, and he wondered what Carl was up to. He'd canceled the reservation at the B&B on Nantucket where they'd planned to spend a romantic weekend celebrating the four-month anniversary of their first date. Now it looked as though the best he could hope for was a phone call.

Get over it. You'll see him soon enough. Summers always flew by, didn't they?

Giving up on the book, Wesley climbed the stairs to the deck and stopped for a moment to gaze out over the water. He'd done some research on the area where they'd be filming, and judging by the enormous container cranes at the edge of the water, he guessed they were making their way down the Cape Fear River, headed toward the Intracoastal Waterway. On a fast boat like this, they'd make it to the island in a few hours at the most.

In the distance, tall clouds dotted the sky. Rain, perhaps, although this time of year, localized afternoon thunderstorms were the norm. Wesley breathed deeply and caught the faint hint of salt on the breeze. He leaned back against the railing and looked up at the flybridge. He'd always wondered what it would feel like to pilot a boat like this from up top.

"Would you care for a drink, Professor?" Jeffrey said from behind him. "The cook has a lovely Waterbrook Sangiovese rosé. Not too sweet."

"I'd love a glass, thank you."

Jeffrey disappeared inside and returned a few minutes later with a bottle on ice and two wineglasses. "Enjoy," he said as he filled the glass and handed it to Wesley.

"Are you joining me?" Wesley said with a gesture to the remaining glass.

"Me?" Jeffrey appeared surprised. "Oh no. I'm on duty."

"Then who…?" Wesley began, but Jeffrey had disappeared belowdecks once again. Wesley chuckled to himself and sipped his wine. "Delicious," he said aloud. The entire scene was surreal. *Gorgeous boat, beautiful scenery, good wine, and me by my lonesome.* In the grand scheme of life, it certainly wasn't the worst outcome. Still, he wished he wasn't alone.

He pulled his cell phone from his pocket and tapped the preset for Carl. If they couldn't be together, at least Wesley could describe for him the alternate universe he'd just stepped into.

It took a few seconds for the call to connect, and Wesley imagined the signal snaking its way down through Florida, then skimming the waves to the southwest, across the Gulf of Mexico, and over to Guatemala.

"This is Carl Stephens. I'm unavailable to take your call at the moment. Please leave a message and I'll get back to you as soon as I'm able."

Figures. Wesley shook his head and disconnected the call. He'd catch Carl another time. He didn't want Carl to feel guilty about the change in plans. It wasn't as if Wesley was suffering here in North Carolina anyhow. He replaced the phone in his pocket and glanced up at the flybridge again. *Why not?* He'd never been particularly shy, and he figured he'd feel more comfortable hanging out with the crew instead of pretending to be some pampered Hollywood celebrity. He refilled his glass and headed up the stairs.

Wesley took in the sleek flybridge with its state-of-the-art instrumentation, radio, and radar. The white seats and console shone like the rest of the yacht, and the panoramic view from high atop the ship had Wesley gasping for breath. The captain sat facing the console, only the top of his head visible over the high-backed leather chair.

"Impressive."

"We aim to please," the captain responded without turning around. His clipped British accent reminded Wesley of a young Peter O'Toole in *Lawrence of Arabia*. "Are the accommodations to your liking?"

"You mean the presidential suite? I only wish I could spend a month or two sailing the Caribbean in accommodations like that." He sighed.

"I might be able to arrange that." The captain spun his chair around so he faced Wesley. Except he wasn't a captain, and he wasn't British at all—

"*Sam*?"

Sam Carr—no, *Sander Carson*, Wesley reminded himself—grinned back at him. It was too easy to forget that the Sam he'd known no longer existed. "That would be me." The British accent was gone, replaced by a hint of a soft southern drawl. Well, at least *that* was authentic.

"What the hell are you doing here?"

Sam appeared entirely unfazed. "Is that any way to say hello to your husband?"

"Ex-husband," Wesley corrected.

"Not for another forty-six days and seven hours." Sam leaned back in the captain's chair, causing the thin fabric of his T-shirt to stretch tight over the muscles of his chest. He looked better than Wesley remembered. No doubt he had some expensive fitness coach he worked with every day to manage pecs like that. His bright blue eyes were as disarming as they'd always been, and the hint of stubble on his strong jaw only made him more attractive. *Like a movie star.* Which, of course, Sam—or Sander—was.

"You haven't answered my question," Wesley said, trying to ignore the jab to his gut at the reminder that their divorce would soon be final. "Why are you here?"

"I had a few days off from shooting, and I thought I'd take her out for a spin. They delivered her last week, and I haven't had a chance to—"

"Wait a minute. You mean she... this is *your* boat?"

"Yep. Bought and paid for," Sam said with pride. "Care to take the wheel?"

"I… no. Thanks," Wesley lied.

The pieces began to fall into place. Marv leaving suddenly. The shoot in North Carolina. Sam wouldn't have had anything to do with Carl's boss's change in plans, but he'd have known who to call to find out about *Wesley's* plans. And Jeffrey. Shit, Wesley remembered where he'd heard that name before: Sam's new personal assistant.

Total setup.

Wesley made a mental note to read his secretary the riot act when he got back to New York. Which would be very soon, if he had anything to say about it. Viv didn't usually handle the details of his personal life, but she had access to his Outlook calendar. Come to think of it, she'd been asking him a lot of questions about his personal life lately. He'd thought it strange when she'd mentioned Sam had hired a new assistant. Stranger still when she'd mentioned his name and blushed. And she'd always loved Sam.

Everyone loves Sam.

"This isn't going to happen, Sammy," he told Sam. "I'm outta here."

"Contract?" Sam said as Wesley turned to head downstairs.

"Contracts can be broken."

"You never read the fine print, do you?" A gleeful grin lit Sam's handsome face.

"What have you done?" Wesley glared at Sam.

"I didn't do anything. The studio's attorneys, though…."

"You set me up." Stating the obvious. Sam was a hell of a lot smarter than he acted. *And way more devious.* "What do you want from me, Sam?"

Sam tilted his head to one side and rubbed his chin as if he were considering the question. "You haven't figured that out yet?" he asked so sincerely it took Wesley by surprise.

Wesley wouldn't dignify the question with a response.

"I want you, Wesley Warren Coolidge. What else?"

CHAPTER THREE

WESLEY SAT on the huge bed in the stateroom and stared at a spot on the wall. *Talk about a sucker.* He'd been a sucker for Sam before, and he was a sucker now. Get too close, and Sam was like a black hole swallowing up an entire arm of the galaxy. Sam burned so fucking bright, you couldn't help yourself.

It's over.

But Wesley knew it was a lie. You didn't get *over* Sam Carr. No one did. You just put enough distance between you and him so you could fight gravity. And for nearly three years, Wesley had done just that.

Someone knocked on the door. "Professor?" Jeffrey said. "Dinner's served on the back deck."

Wesley wished his stomach wasn't already growling. He didn't like to eat before a flight, and he'd left his apartment at seven in the morning. Now it was nearly six at night. *If he's driving the boat*, Wesley reasoned, *he won't be at dinner*. And even if Sam did appear, Wesley figured he'd need to build up his Sam tolerance if he was going to get through the summer with his heart intact.

"Be right there," he answered. He pulled out his phone and was surprised to find it had a good signal. Carl's voice would be a surefire antidote to Sam overload. Wesley tapped the preset and waited.

"This is Carl Stephens. I'm unavailable to take your call, but—"

Wesley sighed and disconnected the call. Carl was probably busy, since it was earlier there than here with the time difference. Carl would see he'd called and call him back.

Buck up. You know Sam better than anyone else. If you can't manage to resist his charm, who can? He could do this. It wasn't as if they hadn't spoken in nearly three years. He'd prided himself on how civil they'd kept everything between them, even after he'd filed for divorce.

Wesley's phone announced the arrival of a text. *In a meeting*, it read. *Will try to call later.*

At least Carl was all right. Wesley stood and inhaled a slow breath before shoving the phone back in his pocket. His stomach rumbled again as he ran a hand through his windblown hair and headed upstairs.

"MIND IF I join you?" Sam slipped into the chair across from Wesley's without waiting for a response.

Wesley had nearly finished his dinner, and the buzz from the wine made him feel mellower and less inclined to argue with Sam. "Who's driving the boat?" He poured himself another glass of wine.

"The captain I hired."

"Oh." Wesley took a sip of his wine and tried his best to appear disinterested.

"You're welcome to take the helm if you'd like."

"Maybe another time." The offer was tempting. The dream of owning a boat like this had been something they'd shared, but engaging with Sam in that way seemed far too dangerous. Sam knew it too. Probably even knew how Wesley was itching to take him up on the offer, seeing as Sam had now asked him twice.

"Wine good?"

"It's your boat. Of course it's good." The wine was excellent. Wesley didn't even want to think about how much it cost. Sam had never cared much about money, but he didn't have a hard time spending it either.

"He's offering 50 percent of future earnings as a settlement," Wesley's lawyer had told him when Wesley filed for divorce. "That's very generous, given neither of you are alleging fault." Wesley hadn't asked for a settlement. He didn't want a penny of Sam's money. His salary was enough to live comfortably—all he wanted was a clean break from Sam.

"I'm glad." Something flickered in Sam's eyes, but it disappeared before Wesley could get a read on the emotion. Sam was a damn good actor, and he rarely shared a feeling unintentionally.

"We aren't headed directly for the island, are we?"

"I thought you'd enjoy the sunset," Sam answered. "We'll have you settled into your bungalow by your bedtime. Promise."

Wesley raised an eyebrow.

"I know you like to be in bed by ten."

"Maybe I've changed," he blustered.

"Oh?" Sam leaned toward Wesley, elbow on the table, his face far too close for comfort.

Wesley feigned interest in his salad, stabbing at a leaf several times and managing only to grind a crouton into tiny bits. When he finally thought he'd skewered the errant piece of lettuce, he put the fork in his mouth and realized it was a spoon. And it was empty.

Sam watched the entire attempt with obvious amusement, the corners of his mouth edging upward in a warm smile. For the first time, Wesley noticed the tiny lines around Sam's eyes. If anything, they made him even more attractive than Wesley remembered. How old would he be now? Thirty-five. Four years younger than Wesley. How was it that some people got better-looking with age? *Unlike the rest of us mere mortals.* Sam leaned even closer and Wesley caught himself wanting to explore those lines with his fingertips.

Focus, Wesley, focus! Wesley took a deep breath and successfully speared a piece of lettuce. Sam leaned back in his chair and took a long sip of his wine.

"So are you going to come clean?" Wesley asked once Sam had retreated to a safe distance.

"How so?"

Wesley chuckled. "The setup."

"Setup? What setup?"

"Fodder for an Academy Award," Wesley said under his breath, knowing full well Sam could hear him. "Who told you I was available this summer?"

"Do you think I put pressure on someone to—"

"What did you promise Viv? A Sander Carson action figure? An autographed limited-edition movie poster?"

"Would you rather spend the entire summer twiddling your thumbs?"

"I'm perfectly capable of finding something to do."

Judging by the way Sam smiled as he drank his wine, he remained unconvinced.

"What did you do to get Marvin to quit?" Wesley pressed.

"Moi?"

"You."

"Can I help it if the man is overly sensitive?" Sam said with a casual wave of his hand.

Sam had always hated silence, and Wesley knew it. Wesley said nothing and, true to form, after a long minute passed without a response, Sam said, "It's hardly my fault props insisted on using nineteenth-century cutlasses with curved blades."

Wesley laughed outright. "Of course not." A quick web search would have revealed that Stede Bonnet lived in the eighteenth century, not to mention Sam knew the difference between the eighteenth- and nineteenth-century blades only too well—over the years he'd attended more than a few of Wesley's lectures on the topic of pirate weapons.

"Of course." Sam wore his who-me expression like a comfy pair of jeans. No doubt Marvin, one of the most intensely passionate pirate history experts Wesley knew, had refused to continue working on the film unless the problem was fixed and the nineteenth-century swords replaced with straight-blade eighteenth-century replicas. Sam had undoubtedly made sure the problem hadn't been fixed. At least not *yet*.

Wesley sighed. "You'll make sure the prop folks get the message *this* time, won't you?"

"Are you implying I was the one who made sure they didn't the *last* time?"

"If the shoe fits."

"Does that mean you're not hopping the next flight to New York?"

"If props cooperates." Wesley had already decided to stay. Sam probably knew it too, but Wesley wasn't going to give him the opportunity to gloat.

"Wonderful. I'll make sure they fix their mistake." Sam refilled Wesley's glass again. What number glass was that? Three? Four? Wesley couldn't remember. Sam had always handled his alcohol better. The rocking of the boat and the excellent food relaxed Wesley. Time seemed to blur, and Wesley imagined himself seated at Sam's side on the ferry to Ocracoke Island, years before.

"I'm glad you came." Sam's eyes looked faraway, and he sounded wistful. He ran a hand through his tousled hair and leaned on one elbow.

Having given up on the salad, Wesley focused on his plate and the slice of key lime pie he'd been debating finishing. He picked up his fork—he made sure it *was* a fork this time—and sank it into the custard. The fork stopped its easy progress at the graham cracker crust, so Wesley pushed harder, sending a bit of the whipped cream upward, where it landed on his beard.

Perfect.

"I like the beard," Sam said. Before Wesley knew it, he reached out and wiped Wesley's face, paused to catch Wesley's attention, then licked his finger seductively.

A memory flickered through Wesley's alcohol-addled brain: Sam drizzling chocolate sauce over his chest, then proceeding to lick it off. Slowly. Paying close attention to Wesley's nipples. The sound of Sam's moans vibrating through Wesley's chest as he arched upward to grind his hard cock against Sam's.

Someone sighed. Wesley's cheeks grew hot when he realized the sound had come from *him*. Damn. He wished Sam were an asshole. It would make this summer *so* much easier. He pushed thoughts of their past from his mind and got to his feet. "I'm beat." He took a step away from the table. The sky blazed fuchsia, orange, and purple as the sun dipped below the horizon. Judging by the waves and the long expanse of water, they were now sailing on the open ocean.

"Good night, Sam." Wesley walked over to the stairs just as the boat cut through a particularly high wave. He stumbled and would have fallen but for two strong arms that encircled his waist. When he turned, his face was inches from Sam's.

This close, with the alcohol and the sound of the wind and the waves, Wesley fought the siren call of Sam's full lips. Sam leaned in, and Wesley found himself closing his eyes in anticipation.

I can't do this. He pushed Sam away.

"Wesley, I—"

"It's over, Sam," Wesley said, mustering as much strength as he could find. "It was over three years ago. You've moved on and so have I." He thought of Carl. "I've found someone new." *I'm not going to fuck that up by getting stuck in the past.*

"I never wanted the divorce." Pain glittered in Sam's eyes.

Wesley drew a long breath. "You never wanted to stay married," he said, then turned and headed down the stairs to the cabin.

"I'M PERFECTLY capable of getting undressed," he told Sam as he wobbled out of the bathroom of his island house some time later. He vaguely recalled getting off Sam's boat and stumbling into a small car that hummed and was open to the elements. A golf cart? He guessed he'd passed out yet again. Or fallen asleep.

Sam eyed him with skepticism. "You still don't do drunk very well."

To which Wesley responded by walking over to the bed and managing—quite well, thank you very much—to catch his arm on the edge of the nightstand as he attempted to pull off his shirt. He didn't like the way the lamp on the nightstand looked anyhow.

It took him a full minute to remove his shirt, but he *did* do the job. Mostly. He couldn't quite get his left arm back far enough. Sure, things would have gone smoother if he unbuttoned it, but what were a few popped buttons in the grand scheme of life?

When he tried to unbuckle the belt on his shorts, he discovered his fingers were stuck between his belt and the sleeve of his shirt. Every time he tried to loosen the belt, he managed only to tighten it. He struggled for several minutes before Sam walked over to him.

"Let me help you."

"I can do it," he snapped, stepping backward as he spoke and falling onto the bed. The fast movement made the queasiness in his stomach rear up like a snake. "Oh shit." He closed his eyes and sucked in air, willing the room to stop spinning.

He struggled back to his feet with Sam's help and ended up with his face inches from Sam's. Sam smelled good, like the ocean at sunset— crisp and clean, with a hint of citrus.

Wesley needed to get away from Sam. He was too drunk, and Sam looked too sexy with his windblown hair and fitted shirt. He pushed Sam away and teetered dangerously.

Chapter Four

SAM CAUGHT Wesley as he stumbled. His plan had worked perfectly and still failed miserably. *I wasn't supposed to let him get* too *drunk.* Wesley had never held his alcohol well, but Sam had hoped that if Wesley relaxed a bit, he might be more open to the idea of them getting back together.

I'm drinking my own Kool-Aid. It would take a lot more than a good Hollywood setup for Wesley to change his mind about their marriage. And whose fault was that?

Wesley had been right when he'd called him out on his bullshit. But Sam had counted on Wesley's forgiveness, not divorce papers.

"Wesley?"

"Go 'way." Wesley shoved Sam and staggered toward the bathroom. He tripped on the edge of the carpet. Sam caught him before he fell.

"You okay?" Sam asked.

"Sammy? You're here?" Wesley looked up at him in surprise. "I missed you. Why didn't you come home?"

Sam swallowed hard and his gut clenched. "I'm here now, Wesley. I'm not leaving you again. Promise."

He'd fucked up big-time. When he'd left for Hollywood, he'd been so focused on his career, he hadn't considered what it might do to their marriage. Wesley had always been there for him—it was part of why he'd fallen so hard for Wesley in the first place. Wesley had encouraged him even when the pickings had been slim. Sam smiled when he remembered Wesley reading scripts with him and how they'd joke that Wesley would make a better romantic lead than any woman.

Smart, funny, clever Wesley, who'd never complained when Sam had begun to get recognized. He'd never complained when they couldn't hold hands in public because being gay would have been the death of Sam's career. Wesley had never asked him to come out. And Sam never did, even after things had begun to change for gay actors.

And I still fucked it up. Wesley had reached out to him, and what had he done? He'd been too busy to call. Too busy to e-mail. Because he knew Wesley would always be there for him. Even though he wasn't there for Wesley.

Wesley smiled and blinked up at him. He reached for Sam's cheek and Sam froze. Their lips were inches apart. All Sam needed to do was lean in and—

And I won't take advantage of him like that. No. He'd do this the right way. He'd treat Wesley well. Give him everything he wanted. Romance him until he couldn't say no.

Starting tomorrow. Tonight he needed to behave himself and make sure Wesley got some sleep.

"Wesley, you need to get into bed." He gently removed Wesley's hand from his face. "Let me get you some pajamas."

Wesley responded with a combination grunt and sigh, then proceeded to fall face-first onto the bed.

"Wesley?" Sam gently rolled Wesley onto his back. He was out cold.

Sam sighed, then got to work on Wesley's clothing. He didn't bother looking for pajamas. Wesley had often slept naked, something Sam had struggled to get used to. It was too fucking distracting. He needed to get out of there before he did something stupid.

As he worked open Wesley's belt buckle, Sam let his eyes wander over the smooth skin of Wesley's chest. In spite of his fastidious attention to his appearance, Wesley had never shaved the hair that dusted the skin around his pink nipples. He'd kept in shape since he'd filed the divorce papers. The neatly trimmed beard and mustache were new, but Sam liked them. Wesley had always had a bit of a baby face, and this new look suited him.

Full professor. He knew how much that meant to Wesley, who'd worked so hard to earn the title. Sam had been calling Viv, Wesley's assistant, at least once a month since he'd been served with the divorce papers. Her updates were the only contact he had with Wesley now.

"He isn't talking much about it," Viv told him when he'd called in early March, "but you can see how happy he is. Since last summer...." She hesitated, and Sam knew she was thinking about the divorce. "He's been working extra hard, you know."

"I can imagine." Wesley had always worked so hard. And after he'd gotten tenure, Wesley had just worked harder.

"He's taking the summer off, though."

"Seriously?" Sam's heart beat faster. If he was taking the summer off, was it possible Wesley was thinking about taking him up on his offer to come to LA and talk things through face-to-face?

Viv laughed. "He and Carl are going to spend the summer in Guatemala. It took a little prodding, but Carl's right. Professor Coolidge needs a break from teaching once in a while."

Sam's chest grew uncomfortably tight. "Carl?" Wesley had a boyfriend? *Of course he can. We're legally separated.*

"Oh, oh, no, I mean," Viv stammered, her voice taking on a note of panicked regret, "I'm so sorry, Mr. Carson, I mean, Mr. Carr, I didn't mean to—"

"Just Sam is fine. And it's okay, Viv. I told you I wanted to know how he's doing." That didn't stop it from hurting like hell, though.

"Oh. Okay." She sounded rattled.

"Please, go on."

"They met during spring break," she explained. "I guess things are pretty serious between them. But they…."

"They what?" he prompted.

"They seem real happy, you know."

"That's great, Viv." It wasn't. It was horrible. Terrible. The worst news. Just what Sam had hoped he'd never hear. Because deep down inside, he hoped—no, he *believed*—Wesley would change his mind. That Wesley would miss him and maybe, just maybe, he'd consider forgiving him. But if Wesley had a boyfriend, Wesley had moved on.

Now, as Sam pulled off Wesley's shorts and boxers, he tried not to linger on Wesley's lean body. He took a deep breath and quickly drew the covers over Wesley. He wanted Wesley, but he wouldn't step over the line. Wesley didn't belong to him anymore.

Chapter Five

WESLEY AWOKE in a strange bed to the mother of all hangovers. His head beat like out-of-tune tympani, his joints ached, and the light streaming in through the blinds hurt his eyes. At least the bed wasn't rocking. *Not a boat.* This wasn't the cabin aboard Sam's outrageous yacht. This was—

The buzz of his cell sounded like fingernails on a blackboard. He meant to shut the ringer off but fumbled and instead ended up answering.

"Wesley?" Sam sounded far too chipper.

"Yeah?"

"Just checking on you."

"Check on me later." Wesley disconnected the call, tossed the phone onto the duvet, and closed his eyes again. How had he ended up here? The last thing he remembered was having dinner with Sam on the boat.

Remember. You need to remember.

He'd definitely drunk too much. He remembered Sam laughing. Or had Wesley been laughing at Sam? He remembered Sam telling someone, "I'll hold on to him if you'll drive the cart."

Cart? *Golf cart.* The only vehicles allowed on Bald Head Island were golf carts and bicycles. He vaguely remembered stumbling up a flight of stairs holding on to something so he wouldn't fall. Holding on to *someone. Sam.* And then....

Shit. Wesley realized for the first time that he was naked beneath the sheets. His face warmed when he realized Sam must have undressed him. Not like Sam hadn't seen it all before, right?

"Wonderful. Just wonderful," Wesley said to himself. His mouth felt like he'd been chewing on sandpaper, and his stomach rumbled like a storm.

The smell of coffee wafted through the open windows. God, what he would do for some caffeine and a few Excedrin. Maybe his neighbor would share. Or maybe the studio had stocked the pantry. Either way, he needed to get his ass out of bed or his head was going to explode.

He wobbled to the bathroom and found it quite large, with a Jacuzzi tub and glass stall. He noticed someone had unpacked his toiletries. Sam, no doubt. He sat down to pee and nearly fell back asleep. When he finally made his way to the sink to splash some cold water on his face, he caught a glimpse of himself in the mirror and cringed.

Reminder to self: don't drink when Sam is around. He repeated this thought several times as he trimmed his beard and mustache. Sam was dangerous enough without the booze.

Wesley made it downstairs a half an hour later, slightly less rickety after having showered and shaved. The smell of coffee grew stronger the closer he got to what he guessed was the kitchen. He walked through the living room into the kitchen and—

"Morning, sunshine!"

Wesley grabbed a countertop to steady himself as his heart slammed against his ribs and his head began to pound again. "Shit. Sam. You scared the crap out of me."

"Sorry." Sam appeared only slightly remorseful.

"What are you doing here?"

"Making you coffee?" Sam offered Wesley a large mug, which Wesley took. The coffee smelled incredible, dark with a hint of chicory. Splash of milk, hint of sugar.

Of course he knows what kind of coffee you like—he made it for you every day for years.

"Thank you." Wesley took a long sip. A few more cups and he'd feel human again.

"One step closer to your happy place?" Sam turned back to the stove.

Wesley ignored the question and drank some more. Sam had always been a morning person. He'd been a night person too, when Wesley really thought about it. Sam was always up. Always happy. *Irritatingly so.* Then again, if those were pancakes Sam was cooking, Wesley was inclined to forgive him his cheerfulness.

Sure enough, Sam handed him a plate full of Sam's special sourdough flapjacks. A small bouquet of wildflowers at the center of the table created a burst of color in the otherwise white kitchen. Sam had probably picked them himself. The flowering stalks of rosemary interspersed with the blooms smelled really good.

Fuck. It was hard to complain when Sam was doting on him. "Sam, I really don't need—"

"I'm just making sure you eat," Sam said, pointing to the table.

Sam had always worried too much about him, like he was some delicate flower in need of protection. The reality was that Wesley had always been as healthy as a horse, and at six feet tall and 190 pounds, he was hardly a shrinking violet. Maybe compared to Sam's six-foot-three-inch frame and 230 pounds of muscle, he wasn't Superman, but....

"Sammy," Wesley warned.

"I know, I know, I'm leaving," Sam said with a dismissive wave of his hand. "I've got an early makeup call anyhow. I just wanted to make sure you had something to eat." He set the remaining flapjacks on the table.

Wesley repressed a sigh. "Thank you." Whatever he and Sam were to each other—or weren't—Sam was a good man.

"Someone will be by around ten to take you to the set." Sam was out the door a second later. "See ya!"

Wesley rubbed the bridge of his nose and released a slow breath. If he was going to make it through the summer, he needed to relax. Sam was old news.

Wesley reached for one of the pancakes and nibbled his way around the crispy edge. *Fuck. The man can cook.* He sighed as he savored the soft interior, allowing the slightly sweet fluffiness to flood his mouth. *Heaven.* Okay, so Sam was old news, but Wesley could still enjoy the pancakes, couldn't he?

CHAPTER SIX

WESLEY FINISHED another pancake and pulled his phone from his pocket. It read 8:50 a.m. That would give him a little time to get his shit together. He smiled and tapped the preset for Carl. He'd always been an early riser, so Wesley guessed he'd be up.

"Wesley?" Carl yawned.

"I hope I didn't wake you," Wesley said.

"Me? Oh, no. Robert gets up before dawn, so I'm working on coffee number two."

"I'm glad." Wesley wasn't going to mention Sam and the pancakes. "I'm on number three."

"You didn't sleep well last night, did you?" Carl asked. "You never do sleep well the first few nights in a new place."

"I sleep better when I have company."

"Get some extra sleep tonight, okay?" Carl said. "You don't need to get sick your first week on the set."

Wesley heard another man's voice—Robert's, undoubtedly—and there was momentary silence on the other end.

"Listen, Wesley," Carl said, "I'm really sorry. Robert and I have an early meeting and I need to get going. Talk to you later."

"Sure. Take care. I lo—"

The call disconnected.

Wesley sighed and set the phone on the table. He ate another pancake before popping his dishes in the dishwasher and putting some plastic wrap over the leftovers.

The kitchen smelled like coffee, but he thought he caught a faint whiff of Sam's aftershave by the stove. Probably just his imagination.

Had he really come that close to kissing Sam the night before? Wesley walked onto the screened porch, where he lay on the comfortable couch he found there. He took a few deep breaths and focused on the soft whirring of the ceiling fan overhead. Leave it to Sam to reduce him to a quivering lump of flesh in spite of his resolve.

He wasn't really angry with Sam. Sam hadn't made any bones about wanting to get him back. Wesley was angry he'd allowed himself to slip back into old habits. Sam was just too damn charming. It was too easy to forget the heartbreak.

They'd met more than ten years before at the opening night party for the school's production of *H.M.S. Pinafore*. Wesley's best friend, Venka Thomason, a professor in the drama department, had guilted him into playing in the pit orchestra when they had too few student volunteers.

Playing was one thing, though. Attending a cast party was completely different. Wesley hated parties. He'd never been comfortable with crowds. He had no difficulty lecturing to a roomful of students, but navigating a social obstacle course without sounding like a blithering idiot wasn't his strong suit.

"Nobody'll think you're rude if you leave," someone said from behind him as Wesley checked his watch.

Wesley, who'd been standing by the doorway to the apartment, turned to face an attractive guy with dirty-blond hair and electric blue eyes. He was perched on the arm of the couch, his bare feet resting on the cushions. Not just any guy, but Sam Carr, the grad student who'd played Ralph Rackstraw, the romantic lead.

"I don't know what you're talking about," Wesley choked out. His cheeks heated at the words.

"First chair, second violins," Sam said triumphantly.

"I… ah… yes."

"Sam Carr," the newcomer said, his gaze never straying from Wesley as he offered his hand. As if Wesley didn't know who he was—since he'd agreed to play in the pit orchestra, he'd watched Sam with more than a little interest. Talented, gorgeous, and entirely out of Wesley's league.

"Wesley Coolidge." Wesley shook Sam's hand, which felt surprisingly soft and warm.

"Nice meeting you, Wesley," Sam said with a hint of what Wesley thought sounded like a southern drawl.

"I need to go." But Wesley didn't let go of Sam's hand, and Sam made no move to dislodge it.

"Oh." Sam finally released Wesley's hand. "Something I said?"

"I… no… it's just that—"

"Good. Wait here." Sam got up and disappeared into the next room without waiting for an answer.

Wesley stared at the place where Sam had been sitting. What was wrong with the man? Wesley had just said he needed to leave, hadn't he? Wesley glanced at his watch again: 11:45 p.m. He'd give himself until midnight, and then he'd leave.

"You *were* hoping to escape."

"Excuse me?" Wesley hadn't even registered Sam's return, which irritated him even more.

"The watch thing. I was right. You were trying to make your escape." Sam looked pleased with himself. He held out a bottle and two champagne flutes. "But I'm glad you didn't."

It took Wesley a moment to register that Sam was offering him a celebratory glass. He'd always been slow at reading social cues, and Sam was operating at warp twelve. "I... ah... I really need to go."

The disappointment on Sam's face took him by surprise. "Do I smell bad?" Sam lifted an arm. One of his biceps strained against the fabric of his flannel shirt.

"Oh.... No. I didn't mean it like that!" Wesley caught a faint whiff of something spicy as Sam lowered his arm. He smelled good, in fact. Really good.

Sam laughed. "Didn't think you did." He poured a glass and held it out for Wesley, who nearly spilled it as their fingers touched.

"I... ah... thanks." He hated that he couldn't get two words out of his mouth without stammering. He half wished he'd made it out the front door before Sam came back. Then again, Sam was good-looking and... *interested*?

Not possible. It didn't surprise him that Sam might bat for his team, but Wesley wasn't exactly the stuff of hotter-than-hell actors' dreams.

"You a student?"

"Assistant Professor."

"Professor," Sam repeated. "Music department?"

Wesley laughed. "Not really."

Sam leaned forward. "Oh, let me guess.... Economics?"

"No, I'm a—"

"Mathematics?"

"No."

Sam frowned. "Hmm."

"I'm a—"

"Don't say it! I'll get it right."

"All right." Wesley finished his second glass of champagne and the current of nerves he'd been swimming against all night finally eased. He was actually starting to enjoy Sam's offbeat manner.

"Physics."

"Definitely not. Calculus was never my strong suit." Seriously, did he look like *that* much of a nerd? But Sam was cute, so Wesley might be able to forgive him.

"I got it!" Sam shouted loudly enough to cause a few guests to turn from conversations. Sam appeared unfazed. "English department. Creative writing."

"Wrong." Wesley smiled in spite of himself.

"Dang." Sam shook his head.

Venka walked over to the couch and winked at him. Wesley should have been mortified. *Maybe it's true what they say about champagne going straight to your head.*

"Sammy," Venka said, "he's a—"

"No! Don't tell me. I'll figure it out."

Venka laughed and several other people came over to see what was happening. They were all enthralled by Sam, watching him as though he held the key to something wonderful. Which Wesley was beginning to think he did.

"I know, I know! Biology."

"Nope." Wesley took the bottle from Sam and refilled both their glasses.

"Botany?"

"Not."

"French."

"Mais non." Wesley set his glass on the coffee table, where it wobbled and nearly fell over. The room had begun to spin a little, but it felt pretty good.

"German?"

"Überhaupt nicht."

Sam laughed and grabbed Wesley's hand. He pulled him to his feet and shouted, "Dance!"

"Definitely not." Wesley laughed as Sam spun him around and the crowd moved out of the way. Wesley caught someone's foot and grabbed on to Sam, who steadied him so he didn't fall.

"You're a mystery man," Sam said, his cheek pressed against Wesley's. "Give me a hint?"

Wesley repressed a shiver as Sam's breath tickled his neck. "Pirates."

"Pirates? Hmmm. Oceanography?"

"No."

"Broceanography?"

"Huh?"

"Surfer dude," Sam shot back.

Wesley laughed again. He'd entirely forgotten about wanting to leave. "Uh, definitely not. I've never even tried surfing." It sounded pretty cool, though.

"Shipbuilding?"

"Come on, Sam. It's as plain as the nose on my face."

Sam pulled back a bit and studied Wesley's nose. Wesley pushed Sam playfully and received a brilliant smile in return.

"I give up." Sam spun him around again.

"History," he whispered in Sam's ear.

Sam laughed, then leaned in and kissed Wesley. The kind of kiss that made Wesley's toes curl and other parts of his body stand up and salute.

Oh crap. Wesley pulled away, only to realize that everyone had been too busy to see the very public kiss. Even so, Wesley knew he should be mortified. But he wasn't. Later, he'd wonder if it was the alcohol or if something about Sam just made him feel as though he was floating a few inches above the floor.

"Professor Coolidge?" The voice brought Wesley back to the present. Jeffrey stood a few feet away.

"Morning." Wesley got to his feet. "Here to take me to the set?" He opened the screen door and ushered Jeffrey inside. Today Jeffrey wore a black shirt with a skull and crossbones on the front. His long, lean legs, visible now that he wore shorts, called to mind a colt ready to gallop. Adorable, but totally not Wesley's type. He didn't want to be reminded of who *was* his type.

"No rush, but the director wants to meet you, and props are asking for help with some of the weapons."

"Let me guess, they've just realized the blades shouldn't be curved."

From Jeffrey's coy smile, Wesley was sure everyone knew what Sam had done. *Leave it to Sam to get away with it.* Sam could charm the pants off a rack at Bloomingdale's.

"Sure. Give me a minute to grab my laptop and I'll be ready. Help yourself to a pancake, if you'd like," he added, pointing to the kitchen table.

Back in his room, Wesley grabbed the case with his laptop and notes he'd made about Stede Bonnet. He caught his reflection in the large mirror near the doorway to his bedroom and paused. The face that peered back at him looked a bit tired but presentable. So why did he feel so completely out of kilter?

You know why. For nearly a year now, he'd successfully avoided Sam. It hadn't been all that difficult, since they lived on opposite sides of the country. For the first few months after Wesley filed for divorce, Sam had called constantly and begged Wesley to reconsider. Sam had finally gotten the message—or so Wesley thought. Now Wesley wondered if Sam hadn't just been waiting for the opportune moment to pounce.

Get me a little off-balance and then worm his way back in.

Wesley sighed as he ran expert fingers through his hair until he was pleased with the result. He wasn't the same uncomfortable and awkward man he'd been when he and Sam had first met. He would act like the successful adult he was. Filing for divorce had been his choice, not Sam's, but it was the right thing for both of them. Wesley had taken charge of his life, and things were finally turning around.

He took a deep breath, then headed downstairs just as Jeffrey finished nibbling on one of Sam's pancakes.

"Damn, these are good. Did you make them?" Jeffrey asked.

"Sam—Sander—made them."

"Omigod, the man can cook too?" Jeffrey held a hand over his heart, waggled his eyebrows, and pretended to swoon.

"I thought you worked for him."

"I do. But I just started a few months ago, and so far he hasn't cooked for me. Nothing wrong with a little hero worship, is there?"

Wesley laughed. He'd gotten used to the Sander swoon, as he liked to call it. When he and Sam had been together, they'd laughed about it.

"I can tell them to get lost, if you'd like," Sam had said the first time he'd been mobbed by fans. They'd taken the downtown A Train for an afternoon at the Brooklyn museum. It was a beautiful spring day not too long after Sam had gotten his first real break.

"I don't mind," Wesley said. He really hadn't. He'd always known Sam would be a success, and he knew the job was about more than just acting. It hadn't been the fans who had fucked up his marriage to Sam. He and Sam had done that to themselves.

"So where's Marnie?" Wesley asked, eager to think of something other than Sam.

"Sam asked me to see to you personally."

"Sam?"

"Sander." Jeffrey grinned broadly. "But I call him Sam."

Wesley stiffened, surprised that hearing Jeffrey use Sam's real name made him jealous. Why should he care if someone else called him Sam? Maybe all of his colleagues did.

"Oh, of course." Wesley offered Jeffrey what he hoped was a pleasant smile before sitting next to him in the cart.

"Most people don't know his real name's Sam," Jeffrey continued without missing a beat. "He's a real nice guy. I'm sure he wouldn't mind that I told you."

So Jeffrey didn't know he and Sam were married. That certainly made things easier. "He is," Wesley agreed. *Too nice, even.* "And my lips are sealed."

"Ready to go? Marnie's working on getting you your own golf cart, but I'll be playing chauffeur until then," Jeffrey said as he turned the key in the ignition.

Wesley said a silent prayer to whatever gods might be listening. "Ready as I'll ever be."

CHAPTER SEVEN

WESLEY GOT his first look at the island on their drive to the beach location. The carefully planted yards gave way to the rugged beauty of the ocean environment as they turned onto a stretch of road more sparsely inhabited. Here, craggy dunes and native plants emerged from the sandy soil in clumps, often leaning in one direction because they'd been buffeted by the constant breezes from the water. Wesley caught the fragrance on the rosemary bushes that flowered along the road. This was a beautiful place, very different from the other islands he'd visited in the area. No wonder pirates like Stede Bonnet and Blackbeard had frequented nearby shores.

"Most of the cast and crew are staying in the same development as you," Jeffrey said as they made their way along the beach road. "Parker, the director, has a house in town, near the ferry landing." The cart slowed as they climbed a small hill, and he pointed to an enormous house with a wraparound deck on the second level. "Sam—I mean Mr. Carson—and I are staying here."

"You're living with him?" Wesley asked with surprise. Not that Sam couldn't date, of course, but the thought that Sam might have found someone else made Wesley uneasy.

Jeffrey giggled. "Separate rooms," he said. "Not that I'd be disappointed if he showed up in mine, you know."

"No, I guess not." Wesley didn't find Jeffrey's answer reassuring. Jeffrey might not look it, but he was smart and clearly on his way up. *Just the kind of man someone like Sam could fall for.*

"Don't get me wrong," Jeffrey continued. "Sam's always been totally professional. I mean, I like him and all. And he's an amazing boss. He found out I was interested in becoming a producer, so he's been taking me to a lot of the high-level meetings. You know, the ones with the director?"

"That's great."

"Yeah, I'm lucky. Not that I wouldn't be lucky to… well, you know… I mean Sam is totally gorgeous, but…." Jeffrey hesitated, then added quickly, "Besides, there's kind of someone I've got my eye on."

"Oh. That's nice."

"I'm not sure he likes me, though, but I kinda think he does." Jeffrey paused, then grinned and began to speak so quickly Wesley could barely follow him. "I mean, he's kind of out of reach, but then again, what does out of reach really mean in a world where there's six degrees of separation? On the scale of an individual, you know, the separation might not even be that much with cell phones and the Internet and—" Jeffrey stopped abruptly and looked at Wesley, red-faced.

Wesley smiled. "Philosophy major?"

"Minor. But how did you…? I mean, is it that obvious?" Jeffrey seemed to realize the conversation had veered far off course, because he added quickly, "Shit. I sound like I'm in high school, don't I?"

"Not at all." Okay, so Jeffrey did sound like a high schooler with a serious crush, but it was kind of cute.

"I guess you could call it admiration mixed with a little like." Jeffrey shrugged. "You know, sort of like when Marguerite first meets Faust and they—" Another abrupt stop. Jeffrey's cheeks were now fuchsia. He nibbled his lower lip, then glanced away and added, "Comparative literature major."

"Nothing wrong with that."

"The set's located at Beach Access #12," Jeffrey continued, although Wesley was sure his pink cheeks had little to do with the ocean breezes. "The ship arrived last week."

"Ship?"

"Parker located an old replica of a pirate ship in Australia about a year ago. Seems she needed a little work on her engines. Between raising money from the backers to have her repaired and sailing her halfway around the world, it took a little time for her to get here."

Wesley smiled. "At least she *has* engines. Back in the day, a passage like that would have been nearly impossible."

"Are you really a pirate expert?" Jeffrey asked.

"I guess you could call me that. I specialize in American history. But I've always been fascinated by pirates."

"Sam said you've consulted on other films."

"A few." The last time had been nearly six years ago. Back then, things between him and Sam had been good. They'd spent a wonderful summer in the Caribbean. It had been one of the happiest times of Wesley's life. "Recently I've been too busy teaching to do much consulting."

Jeffrey rounded the corner after another hill and pulled the cart onto the side of the road, where a half-dozen carts were already parked.

"The beach access is right there." He pointed to a sign about fifty feet away. "You might want to take your shoes off."

Wesley slipped off his loafers and followed Jeffrey to a boardwalk. They climbed up stairs and over a large dune, then began to descend toward the beach. Wesley saw the ship immediately, a three-masted beauty moored in a small cove near where a dozen or so trailers were parked on the sand. A historically accurate reproduction of the *Queen Anne's Revenge*. The *Queen Anne's Revenge* wasn't Stede Bonnet's ship—that was her predecessor, the *Revenge*—but she was similar enough that Wesley nearly sighed with relief as he approached the vessel. One less thing to worry about.

"What do you think of our old girl?" said a woman's voice from behind Wesley.

"She's a beauty." Wesley turned to face a tall woman with long salt-and-pepper hair pulled into a high ponytail. Dressed in a pair of jeans rolled at the ankles and a shirt tied at the waist, she looked to be in her midforties. Quietly confident and friendly.

"Parker Vance," she said as she extended her hand.

"You're the director."

She chuckled as they shook hands. "Most people assume I'm a man." She shrugged and added, "I don't mind. I prefer to keep a low profile."

"Wesley!"

Wesley looked up to see someone waving at him from atop the mizzenmast. Sam grabbed one of the ropes and jumped into the air, swung like an aerialist, and landed gracefully on the deck.

"He's going to give me a fucking heart attack," Parker said with a hand against her chest.

Wesley was thinking the same. He knew Sam loved to do his own stunts, but Wesley had always refused to watch him film them. Sam had never seen the irony in his mother-hen approach to Wesley.

"So what do you think of the ship?" Sam asked as he trotted over.

"She's perfect." Wesley smiled at Parker. "Well worth the wait."

"You heard about her trip from Australia?" Parker asked. "It set us back six months in filming, but it was the best thing that could have happened. The actor who'd been signed to play Stede Bonnet had to pull out because of a scheduling conflict." She smiled at Sam. "We couldn't believe our luck when Sander's agent contacted us."

"Very lucky," Wesley agreed, knowing full well luck probably had nothing to do with it. Sam winked at him, confirming Wesley's suspicions.

"I'd like to run through the next scene," Parker said as she glanced down at her clipboard.

Sam turned to Jeffrey. "Give him the VIP tour, okay? I'll try to catch up with you both later."

Jeffrey smiled broadly. "This way, Professor."

"Please call me Wesley."

Jeffrey looked to Sam, who nodded his approval. "Okay, Wesley. This way."

WESLEY FINISHED his tour of the set about an hour later. How could he not admire the extent of Sam's subterfuge? The number of obvious historical errors was stunning. Poor Marv Hatfield hadn't stood a chance. Marv had probably left the project with a hefty check—Sam was nothing if not a gentleman—but Wesley guessed Marv's ego had taken a bruising.

"Wrong flag," Wesley told Jeffrey, who had been taking notes as Wesley discussed what he'd seen with Bob Fleming from props. "The flag attributed to Stede's ship had a skull, crossbones, a heart, and a dagger. That one's from the *Queen Anne's Revenge*. Blackbeard."

The wink and nod this statement garnered made it clear the prop master knew perfectly well the details were completely wrong. How many people were in on the ruse? *Leave it to Sam to charm the pants off them all.*

"And the name of his ship was the *Revenge*," Wesley added for good measure. "Not the same as Teach's."

"Didn't I tell you he'd be perfect for the job?" a familiar voice said from behind him.

"You were right," Bob agreed.

Wesley took a deep breath and smiled at Sam. "Good to see you, Sander."

"And you, Professor." Sam bowed formally and removed his tricorne hat to reveal the rest of a long, curly wig.

"I'd better get back to work," Bob said with a snort. "You gentlemen enjoy the rest of your afternoon."

"No doubt we shall meet again." Sam waved as Bob disappeared into the shop.

Sam's British accent was spot-on. Not what one might associate with a man who'd lived in England in the eighteenth century, but the perfect combination of clipped British speech with a touch of Barbados, the island where Stede Bonnet had been born. No doubt Sam also knew the stories that Bonnet's foray into pirating came about because of an unhappy marriage or a psychological disorder. Sam had always been a stickler about research.

Wesley raised an eyebrow and gestured to the flag. "Your handiwork?"

"They'll replace it, of course." Sam grinned. "They'll use CG to fix it in the scenes we've already filmed."

"And the weapons?" Wesley asked.

"Fortunately we haven't filmed any fight scenes yet."

Before Wesley could respond, one of the assistants handed Wesley a tablet with photographs of costumes, and he began to page through them. Not good. Instead of the long justaucorps jackets worn during Stede Bonnet's lifetime, the pirates were all dressed like something out of an Errol Flynn movie, with pantaloons and shirts that laced closed. This would take more than CG to fix.

"Lunch?" Sam asked after Wesley had finished reviewing the pictures.

"I'm going to need to speak to the costume designer about replacing most of these," he told the assistant.

"Of course, Professor," the assistant replied. "I'll make sure Amy Gilcrest, the costume supervisor, knows. She went to Wilmington to pick up a few things. She should be back late this afternoon."

"Perfect," Sam said as the woman left them alone. "You can have lunch now and meet with Amy later."

"I ate breakfast three hours ago."

"Drinks?"

"Sam, it's noon and I'm working."

"Okay, so no lunch and no drinks. Walk with me?" Sam persisted. "We can check out one of the other locations." When Wesley didn't immediately answer, he continued, "For historical accuracy, you know?"

"I don't think I—"

"Okay if I borrow Wesley?" Sam asked Parker, who was looking through a script.

"I need him back after lunch to meet with the set designer," she said. "And I want to introduce him to Cyrus. He's coming in on the four-thirty ferry."

"I'll have him back in plenty of time. Promise." Sam led a reticent Wesley away from the set.

"Cyrus?" The name sounded familiar.

"Cyrus Eastman's the producer. He produced my first film."

"Oh." Wesley followed Sam to his trailer, where a man who introduced himself as Chaz helped Sam out of his wig.

"Wouldn't it make more sense to stay in costume if you're shooting this afternoon?" Wesley asked, hoping to avoid spending any more time with Sam.

"Nah." Sam smiled and thanked Chaz. "We won't be getting to my scene until sundown."

Chaz left the trailer, and Sam began to take his costume off.

"Shouldn't someone be helping you with that?" Wesley asked, keenly uncomfortable with Sam undressing in front of him.

"Probably." Sam grinned and hung his jacket on a hook by the door.

"I'm going to get something to drink," Wesley said as Sam began to pull his shirt over his head.

Sam's throaty chuckle seemed to follow Wesley all the way to the kitchen, where he found a bottle of water in the fridge and sipped nervously on it. Sam Carr was the most attractive man Wesley had ever known. The last thing he needed was to fight his own body's reaction on top of all his other feelings.

"Ready?" Sam asked as he joined Wesley in the small kitchen a few minutes later.

"Sure. Lead the way."

"My pleasure."

They walked out into the blinding sunshine. In spite of the sun, the breeze off the ocean made it feel quite comfortable.

"You're entirely obvious, you know," Wesley said as they made their way past the cluster of trailers and a set that looked like the outside of a run-down tavern.

Sam shrugged. "You'd see through me anyhow." He led them between two houses and onto the road. "Besides, I'm not hiding anything."

Wesley ignored this. "Where are we going?"

"You'll see."

Wesley shook his head. "You always enjoyed surprises more than I did."

"Maybe that's because I didn't surprise you enough." Sam's eyes sparkled with mischief. His expression reminded Wesley of the kid on the airplane with his finger up his nose.

"So how have you been, Sammy?" Wesley asked as they ambled along the road. From time to time, golf carts whizzed by them, headed toward the harbor.

Sam shrugged. "No complaints. I'm keeping busy."

"Sander!" someone shouted. One of the golf carts slowed, and a woman waved and blew Sam a kiss.

"Hey, Rachel!" Sam reached out, and she brushed her fingertips against his.

"You joining us for drinks tonight?" Rachel asked.

"Thanks, but probably not. I've got an early call in the morning."

"You sure?" she pressed.

"Sure."

She pouted, then waved as she drove off.

"Sorry about that," Sam said.

"There's nothing to apologize about. It's part of your job."

"Wesley, I—"

"Water under the bridge." Wesley tried to push back the memory of watching the interview with Sam nearly three years before. He'd nearly missed it. He wished he had. The interview had been the last nail in the coffin of their marriage—a reminder that even though he loved Sam, the gap between them was too wide to bridge.

"Professor Coolidge," Viv had shouted through the phone. "Sam—I mean Sander—is on *Night Out Hollywood* right now. Channel eleven."

Wesley had known about the interview and he'd told Sam to let him know when they'd be airing it, but Sam had forgotten yet again. Wesley knew Sam was busy, and he tried to brush this off as he'd brushed off a half-dozen other things Sam had promised to do but forgotten. At least he'd brushed them off when he'd spoken with Sam. Underneath it all, though, he'd begun to wonder if Sam regretted their long-distance relationship or, worse, their marriage.

"We've been seeing you all around town with your costar, Melanie Foster," the host was saying as Wesley turned on the TV.

The camera panned to Sam, who smiled affably and said, "She's a lovely woman."

"Sander," the host pressed, "you know you've been seeing each other for some time now. Rumors are that it's pretty serious between you."

"I'm not one to kiss and tell, Tammy," Sam said with a roguish grin.

Wesley knew the studio had arranged the "dates" for Sam and his costar. Sam had warned him they might, and he'd reassured Wesley they were nothing. Wesley hadn't been worried. He knew Sam, knew that although he loved women, he'd never been sexually attracted to them.

"So there's no one who owns Sander Carson's heart?" she pressed.

Sam looked directly into the camera and said, "No. No one."

Wesley stared at the screen. How long had it been since he'd spent more than a fleeting weekend with Sam? They hadn't even celebrated their anniversary together the past two years. He'd gotten so used to Sam's absence, he'd found himself telling one of the new hires at the university that he lived alone. And he did, for all intents and purposes.

The ache in his chest intensified. He picked up his cell and tapped the preset.

"*Hey. This is Sammy. Sorry I can't take your call. Promise I'll call you back when I can.*"

"Hey, Sam. It's me. Nothing important. I just wanted to hear your voice." Wesley disconnected the call and set the phone down. He walked over to the window and gazed out at the gray sky. It had been raining all week.

He tried to stem the tears that pricked at the corners of his eyes. He'd gotten good at rationalizing them away. But this time they fell unimpeded, running over his cheeks like the drops of rain on the window. *Time to let him go.*

"Wesley?"

"Oh. Sorry." He'd let his mind wander. He needed to let their marriage go. He thought he had, but seeing Sam again was harder than he'd expected. *Then again, you didn't expect that you'd have to spend time with him again.*

"You okay?" Sam furrowed his brow.

"I'm fine. Thanks."

"Listen, Wesley, I—"

"Don't sweat it, Sammy. I know you meant well." He could be friends with Sam, even if they weren't together. Whatever had happened between them, Sam was a good man.

They walked in silence for a few more minutes, turning off the road onto a dirt path through dense vegetation. "Just a bit farther," Sam said.

Wesley flicked away yet another mosquito. He'd need to buy some spray in town or he'd be one big bug bite. Sam, as usual, appeared entirely unaffected.

"You're just sweeter than I am," Sam had told him as he'd handed him a bottle of calamine lotion on the second day of their honeymoon in the

Dominican Republic. He'd then proceeded to kiss every one of Wesley's bites. The calamine had been forgotten, but the sex was great.

Stop it! This was exactly what Sam was counting on. Wesley couldn't be weak. The divorce was the best thing for both of them. Now if he could only convince Sam.

"Whatcha think?" Sam pointed to a tiny cottage in the middle of a clearing. "We got special permission from the island to build it."

"Nicely done." The building was impeccably rendered to look as though it had been built in the early 1700s, with a sloping roof and rough timber siding.

"Wait until you see the inside." Sam beamed as he opened the door. The interior was a perfect reproduction of the kind of home Wesley expected to see for the time period in which Stede Bonnet had lived. Wooden beams crisscrossed the ceiling over a rustic four-poster.

Wesley ran his hand over the mattress and grinned when he realized it was made of straw. "You did your homework."

"I've been known to," Sam replied.

"When you want to."

Sam shrugged.

"It's perfect."

"I'm glad you think so. We'll start filming some of the scenes here next week." Sam walked over to the bed and lay down on it.

"Sammy, I...."

"I know." Sam sighed. "Can't blame me for trying, can you?"

"I'm flattered." He was.

"But?"

Wesley pressed his lips together and tried to gather his thoughts. "But I'm not going to lie to you. I've moved on."

"So you say."

Wesley sighed and shook his head. "Sammy. Let it go."

"Leave me with my little fantasy, then. And there's nothing wrong with my enjoying your company, is there?"

"No. I guess not." He could never hate Sam, no matter what had happened between them.

Sam hopped off the bed and grinned. "Good. But since I promised to have you back after lunch, we should probably get going."

"Sure." Maybe this would be their opportunity to work out what being just friends might feel like.

CHAPTER EIGHT

"SO GOOD to meet you, Wesley," Cyrus Eastman said as he shook Wesley's hand. A well-built man with spiky silver hair, electric blue eyes, a gold stud in his left ear, and perfectly bronzed skin, Cyrus looked like a cross between Jack LaLanne and Paul Schaffer. Buff Hollywood meets nebbishy New York, edges smooth as silk.

"The pleasure's all mine." Wesley found himself drawn to Cyrus's quirky charm.

Cyrus put an arm around him and began to walk him down the beach toward the trailers. "Are they treating you all right?" he asked.

"Better than. Thank you."

"Good, good." Cyrus waved at someone walking by. "Sander said you were the best man for the job." He stopped walking and faced Wesley, his expression suddenly serious. "I rescued this little picture because Sander agreed to star in it. To be honest, it's a total piece of shit. No idea why he thought it was worth salvaging."

Wesley wasn't about to share the answer to that particular question. "I appreciate the vote of confidence," he said blandly.

"…be right back," someone said as they stepped between the rows of trailers and collided with Cyrus. Wesley realized the someone was a very flustered-looking Jeffrey, who stared up at Cyrus and straightened Cyrus's sunglasses, which were slightly askew. "Omigod. Mr. Eastman! I'm so sorry, I—"

"It's all right…. You're Sander's assistant. Jeffrey, isn't it?"

Jeffrey's lips parted, but no words issued from his mouth. Finally, he nodded.

Cyrus smiled and patted Jeffrey on the head. "Relax, Jeffrey. I don't bite. Promise."

Jeffrey swallowed hard and seemed to collect himself. "Sander's inside. He said you might be coming by. I was just going to soda some grub. I mean grub some suds. I mean grab some grubs."

"You mean grab some sodas?" Cyrus prompted.

Jeffrey nodded, then shoved his hands in his pockets and waited, seemingly unsure of what to do next.

"Sounds great. We'll see you in a few minutes, then," Cyrus said.

"Sure." Jeffrey's smile lit his entire face. He was gone a moment later in a flurry of movement and sand.

"Adorable." Cyrus watched Jeffrey trot off down the beach.

Wesley was pretty sure he'd just met the object of Jeffrey's crush. Wesley chuckled to himself and wondered how long it would take the two of them to realize the attraction was mutual.

BY THE time Jeffrey dropped Wesley off at his house, it was nearly nine o'clock. The only grocery store on the island had closed long before, so Wesley figured he'd take a shower and head to one of the restaurants he'd seen near the ferry landing.

Wesley paused for a moment on the front porch to watch the last hints of fuchsia and purple on the horizon. Whatever the insanity he'd stepped into, Bald Head Island was a beautiful place to spend the summer. He'd watch them film the next morning, then maybe see if he could rent a bike in town and explore.

He unlocked the front door and kicked off his shoes. He wriggled his toes to get rid of some of the sand that had stuck to them, then laughed and shook his head. What did he care about a little sand in the front hallway? This was an island. Sand was *good*. Far better than New York City in the heat of the summer.

The thought reminded him he needed to call Carl. *Later. It's an hour earlier there—he's probably eating dinner.*

He emptied his pockets and set his keys and his phone on the side table, then padded into the kitchen barefoot, pausing on the soft shag rug by the fridge. For the first time, he noticed the kitchen smelled good. Really good. In the dim light from the hallway, he realized there was something on the breakfast table. He walked over to the entryway and flicked on the light.

The table had been set for one. A bottle of wine chilled in a small bucket on the counter. Several pans waited on the stove, next to which there was a note. He recognized the handwriting immediately.

Hope you don't mind. I guessed you didn't have time to shop. Meat's warming in the oven. Just heat the sauce. The risotto should still be warm. Dessert's in the fridge.—S

Mind? How could he mind? Wesley opened the oven and glanced inside. Two beautiful lamb chops waited there, perfectly seared. His favorite. And Sam's risotto....

Sam had always had dinner waiting for him when they'd first moved in together. Back then Wesley had spent long days teaching and evenings working on a book about the lives of seamen in the southeastern United States. The book had ultimately been Wesley's ticket to a promotion to associate professor when he'd landed a sweetheart of a grant to study several sites in South Carolina.

"You don't have to do this, you know," he'd said as he set his briefcase on the floor outside the tiny kitchen. "I really don't mind cooking dinner."

Sam had swept him into a bear hug that had ended in the sweetest kiss. "I like doing things for you," he'd said against Wesley's ear in that deep voice that made Wesley's knees wobble. "And after dinner, I'd like to do a few *more* things for you."

Wesley smiled at the memory as he sat down to his dinner. Even reheated, the food was perfect as always. Damn, he wished he could hate Sam. That would be so much easier. He could almost see Sam seated across from him at the breakfast table, chin in his hands, watching him intently as he said, "Marry me, Wesley."

Wesley remembered the look on Sam's face when he proposed— focused like an Olympic ski jumper poised at the top of the highest jump, at once terrified and thrilled to be taking his life into his hands.

"Marry you?"

"Why not? It's been six months since you said you'd think about it. We've been living together for a year now, and you haven't strangled me yet." Sam was *so* fucking good at the lost little boy look. Any look, really. He was a far better actor than the "I'm just okay" he claimed to be. And he was anything *but* lost. If Wesley knew Sam, he'd been thinking about this for months now, and he'd developed a plan of attack weeks before.

"That sounds like a perfect reason for until death do us part."

"Think about it, Wesley," Sam persisted. "Waking up to me every day. And I could make breakfast for you every morning."

"You do that already." Wesley knew how the conversation would end, but he wasn't going to let Sam claim victory too soon.

Sam frowned. "You really like to torture me, don't you?"

Wesley leaned across the table and stole a kiss, lingering only long enough to make Sam crazy. "Be honest," he teased, "you love it when I play hard to get."

"I could just tie you up and force you to marry me."

"You could tie me up anyhow." Wesley waggled his eyebrows.

"Deal."

"Figuratively speaking, of course."

Sam smirked. "I know what you're doing, you know."

"Oh? And what would that be?" Wesley asked.

"Trying to get me to forget what I asked you."

"Me? Never."

"I wasn't kidding, Wesley," Sam said, his expression once again serious. "I want to marry you."

Wesley smiled, then drew a long breath. "Okay."

Before he could even comprehend what he'd just agreed to, Sam grabbed him in a bear hug and whooped so loudly Wesley was sure their downstairs neighbor would be pounding on the front door in short order.

"God, Wesley," Sam said after he'd kissed Wesley until his lips were numb. "I love you so much. You don't even know."

Wesley realized he was smiling at the memory. Far better than the usual struggle against his tears. Maybe being here with Sam would be good for them both.

That thought led to another: he'd forgotten to turn the ringer on his phone back on. Maybe Carl had called him back. Talking to Carl would help Wesley focus on something other than the past.

He pulled the cell from his pocket and unlocked it. Nothing from Carl. No messages. No texts either. Wesley brushed away the thought that maybe Carl didn't want to talk to him. The man was busy. And with his boss watching him work, of course Carl didn't have time to drop everything and return Wesley's call. But what if something had happened to Carl? Maybe he was hurt and that was why he couldn't call. Or maybe—

Stop it. Robert's with him. If something was wrong, Robert would know to call.

Wesley hesitated a moment longer, then decided to shoot an e-mail to Viv. She was friends with Daria, Robert's assistant. If there was something wrong, Viv would find out for him.

Wesley tapped the icon for his e-mail and found more than two hundred, a third of which were junk and another third of which were about changes to the university's employment policies and accounting practices, or reminders from the department chair about something he'd been volunteered to do at the last faculty meeting and he'd forgotten about. The usual. His mother had sent him a silly video of a cat that danced and hiccupped, and a second e-mail that included a grumpy cat meme with the word "history" in the quote.

Wesley rubbed his face and refilled his glass. The wine was really good. He finished reading through the list of e-mail, then wrote a quick message to Viv asking her to check on Carl for him. Finally relaxed for the first time that evening, he got up and set his dishes in the sink. He'd deal with them in the morning. He peered into the fridge and found a ramekin with what he guessed was a crème brûlée. It smelled faintly of coconut. Another of his favorites.

He knew he shouldn't be surprised about any of it. Sam had been nothing but honest about his motives. Wesley had forgotten just *how* persuasive the man could be.

He let the sweet custard dance on his tongue and sighed out loud, then chuckled at himself for being such a pushover. He could get through this, torture that it was. He laughed again, but this time felt suddenly sad. If only Sam didn't always remind him of the good times. It would be hard to keep things in perspective, and too easy to fall back into Sam's arms.

CHAPTER NINE

WESLEY WOKE the next morning and headed out for a run at sunrise. Between Sam's food and the two glasses of wine he'd allowed himself, it took him nearly a mile before he felt human. He made his way down the road that paralleled the beach and toward the center of the island, where the trees grew in a tangle of greenery that reminded him of the tropical rainforest he and Sam had visited on their trip to Puerto Rico ten years before. From time to time, the scents of jasmine and rosemary tickled his nostrils. Several golf carts whizzed by him, occupants waving as they passed. Wesley thought he saw Jeffrey in one.

Such a gorgeous day. He could almost wrap his brain around surviving a summer alongside Sam in such a beautiful place. Once Sam got the message that Wesley wasn't interested, that is. That particular detail might take a bit more effort.

Wesley turned onto the small road that wound its way by the ancient lighthouse and slowed to get a good look. Jeffrey had said it looked like a cross between a Lego and a half-peeled potato, and the analogy was pretty much spot-on. Its mottled brown-and-tan surface of sand and lime covered the brick structure beneath, and the stout turret shape was pretty much what Wesley expected from a lighthouse built in the late 1700s. The modern navigation beacons on the Cape Fear River had long since rendered it obsolete, but "Old Baldy," as the locals affectionately called it, was a charming relic.

"Cyrus suggested we film here, but I told him the lighthouse was built long after Stede Bonnet was executed."

Wesley shook his head and turned to see Sam standing about ten feet behind him. Dressed in running gear, his wavy hair falling in damp curls onto his forehead, he'd clearly been out on a run himself. "But you neglected to mention to Cyrus that the weapons they were using are anachronistic."

"Figured I'd leave that to the expert," Sam replied with a smirk.

"You're so obvious."

"I have nothing to hide."

"How did you know where to find me?" Wesley asked.

"Process of elimination."

"Jeffrey told you."

"Could be."

Wesley chuckled and trotted off down the road, pausing momentarily to shout back at Sam, "You coming? Or are you going to slow me down?"

"I've gotten faster," Sam said as he caught up with Wesley.

"Oh?"

"Want me to show you, cheetah boy?"

They'd loved to race through Central Park when they'd lived together in New York. Wesley had always won. Sam had called him his sexy little cheetah.

Fine. Nothing wrong with a little challenge. "Bring it on, muscle man," Wesley teased.

The grin on Sam's face told Wesley he liked that Wesley had noticed how he'd bulked up. Sam wasn't particularly vain, but he worked hard to sculpt his body, and he appreciated it when other people complimented him on it. "You're on."

"Ferry landing. In three, two, one!" Wesley sprinted down the main road that led to the marina with Sam at his heels.

Several golf carts that passed them pulled onto the shoulder to watch them run, their occupants no doubt having recognized Sam. This attention only inspired Wesley to give it his all. With the ferry landing in sight, he turned to Sam, who'd been running shoulder to shoulder with him. "Not bad, Sander," he said with a wink.

Sam laughed, and several bystanders whistled and whooped as they rounded the parking lot for the harbor. With about a hundred feet to go, Wesley waved at Sam, then let go with everything he had. He reached the dock several seconds before Sam, and they both collapsed onto the ground, alternately gasping and laughing. Someone shouted, "That's Sander Carson!" and a crowd soon gathered around them.

"Damn… Wesley," Sam said between gasps. "Can't… believe… you… beat… me."

"I've… gotten… faster too." Wesley sat up and pulled a leg to his chest to stretch his protesting thigh muscles. He didn't mention that after he'd filed for divorce, he'd bumped up his daily run in the park from five to ten miles. The running had kept him sane and focused.

"Breakfast on me?" Sam asked as Wesley offered him a hand up.

"Sure."

Sam's hand felt warm and familiar. Their gazes met briefly, transporting Wesley back to their life in New York. Sam's work on the set of the soap began very early, but they ran together every morning in Central Park, even when the sun hadn't yet risen. Cold mornings when Wesley could see his breath. Summer mornings before the millions of air-conditioning units heated the air between the skyscrapers like a convection oven. Beautiful spring mornings when the smell of cut grass from the Great Lawn mingled with cherry blooms. Sam's scent after a shower, when the droplets of water glistened on his skin, and his smile and sweet kiss before he headed to work, kept Wesley going, even when his work overwhelmed him.

They'd spent summer weekends at Jones Beach until Sam had become too familiar a face. Then they'd rented a house on Fire Island and escaped the crowds and the city.

"Sometimes I wish we could just stay like this," Sam had said as they'd lain in the sand on a bright August day. They hadn't dared hold hands in public, but Sam's bare foot pressed against Wesley's was enough of a touch to keep Wesley going. Later, they'd eat dinner side by side on the deck overlooking the ocean, Sam having cooked another amazing meal.

The memory made Wesley's chest ache.

"I'll take the pancakes," Sam told the server, his words bringing Wesley's focus back to the present. To their left, a woman held up her phone and snapped a photo of Sam, who smiled without missing a beat.

"I'll have the Old Baldy breakfast," Wesley said.

"Grits?" the woman asked.

"Sure." Wesley saw Sam was grinning. "What's so funny?"

"Just that the Northerner is eating grits."

"I'm sure they're not as good as yours," Wesley replied as he poured some milk into his coffee. He took a sip, then added, "And the coffee is *definitely* not as good."

"Then you'll just have to stop by my place tomorrow morning for coffee."

Wesley smiled, but he knew he wouldn't. He didn't want to lead Sam on. He hoped he hadn't done something to give him the wrong impression. "Listen, Sammy, I—"

"So how's it going? With props?"

"Good. But I know you're changing the subject."

Sam shrugged. "Can you blame me?"

Wesley chuckled. "I guess not. You've got chutzpah."

"I'm glad you decided to stay."

When the waitress deposited their breakfasts on the table, she said, "Mr. Carson, would you mind if I take a photo with you?" She handed Wesley the phone without asking if he'd mind taking the picture.

"Talk like a pirate! Say 'argh,'" Wesley said.

"Argh!" they both said. The waitress laughed, and Wesley snapped the pic. "Thank you so much." She blushed as Wesley handed her the phone, then trotted off to show one of the other servers the photo.

One of the busboys nibbled on his lower lip while another unabashedly ogled Sam. The hostess, who must have just realized who Sam was, giggled and whispered something to the waitress, who nodded.

The woman at the table next to theirs pulled her phone out of her purse and pretended to talk on it while she snapped a photo of Sam. Sam saw this too, because he turned and smiled at her, causing her to nearly fall out of her chair and fumble the phone. Sam waited patiently until she picked the phone up and aimed it at him again. He smiled as though she was the only person in the room.

The man seated with the woman looked irritated, but his angry look turned into one of surprise after the woman whispered something in his ear. He walked fearlessly over to Sam and took a selfie without saying a word. Sam smiled again and appeared entirely unoffended as he autographed a receipt the man dug out of his pocket.

"Sorry about that." Sam appeared genuinely contrite.

"No need to apologize." Wesley sipped his coffee.

"No, really. I know how hard it must be—"

"Hey. Sammy. It's me? Remember?" Wesley pressed his lips together and shook his head. "This stuff? I never had a problem with it." He'd accepted the hero worship as part of Sam's work. The distance, though....

"I want to make it up to you." Sam looked so damn earnest.

"Let's just work on the friends part, okay?" Wesley knew that wasn't what Sam wanted to hear. He also knew he should be running away from Sam really fast.

"I want more," Sam said. Before Wesley could object, Sam added, "But I'm really glad you decided to stay. I've missed you."

I've missed you too, Sammy. I've missed you too.

CHAPTER TEN

STEDE BONNET walked down the narrow cobblestone street and glanced at his reflection in one of the store windows. He deftly straightened his collar and removed his hat to smooth his hair. He smiled and pressed his lips together, his pride obvious. He twirled his hat and replaced it on his head, taking care to ensure it was straight, then glanced around and rested his hand lightly on the hilt of his weapon.

He entered the lively tavern holding his head high, knowing he was the center of attention, confident and a bit cocky. He took his time, making sure everyone got a good look at him, the hint of a smile playing on his handsome features as some of the men whispered to each other.

One of the whores he'd seen before, a pretty thing with long black hair and lips the color of blood, sidled over to him and nearly tripped on her long skirt. She muttered something that sounded a lot like "shit" under her breath, but Bonnet was undeterred. The barkeep filled a tankard of ale, but when he went to set it down in front of Bonnet, he placed it directly on Bonnet's hand, and half of it spilled onto the bar. Bonnet nodded to the bartender before taking a long drink.

"Another drink," Bonnet said as he wiped his hand on his shirt. "For the beautiful woman."

"I'd rather drink from your lips," the woman said, her wide smile revealing a set of perfect and brilliantly white teeth.

"No doubt your lips taste like honey. But I am a married man."

"Master Bonnet"—the wench pouted as she hiked up her skirts and flashed the frilly garter on her upper thigh—"you are too much of a gentleman."

"Sweetheart, I'm not too much a gentleman that I can't appreciate a beautiful woman's charms." Stede ran his hand over the woman's thigh and snapped the garter belt.

"And… cut!"

Wesley rubbed the bridge of his nose, then covered his mouth with his hand to suffocate a laugh. After breakfast with Sam, he'd spent the morning going through the weaponry with one of the props staff. He had finally made it to the set about an hour before and had been watching them film for the past thirty minutes. It was all he could do not to roll his eyes. He'd never seen—or heard—anything as horrible. Cyrus was right. The script was a piece of shit. Worse than shit. Was there such a thing as a D movie?

"Mr. Carson?" The actress still hadn't covered up her leg as she planted a huge kiss on Sam's cheek. "You were magnificent."

Wesley caught Sam's eye and did his best to keep a straight face. Sam managed a lopsided grin before signing the script the woman shoved into his hands.

Time to go. Wesley went to find someone from wardrobe. The wench's costume would have been perfect... *if* they had been filming a scene at the Moulin Rouge in Paris. He wouldn't even touch the rest of the disaster he'd just witnessed.

"Excuse me," he said to one of the assistants. "I'm looking for—"

"Wesley!"

Wesley took a long breath. "Sa—Sander."

Sam wrapped an arm around his shoulder and led him into a trailer a few yards down the beach. Wardrobe would wait. Wesley doubted the actress would mind having to do another take of the scene, as enthralled as she'd been with Sam.

A blast of icy air hit Wesley as they walked inside, and Sam closed the door. The hairs on the back of Wesley's neck stood at attention and he shivered.

Sam set his tricorne hat on the table. "Well," he said with eager anticipation, "what did you think?"

"I... ah... words can't express... ah... you were very... er... serious."

Sam erupted into laughter. "Biggest pile of shit ever, isn't it?"

"You were pulling my leg."

"Don't I always?" Sam grinned and scratched his head underneath the long wig.

"What the hell are you up to, Sammy?" Wesley demanded. "I thought you could pick and choose your gigs these days. This is like amateur hour. *The Gong Show. American Idol Rejects.*"

Sam studied his reflection in a mirror on the door to the bedroom, lifted the curls that covered his ear, and said thoughtfully, "I'm thinking I might have my ear pierced. What do you think?"

Wesley ignored the question and glared at Sam.

Sam shrugged. "Parker's a friend."

"Even *that* doesn't explain it." Wesley knew the real reason Sam had taken the gig, and he knew Sam knew he knew it too. He was flattered Sam had gone to such lengths to try to change his mind about the divorce, but he worried what effect they might have on Sam's career.

"Parker thinks it's shit too."

"Which *really* explains things." Wesley rubbed the bridge of his nose in frustration. "I've seen some of her movies. She's an A-list director."

"Parker took the gig to help a friend out."

Wesley supposed that made a modicum of sense. Especially if Sam was the friend in question. "It's still crap, though. It could hurt your career if you're—"

"I'm working on something to clean things up a bit." Sam appeared entirely unconcerned.

Wesley frowned. He'd seen that look before. "What kind of something? This clusterfuck needs CPR. Or maybe a complete brain transplant."

"You'll know when you hear about it."

Wesley's gut clenched. If Sam was insane enough to take a job just to try to repair their marriage, what other crazy idea did he have up his sleeve? No matter what had happened to them, Wesley knew how much Sam's career meant to him. "Sammy, something this bad will ruin—"

"Parker says Cyrus is staying for a few weeks to watch us film."

It wasn't worth pressing Sam on this. Whatever he had planned, Wesley would hear about it eventually. Sam wasn't so insane that he'd tank his career to get their marriage back on track. At least Wesley didn't *think* Sam was that off his rocker. "I've got a meeting with Amy about the costumes in ten," he said, knowing he'd get nowhere until Sam wanted to come clean.

"Lunch?"

"You just bought me breakfast. If you're trying to fatten me up so you can beat me the next time, you're barking up the wrong tree."

"You have to eat," Sam pointed out.

"I'm probably just going to grab a sandwich. The caterer's food looks pretty good." He didn't need to spend any more time with Sam than absolutely necessary.

"Sure. Dinner tonight, then?"

"Sam, I—"

"I promise I'll be a perfect gentleman." Sam grabbed his hat from the table and bowed low.

"Master Bonnet," Wesley said, imitating the wench in the scene they'd just filmed, "you are too much of a gentleman."

Sam snorted, surprising Wesley into his own laugh, which quickly turned into a cough when he breathed wrong.

Sam tapped Wesley on his back. "It really is shit," he agreed after Wesley stopped coughing.

Wesley pulled quickly away to avoid prolonging the physical contact.

"So you'll join me for dinner?" Sam asked again.

Sam wouldn't drop it until he caved. "Sure." Breakfast after their run had been nice, and Sam had been well-behaved. Much as Wesley didn't want to admit it, he was enjoying Sam's company.

Sam's face lit with pleasure. "My place, then. Eight?"

"I'm not sure that's a good place—"

"Jeffrey can chaperone."

Wesley laughed outright. "Okay, okay. You win."

"I always do," Sam said with a crooked grin.

A minute later, with his feet in the sand and the hot sun beating down on his shoulders, Wesley sighed and headed for the wardrobe trailer. Needing a little boost before he had to face Sam again, he pulled his phone from his pocket and tapped Carl's number.

"Hello?"

"Carl? Oh, thank goodness! I've been trying to catch up with you for more than a week."

"Wesley… ah, yeah," Carl said. "Sorry. Rob and I spent the week at a clinic in Calhuitz. Up in the mountains. Not much cell reception."

"It's okay. I understand. How are things going with the research?"

"Great. Rob thinks we'll be getting some more funding for the project from Washington."

"Terrific news."

"How about you? Heard anything more about the big grant?" Carl asked.

"Nothing." Wesley had done his best to ignore the anxious buzz of anticipation. "The Restus Foundation said they'd be letting folks know very soon. I guess they had more submissions than expected this year."

"You'll get the grant. I'm sure of it. And when you're rich and famous, I'll tell everyone I knew you when."

Wesley laughed. "Hardly rich. But a little recognition would be nice." It felt good to know Carl believed in him, though.

"You'll get it," Carl repeated. "And when I get back to the States, you and I can celeb—" Someone speaking in the background interrupted

Carl. "Yeah. Sure. I'm coming. Ah, listen, Wesley," Carl continued after a moment, "I've really got to run."

"No problem. Listen, I'd really like to talk to you," Wesley said. With the onslaught of Sam's attentions, he needed more than just a few minutes with Carl to keep him sane. "I'll give you a call—"

"No need," Carl interrupted. "I'll call you over the weekend when I have a minute."

"Sure." That would certainly make it easier. "Can't wait to hear what you've been up to."

"Gotta run, Wesley. Talk to you later."

"Love y—" The sound of the call disconnecting and a blast of static cut short Wesley's words. He pocketed the phone and climbed the stairs to the trailer. Hearing Carl's voice reinforced the fact that he shouldn't be enjoying himself in Sam's company. He really should tell him he'd changed his mind about dinner.

Wesley wished he was in Guatemala with Carl. *Anywhere but here.*

CHAPTER ELEVEN

"I'M GLAD you came," Sam said as he opened the door to let Wesley inside.

In the end, Wesley had given up trying to pull out of dinner at Sam's. Jeffrey had come by to drop off a golf cart for Wesley to use in case he wasn't available to drive Wesley around.

"Sam said to let you know I'm joining you for dinner," Jeffrey told him as he showed Wesley how to use the cart and handed him a set of keys. "I hope you don't mind."

Wesley reassured Jeffrey that he didn't. At least Sam's promise of a chaperone had been on the up and up. Having Jeffrey there would mean Sam would tone things down—Sam might want him back, but he wasn't out in Hollywood.

Wesley handed Sam the bottles of Saint-Émilion he'd found at the island's only grocery store. "For dinner."

"My favorite. Thank you."

"You're welcome. I was impressed with the selection. Clearly the islanders have good taste." The formal exchange felt entirely wrong, but Wesley supposed Sam was doing as he promised and behaving "like a gentleman." As strange as it felt, it was easier this way.

"Come on in." Sam gestured Wesley into the foyer, an immense space with a ceiling that reached up to the roof. "I told them the place was too big," Sam said, as if guessing at Wesley's thoughts, "but they insisted I stay here. Jeffrey has the entire southern wing of the house to himself."

Wesley followed Sam into the dining room, where Jeffrey was humming Madonna's "Like a Virgin" and dancing around as he set the table.

"Someone's happy," Sam said under his breath.

"I *heard* that," Jeffrey shot back as he twirled around and put a spoon at the edge of one of the place settings. "Would you prefer I sing opera?"

"You listen to opera?" Wesley asked.

"My mom loves it," Jeffrey said and began to sing "La donna è mobile" from Verdi's *Rigoletto* in passable Italian.

"Jeffrey's got a crush." Sam grabbed a corkscrew from the side bar and worked open the wine.

"Nothing wrong with that." Wesley smiled at Jeffrey.

"You going to tell us who you're crushing on?"

Jeffrey glared at Sam.

"Ignore him, Jeffrey," Wesley put in, chuckling. "Sam likes being a pain in the ass."

"Do not," Sam protested.

Jeffrey giggled as he filled the water glasses. "You two have known each other for a while, haven't you?"

"Long enough," Wesley said with a barely repressed smirk.

"I'm not keeping it a secret," Jeffrey told Sam. "I just don't want to jinx it. If you know what I mean."

"Seems reasonable." Wesley took the wine Sam offered and sipped it.

The doorbell rang and Jeffrey nearly jumped in surprise.

"That will be our fourth guest," Sam said as he handed a glass to Jeffrey.

"Fourth?" Jeffrey frowned. "But I only set the table for three."

"I guess you'll have to set another place, won't you?" Sam winked at Wesley and headed for the front door.

Wesley followed, whispering, "What are you up to?"

"Not telling." Sam pointed at his own lips to demonstrate how tightly sealed they were.

Wesley rolled his eyes. "Some things never change."

Sam shrugged and opened the door.

"Good to see you, Sander. Wesley." Cyrus Eastman's earring—a diamond stud this time—glinted in the light from the entry.

"Glad you could make it on such short notice," Sam said as they all walked back to the dining room. "You've met my assistant, Jeffrey, haven't you?" he added as Jeffrey walked back in, hands full.

Jeffrey nearly dropped the plate and silverware he'd been carrying. "M-M-Mr. Eastman," he choked out.

Wesley did his best not to laugh. *Leave it to Sam to play Cupid.* Sam was an incurable romantic.

"Call me Cyrus. Please."

Jeffrey nodded and blushed to the roots of his blond hair. "Of c-course. Mr. Cyrus—Cyman. I mean, Mr. Eastman. I mean…. Ah, excuse me." He trotted off to the kitchen, Cyrus watching him with keen interest.

"Lovely," Cyrus said, gaze focused on Jeffrey's adorable backside so it was clear the comment had nothing to do with the perfectly set table. He glanced at Sam and added, "And he's as sharp as they come. Did you know he helped Parker set up a shot yesterday? You should have seen her face when she realized he'd nailed it."

Wesley smiled. "I'm not surprised." Sam had always had a canny business sense, even though he pretended otherwise. Jeffrey was clearly a winner of a hire.

"Wine?" Sam asked as he held up the bottle.

"Thank you," Cyrus said.

Ten minutes later they all sat around the table as Sam served them bowls of fragrant fish and shellfish from a huge pot of bouillabaisse. The scents of fennel and broth wafted from the pot, and Wesley's stomach growled in appreciation. It was one of Sam's favorite dishes, something he'd made for them when they'd spent a week on Hatteras Island years before.

"I didn't realize you could cook," Cyrus said appreciatively. "I'm impressed."

"This was a joint effort," Sam explained and inclined his head to Jeffrey. "Jeffrey managed to scare up some beautiful flounder from a fisherman over in Southport, and we found some local clams and shrimp on the island."

Wesley lifted his glass. "You've outdone yourself, Sander."

"Thanks. And please, call me Sam. All of you." He gazed directly at Wesley and added, "There are no secrets here." These words had Wesley wondering what other truths Sam had shared with Jeffrey and Cyrus.

"Indeed," Cyrus put in. "Except perhaps that you're an excellent cook."

"To good friends," Sam said and raised his glass. "And to second chances."

Wesley did his best not to telegraph his discomfort with Sam's toast.

"So... ah... Cyrus," Jeffrey began after they'd all been served. "How long do you plan on staying this time?"

"I'll be here through the end of the month." Cyrus sipped thoughtfully on his wine, then turned toward Jeffrey. "Of course, I can always extend my stay. Should there be something to keep me here." Jeffrey blushed again and coughed on his wine. "I haven't seen much of the island."

"I'd love to take you around," Jeffrey said so quickly it took Wesley a moment to discern what he'd said. "We could visit the conservancy. There are some interesting ruins from the confederate occupation of the island."

"Perfect." Cyrus leaned over and touched Jeffrey's wrist.

Wesley glanced at Sam, who wore a look of smug satisfaction. Sam had always been good at reading people, and for the most part, Wesley had benefitted from that ability.

"So, Wesley," Cyrus said after a long moment. "How are you enjoying your stay?"

"It's a beautiful island, and the house is very comfortable." Wesley figured he should probably avoid the subject of work, and especially the sorry state of the shoot, with all the changes the crew were scrambling to accommodate on his account.

"Indeed. Very romantic, don't you think?" Cyrus winked at Jeffrey, who looked as though he were about to bounce out of his seat.

"I wouldn't know," Wesley admitted. "Although it's a perfect location to film. We don't have any evidence that the gentleman pirate himself ever frequented these shores, but it's certainly possible." Shit. He sounded just like a professor, didn't he? He'd never been very comfortable with Sam's Hollywood friends and colleagues.

"Parker tells me you've been whipping the props and wardrobe folks into shape."

"I… ah, well, there were a few things that needed immediate correction." Wesley finished the rest of his wine and was thankful when Sam immediately refilled it.

"It's what I'm paying you for," Cyrus said with a dismissive wave of his hand. He leaned in and added in a conspiratorial whisper, "To be honest, I thought the script was a piece of shit when I read it. But with Sam coming on board…."

"I've got a few ideas about the script." Sam's charming smile appeared entirely casual, but Wesley had the sense he'd planned to speak to Cyrus about it all along.

"I look forward to hearing them." Cyrus held out his glass, and Sam emptied the remainder of the bottle into it.

Jeffrey was on his feet an instant later. "I'll get more wine from the pantry. I think there's a lovely bottle of 2011 Meursault Sander's been waiting to open."

"Excellent," Sam said.

Jeffrey nibbled his lower lip and locked eyes with Cyrus before walking into the kitchen.

Cyrus smiled at Sam. "You were right. He's perfect." Cyrus turned to Wesley and added, "Sam's such a good judge of character. He's been telling me about Jeffrey for the past few months. Ever since Antonio up and left me." Cyrus blinked back a few tears, then dabbed the corners of his eyes with his napkin. "I have no doubt he was right about the film as well."

"So you signed on after Sam?" Wesley asked.

Jeffrey came back into the room carrying two more bottles, which he set on the side bar and began to open.

"The original backers pulled out after Van Carrington walked off the set and took the director with him. When I heard Sam had agreed to sign on, I called Parker and convinced her that we could do something with it." Cyrus sighed. "She agreed, so long as I agreed to pay to have someone sail the ship here."

"The replica of the *Queen Anne's Revenge*?"

"I know it's not Bonnet's ship," Cyrus explained as Jeffrey sat down, "but your predecessor agreed it was a good substitute."

"About that." Wesley swirled the wine around in his glass. "I was surprised to hear Marv left. Seems it happened very suddenly." He glanced at Sam, who conveniently picked up the basket of bread, took a piece, then passed it to Jeffrey.

"It did." The edges of Cyrus's mouth curved upward. "Seems he and my star had a bit of a disagreement about weaponry."

"They did, did they?"

Sam still wasn't looking at him.

"So," Sam said, changing the subject, "I hear you've approved new costumes for the women."

"I have." Wesley speared a shrimp and eyed it with feigned interest. "I think we're on the right track now."

"Sam says you've known each other a long time," Cyrus offered casually.

"More than ten years," Wesley said. He'd leave it at that.

"That's a story I'd like to hear." Cyrus leaned over to Sam. "About how you two met."

Wesley stiffened but said nothing. He'd let Sam make up whatever cockamamie story he wanted. He was sure it would be entertaining.

"We met when I was a grad student," Sam said. Not a story. The truth. *Now this is interesting.*

"You met in school?" Jeffrey asked excitedly. "What school?"

"New York University," Wesley interjected. He figured it couldn't hurt to tell the truth, since Sam had offered up that much of their past.

"I was a grad student. He was a baby professor." Sam looked as though he was having way too much fun.

Wesley had heard Sam tell the story of how they become "roommates" before, of course. Sam always began with the truth, but somewhere along the line, he would embellish and Wesley's nonexistent sister or cousin would become the object of Sam's affections. Their cover story. The one they told the public.

"So you two *dated*?" Jeffrey asked, wide-eyed.

"I… well…," Wesley stammered. That wasn't part of the cover story.

"Yep."

Wesley stared at Sam. He didn't think Sam was out to anyone in Hollywood.

Jeffrey clapped his hands together with glee. "I was right!" he shouted triumphantly. "You *are* gay! Both of you."

Cyrus didn't look in the least bit surprised.

"We are," Sam confirmed. "In fact," he added with a devilish smile, "Wesley is my husband."

CHAPTER TWELVE

"OMIGOD, OMIGOD," Jeffrey chanted as he helped Sam wash the dishes after Wesley and Cyrus left. "I can't believe I was right!"

"You knew I was married?" Sam teased.

"I… ah… no. But I thought maybe you were queer."

Sam laughed and patted Jeffrey on the head with a soapy hand. "Yeah, well, we're about to get divorced." He'd seen the look on Wesley's face when he'd dropped the bombshell. He wasn't sure if panic was a good or a bad thing.

"Oh. I wondered why Wesley wasn't staying here. So that's why he changed the subject and looked like he was going to kill you?"

"Probably."

"And you don't want to get a divorce."

"Not particularly." He'd hoped letting other people he trusted know about them might help him convince Wesley not to go through with the divorce. But he'd gotten nowhere fast. He needed to bump up his game. When summer was over, his marriage to Wesley would be over too.

Jeffrey began to dry another pan. "Thanks for inviting Cyrus tonight. I know you said you ran into him on set, but I think you planned it."

"And if I did?"

Jeffrey shrugged. "Either way, I'm good."

"Cyrus is a good friend. I think you're a good match."

"And what about you?" Jeffrey flicked the towel he'd been holding.

"I'll be okay." Sam grinned. "Haven't given up yet."

Jeffrey tilted his head to one side as if considering something. "You know," he began as he dried the pot Sam handed him, "assistants are supposed to help their bosses."

"They are?" Sam kept his expression solemn.

"Yes. And, well, I might have a few ideas about how you can win him back, you know."

"You might?"

Jeffrey nodded.

"All right."

"You'll let me help?"

The kid was damn cute when he got excited about something. He was also damn good at his job—the best assistant Sam ever had. Clever and entirely unorthodox. "I might."

"What are you thinking?"

"Something big and romantic," Sam said. "You know, the over-the-top kind of gesture you'd see in a romcom,"

Jeffrey frowned. "I don't know about that."

"Really?" Sam chuckled. "Wesley isn't immune to romance just because he's the academic type."

Jeffrey took another plate from the strainer and began to dry it. "I don't know him as well as you do, of course," he said with a quick glance at Sam. "He just... I don't know... I guess he seems a little skittish."

"He's not going anywhere." Sam used the back of his hand to wipe away some bubbles that landed on his nose.

"Yeah. I guess not." Jeffrey appeared unconvinced. "Still, sometimes romance is about the little stuff."

"Sure. But I've done a shit job of being a husband to him. I've got a lot of making up to do." Wesley had always enjoyed when Sam bought him flowers or gave him gifts, hadn't he?

"What happened between you?" Jeffrey asked. "I mean, if things were so bad that you're getting divorced, why...."

"Why aren't we at each other's throats?"

"Yeah." Jeffrey shrugged. "I don't know, it's just that you seem to *like* each other."

"We do."

"I don't get it." Jeffrey put the wineglasses back in the cabinet and leaned on the counter.

"Sometimes I don't either." Sam sighed. "It's my fault things are the way they are, though. When I left New York to work in LA, I wasn't very good at the husband stuff. I didn't see Wesley much. I think he was lonely."

"I don't think flowers are husband stuff."

Sam chuckled. "A man can buy his husband flowers."

"That's not what I meant." Jeffrey looked a bit sheepish, but he persisted, and Sam had to give him credit. "I've never been married, so maybe I'm wrong...."

"Go ahead." Sam offered Jeffrey a reassuring smile. "You're not overstepping if I ask for your opinion."

Jeffrey pressed his lips together, hesitating a moment before saying, "I just meant that the romantic stuff isn't the only thing people want from a husband."

"Agreed." He couldn't help but think of how young and naïve Jeffrey was. Sure, it was true, but he wasn't going to risk losing Wesley for good by being too subtle, either. There'd be plenty of time for the little stuff later. *Once I get Wesley back.*

CHAPTER THIRTEEN

WESLEY ROLLED over and glanced at the bedside clock. Five a.m. He'd woken up a half-dozen times before, in between hours of tossing and turning. He'd have liked to blame the alcohol, but the truth was his brain simply wouldn't shut down. The words "Wesley is my husband" kept replaying in an infinite loop all night long.

Nearly ten years together and this was the first time Sam had mentioned their marriage to anyone except their closest friends. And with those four words, Sam had once again upended Wesley's ordered universe. It didn't matter that it wasn't enough to make up for the years of being estranged—Wesley couldn't deny the effect those words had over him.

The echo of a memory tugged at Wesley's mind and wouldn't dislodge itself. Sam excited about his first big film—the film that had made him a household name. "It's not Shakespeare," Sam said as he set the bottle of champagne on their rickety breakfast table after Wesley got home from the university. "But if I do a good job, there'll be more work."

"Congratulations." Wesley kissed Sam. He'd been truly happy for him; he'd never wished Sam anything but success.

"There's one hitch," Sam said as he cooked them dinner. "I'll need to stay on the West Coast. British Columbia and then in LA for the sound stuff. Just a few months."

"I figured you wouldn't be able to commute from here if you got the gig." Wesley had been prepared for that part of the deal. "Maybe I can come out for a weekend or two. There are some good deals on flights."

Sam had hugged him so tight, Wesley could still remember how it had felt. He'd believed, like Sam, that they'd make it work. But neither of them had considered how exhausting the trips from New York to LA would be. Wesley had nearly slept his way through his Monday morning class—he sure hadn't slept on the red-eye.

"It's okay," Sam had said after the fourth or fifth weekend Wesley commuted cross-country and ended up with a case of bronchitis that had knocked him on his ass for nearly a week. "I know it takes a lot out of you."

Sam had managed to get away for four days about halfway through the third month of filming. The weekend together in New York had been amazing, and Wesley had forgotten about the weeks alone. They'd parted at LaGuardia with a kiss in the men's room, and Wesley knew they'd be fine. But that first movie had led to more. With some, Sam had weeks of downtime between. With others....

"I'm not going to be able to make it back this weekend," Sam told him by phone the Thursday before he was to fly back to New York.

"I'll come to you, then," Wesley offered.

"Nah, don't sweat it. I've got this premiere I'm supposed to go to. You know, I'm supposed to get my face in the tabloids." Sam hesitated, and Wesley waited, knowing Sam wouldn't be able to tolerate the silence for long. "Yeah, they want me and Danielle Hartfield to make an appearance. Just for show."

"I trust you, Sammy."

"Thanks."

Wesley ignored the photos in the gossip magazines. He didn't doubt Sam. But three months apart soon turned into a year, then two. Often Sam's schedule didn't jibe with Wesley's, and Sam would come back to New York only to putter around the apartment. You could only work out so many hours, Wesley reasoned, before you needed something else to keep you going. And when Sam headed back to LA, Wesley stopped seeing him off at the airport.

"I'm going to tell Corliss I want the summer off," Sam announced toward the beginning of the school year, the third year they'd been apart.

"Isn't that risky?" Wesley asked. He could take the summer off from teaching, but he'd overheard the conversations Sam had with his agent about his schedule. He'd heard Sam press her for work, even small roles with some of the smaller films.

"I don't give a shit. This isn't what I want. Not for my career and not for us."

"I've applied for a job at UC San Diego," Wesley told him.

"Tenure-track position?" Sam asked brightly.

"No, but there's always the possibil—"

"You are *not* giving up tenure for me." Sam looked genuinely upset. "You worked so fucking hard to get where you are." Wesley shrugged and pretended he didn't care. But Sam knew him too well. "No fucking way, Wesley. I won't have you do that."

But Sam's schedule didn't change, and his plans of a summer off evaporated with a role his agent said would be a great way to break into more serious roles. "I can't come this weekend," Sam would say more often than not. Wesley had gotten used to it. When Sam was with him, Wesley was happy. But monthly trips turned into trips every two or three months. Messages left on cell phones when their schedules didn't match up. More than anything, Sam seemed happy. He didn't seem to need Wesley, which left Wesley feeling worse than just being lonely.

And finally that moment came when Wesley couldn't hang on anymore. Not even for the man he still loved.

Ancient history. Hell, he should know. History repeated itself unless you learned from it.

Wesley sighed and sat up in bed. He needed to go for a run. It didn't matter that he'd run the day before, he needed to clear his brain of Sam. He couldn't focus on anything *but* Sam—the sincere, even apologetic expression on his face as he'd told Cyrus and Jeffrey about the marriage. The way being with Sam was so *comfortable*. Familiar.

Of course it's familiar. It's Sam.

BY THE time Wesley made it back to the house, the sun had just emerged on the horizon. He lingered for a few minutes on the front porch and watched a gray heron gracefully dip its long neck into the creek that ambled alongside the house.

Wesley stretched his legs on the railing. He felt calmer than before. Levelheaded. After all these years, the only person who could really ruffle his feathers was Sam. He'd had his share of run-ins with some of the other faculty at the university, dealt with difficult students and ornery helicopter parents, even managed to debunk a major paper in an esteemed history journal without missing a beat. But Sam always set him spinning like one of those rides at an amusement park. A tilt-a-hurl that left you breathless and struggling to keep down your lunch.

Wesley pulled the key from his pocket and was just about to insert it in the lock when he realized the front door was open. Strange. He was sure he'd locked it, because he always laughed at himself when he did. He doubted there'd ever been a break-in on the island. He walked inside, set the key on the front table, then realized the entire entryway was lined with flowers. Bouquets of flowers. Flowering plants. And a trail of rose petals that led to the kitchen.

Holy shit. The place looked like a cross between a funeral home and a honeymoon suite from a bridal magazine spread.

"Sam." The smell of bacon wafted in from the kitchen, and his stomach rumbled its approval.

"At your service." Sam grinned up at him from the stove.

The kitchen table was set with a linen tablecloth, crystal stemware, and china that looked vaguely familiar. A single setting. "Impressive." Totally over-the-top. *And totally Sam.* "Does props realize you borrowed their dinnerware?"

Sam shrugged. "Momma Carr brought me up right," he said as he laid on the Southern accent. "She always told me you catch more flies with honey than vinegar."

"I'm a fly now?"

"In a manner of speaking." Sam winked at him.

Wesley rubbed his mouth and tried not to laugh. "I'm not going to starve, you know. In fact, if I keep eating your food, I'm going to need to run a marathon every day."

"I told you, Momma brought me up right. I dragged you out here. I'm going to make sure you eat well."

"Sammy, I told you I—"

"Not listening." Sam began to hum "Disco Inferno" and dance as he snagged a few strips of bacon and set them on a paper towel.

"You never did have any taste in music."

"Disco is the classical music of the seventies." Sam whirled around and stuck the spatula in the air. He didn't have any taste, but the man could *move.*

"And John Travolta is Baryshnikov. Yeah, I know."

Sam pursed his lips, then cracked an egg into the pan, switching from The Trammps to the chorus of "Stayin' Alive."

Wesley rolled his eyes and grabbed a bottle of water from the fridge.

"Sit," Sam commanded.

"You can join me." Wesley gestured to the other chair.

"Nope. I know there are limits. I wouldn't want your boyfriend—Chris, was it?—"

"Carl." As if Sam didn't know his name!

"—Carl to get the wrong idea."

"He wouldn't. He'd know exactly what you're up to." Wesley pointed to the chair again. "Sam, seriously, I don't want you waiting on me. Join me? Please?"

"Okay." Sam had probably planned this too, but Wesley didn't mind.

"How is Momma Carr doing these days?" Wesley asked after they both had a plate full of food in front of them.

"She has a boyfriend. Ralph Watson. He's an accountant. They met at church."

"That's great news. Sounds like she's finally been able to get over losing your father."

"Dad would have liked Ralph," Sam said with a slightly sad smile. "He'd be happy she's not alone anymore."

"You must miss him." Wesley had been at Sam's side for his father's funeral. They'd only been together a few months, and Wesley had been surprised Sam wanted him to tag along.

Sam nodded. "I remember when I got my first real acting job, how I wished he could have seen it. He worried I wouldn't be able to make a living at it."

Without thinking, Wesley reached across the table and touched Sam's hand. "He'd be really proud of you." Wesley withdrew his hand quickly.

"Thanks."

"I'm sure it's been—"

"Jeffrey couldn't stop talking about Cyrus last night," Sam said.

The abrupt change in topic didn't surprise Wesley. They'd never really talked about Sam's father's passing, although Wesley had tried to get Sam to open up about him. Things hadn't changed. Sam still avoided difficult topics.

Wesley wouldn't press. That wasn't his role anymore, and Sam had never been comfortable leaning on him anyhow. That was the problem, after all. "I had to cut Cyrus off. He cornered me outside after dinner when I was getting ready to drive home. He wanted to know if I could ask you to set them up on a date." Wesley chuckled. "Talk about a roundabout way to ask someone out."

"I'll take care of it. Jeffrey would be good for him. The way Cyrus has been moping since Antonio left him last year, I was thinking of fixing him up. This makes it easier."

"Still an incurable romantic, aren't you." Wesley swallowed a sigh.

"Anything wrong with that?"

"No. It was one of your best qualities," Wesley admitted. Sam had never missed an anniversary or birthday. He even sent Wesley flowers to commemorate the day they'd met. Wesley wished that had been enough to keep him going through the lean times. "But Sammy?"

"Huh?"

"This…." Wesley gestured to the flowers and shook his head. "I'd really rather you don't. It's lovely, but…."

"But you've moved on. Yeah. I get it. Fair enough." Sam's smile didn't reach his eyes. He got to his feet and began to clear the table.

"I can do that," Wesley said.

"Nah, this one's on me." Sam turned on the water and washed the skillet. "Wesley?"

"Yes?"

"Do you love him? Chris?"

"Carl," Wesley corrected again.

"Do you love Carl?" Sam didn't look at him as he loaded the plates into the dishwasher.

"He's a great guy."

"That's not an answer," Sam replied, still not meeting Wesley's gaze.

Sam was right. Why had he hesitated? Carl was a great guy. They had so much in common. He was good-looking and intelligent. He wanted the same things Wesley wanted from his life.

Wesley sure as hell didn't want to give Sam hope where there was none. "Yes," he said quickly. "Of course I do."

"Oh. That's good." Sam didn't sound at all convinced. And he still didn't look at Wesley. "I want you to be happy, Wesley. Whatever happens."

"Thanks." Well, he *was* happy. Wasn't he?

CHAPTER FOURTEEN

"THAT'S IT!" Parker shouted after they'd finished filming. She wiped her face with the back of her hand and shook her head. "Too fucking hot."

Sam laughed and handed his hat to Rosie, the wardrobe assistant, and scratched idly at his scalp. It felt like 102 degrees in the shade, and the humidity could only have been higher if it rained. Jeffrey, whose blond curls were plastered to the back of his neck, offered Sam some water.

"Thanks," Sam said after chugging the bottle and retrieving another. "Ten minutes more and I'd have melted." Sam waved at Wesley, who walked over to the ship. His shirt was stuck to his skin, his nipples and the faint outline of his pecs visible. Tendrils of his dark hair clung stubbornly to the back of his neck. He looked damn good. Too good. "How the hell did pirates survive in wool?"

Wesley laughed. "I doubt they'd have been wearing their jackets in this heat."

"Tell that to Parker."

"And let you off the hook?" Wesley raised an eyebrow. "What's it worth to you?"

"Dinner?" Sam offered. He'd backed off Wesley a bit the past week, not wanting to send him running off to track down the boyfriend. But he figured it was time to up the ante, and Jeffrey had suggested cooking for Wesley might be a little too much. Maybe a more social setting would work better, one with more than just the two of them together in close quarters.

"Sam. I really don't think—"

"Cyrus is throwing a little party. You won't be the only guest."

"Oh. Okay." Wesley was visibly relieved. Not that Sam had figured Wesley would be a pushover, but a wary Wesley was going to make this a lot harder. "Where is Cyrus's house?"

"A few blocks from yours. But this party's on the boat."

"*Your* boat?"

"I promised him a sunset sail." Sam did his best to sound nonchalant.

"I guess that would be all right."

"Sander!" Jeffrey waved from the steps of Sam's trailer.

"Come with me?" Sam asked. When Wesley hesitated, he added, "At least cool off for a bit and get something to drink, okay?"

"I don't know. I really need—"

"At least come out of the heat and cool off."

"I... sure." Wesley followed Sam to the trailer, where Jeffrey held the door for them.

"You might need a gas mask," Sam joked as he peeled off his wool jacket and handed it to Rosie while Jeffrey poured a glass of water for Wesley, who was seated at the kitchen table. "No wonder nobody lived very long in the 1700s. They probably shriveled up and died in the heat."

Rosie laughed. "We'll get it fumigated, Mr. Carson." She helped Sam out of his pants and shirt, then bundled them up and left them alone.

"Have a drink of water," Sam told Wesley, who was starting to look a lot less like he was on the verge of melting.

"Thanks." Wesley raised his glass and smiled as Jeffrey set a pitcher of ice water in front of him.

"WHERE'S WESLEY?" Sam asked Jeffrey after he'd showered and changed into a T-shirt and shorts.

"He said he was going to check on a dagger or something, then head home. I told him I'd be by to pick him up around five."

"Good." For a moment there, he'd worried Wesley might change his mind. He grabbed a comb from the makeup table and worked it through his hair. It had gotten longer over the past month, and one of the makeup assistants had joked that by the end of shooting, Sam might not need the wig. "So how are the plans coming?"

"Everything's a go. Parker agreed to help, and the caterer was already setting things up last time I spoke with them," Jeffrey explained. "The special effects guys are taking care of the rest. Luis and the other crew had already washed the boat down. They said they're going to make her shine. We have fifteen RSVPs, but we'll have enough food for double that, just in case."

"That's terrific. I can't believe you managed to pull it all together so quickly."

Jeffrey didn't look all that pleased.

"Something wrong?"

Jeffrey shrugged and shifted from one foot to the other.

"Come on, Jeffrey," Sam pressed. "You know I want you to tell me what you really think."

Jeffrey inhaled slowly, then met Sam's gaze. "I think this is—might be—a mistake."

"A mistake? Why?"

"I don't know, it's just…. What if it backfires?"

"Backfires?" The entire setup was perfect. Romantic and—

"What if it's too over-the-top?" Jeffrey said. He glanced away for an instant, clearly uncomfortable. "Wesley seems a little… I don't know…."

"It won't backfire." Sam was sure this would work. What could be more romantic than a sunset cruise with a little entertainment to sweep Wesley off his feet? Wesley had always loved grand gestures of Sam's affection.

"I guess not."

"Listen," Sam said, "this is on me. Whatever happens, you did an amazing job."

"Thanks."

"Remind me to double that bonus I promised you," Sam said.

Jeffrey blushed as he always did when Sam complimented him. "Actually," he said awkwardly, "I was hoping I might take tomorrow off."

"Oh? Why?" Sam was pretty sure he knew the answer.

The flush on Jeffrey's cheeks grew darker red. "Cyrus asked me to spend tomorrow with him shopping in Wilmington. Marnie said she'd be available in case you needed anything, so you don't have to worry about—"

"You got it." Sam winked and added, "But you're still getting a bonus." This was going to be great. He was absolutely sure of it.

WESLEY THANKED God for the breeze as he and Jeffrey rode toward the marina in Jeffrey's cart. "Sam doesn't get to show off his boat very often," Jeffrey said, his constant chatter a relief to Wesley, who wasn't feeling all that talkative or in a party mood. He'd tried once again to reach Carl and had ended up leaving yet another message.

"Oh?"

Jeffrey nodded. "He bought her about six months ago, and this is only the second time he's been able to sail her. His crew keeps her clean and meets up with him whenever he has time off, but his schedule has been pretty crazy."

"He mentioned this film was a last-minute gig."

"Yeah. Sam was supposed to take all of June and July off. He's been working pretty much nonstop since last year, or at least that's what Diana, Sam's last assistant, told me," Jeffrey continued.

This didn't surprise Wesley. "He doesn't have much fun, does he?"

Jeffrey shook his head. "Not much, I guess. He doesn't date, if that's what you mean."

So much for being subtle. Jeffrey was definitely smarter than he let on. Clearly Sam had filled Jeffrey in on more of the details of their relationship. "I know the studios love to invent relationships," he said offhandedly.

"I guess. Sam told them to fuck off, that he wasn't going to do that bullshit for the studio or anyone. His agent was really pissed." Jeffrey pressed his lips together. "I guess now I know why."

"Oh?"

"He didn't want it to look bad. For you, I mean." Jeffrey stared straight ahead.

Way too close to the truth.

"Sorry. I probably shouldn't be telling you all of this," Jeffrey added quickly.

"Don't apologize. I was married to Sam, remember?"

Jeffrey giggled, then grew more serious. "I know it's probably none of my business," he said.

"But you want to know why we're getting a divorce?"

"Yeah. I mean, you two seem so… I don't know…. You like each other."

Wesley laughed. "Sometimes things just don't work out the way you thought they would," he offered, dodging the question.

"I'm sure having Sam on the other side of the country was rough."

"I can't say that was fun," Wesley said. "But it was more than just that. I guess you could say we drifted apart." He wasn't very good at articulating the point, partly because he wasn't really sure himself what had happened. He'd come to believe what had happened didn't matter all that much. He and Sam just weren't good for each other.

If Jeffrey understood, he didn't say, because at that moment they pulled into a parking spot near the docks and got off the cart. "The boat's over there." Jeffrey pointed to the dock nearest to the bar.

"Welcome aboard." Sam offered his hand to Wesley as he climbed the stairs to the deck. Wesley took Sam's hand, and as always, the brief contact had Wesley taking a deep breath to head off his body's reaction. This time, however, Wesley realized he felt a little guilty for it.

Sam released his grip on Wesley a moment later, and Wesley and Jeffrey followed Sam onto the foredeck, where several large tables were set with hors d'oeuvres and several waiters dressed all in white offered drinks to the guests. Wesley counted more than a dozen guests, many of whom he recognized from the set.

"Good to see you, Wesley," Cyrus said as he leaned in and kissed Wesley on both cheeks in the European manner, then made a beeline for Jeffrey. No European greeting there—Cyrus kissed him on the lips, much to Jeffrey's surprise and obvious pleasure.

Wesley glanced at Sam for his reaction, but realized Sam was looking directly at him. Desire flickered over his rugged features, but it vanished a second later as he flagged down a server and snagged two drinks.

"I'm glad you came." Sam handed a glass to Wesley.

"Thanks." Wesley took a quick sip of the wine. "Are you sailing her tonight?"

"I'm a passenger for this trip." Sam waved to a few of the guests making their way up the gangway. "I hired a crew." He pointed to a man dressed in a white shirt and shorts who secured the opening in the railing and got to work on the ropes.

"I thought you had your own crew," Wesley said.

"I gave them the month off. I'll be too busy shooting to sail much, and I can single-hand her if I do find time. You're welcome to join me, you know. Give her a whirl?"

The offer was more than a little tempting. Wesley hadn't piloted a boat in a few years, and this boat was something out of his wildest fantasies.

Someone giggled, and Wesley turned to see Cyrus hand Jeffrey a drink complete with umbrella and a fruit spear. "Jeffrey and Cyrus are inseparable, aren't they?" Wesley said as he watched the two men climb the stairs to the upper deck, arm in arm.

"I've never seen Cyrus so happy." Sam smiled. "Hard to believe they've only known each other for a few days."

"You thinking things between them might get serious?"

Sam sighed theatrically. "I think so. I may end up losing a good assistant if things keep going like they are."

"I thought Cyrus has a place in LA."

"He lives most of the year in Manhattan. His mom's in a home on Long Island, and he visits her as much as he can," Sam explained.

A long blast of the ship's horn nearly made Wesley jump.

"That means we're leaving," Sam said, beaming. "Best view is on the foredeck. Join me?"

Sam's gentle touch to his shoulder took Wesley by surprise, but he schooled his expression and hoped his response wasn't entirely obvious. "Sure," Wesley said, and they headed to the front of the ship, Sam greeting some of the guests on their way.

They arrived at the bow just as the boat pulled out of the short channel from the marina and onto the Cape Fear River. Wesley walked over to the railing and peered out at the island as it grew smaller. He sighed and inhaled the salty air.

"How long has it been since you've last sailed?" Sam asked.

"Nearly five years."

"Ocracoke." Wesley caught a ghost of a smile on Sam's lips and guessed it mirrored his own. The boat they'd rented hadn't been nearly as big, but Wesley could still remember the powerful vibrations of the engines as he'd steered her easily through the zigzagging channel.

"I could take you there over July Fourth," Sam added.

"I don't think that's such a great idea, Sam."

"Why not? You love to sail, and there's plenty of—"

"Let it go, Sammy. Please?" The offer was far too tempting.

Sam appeared undaunted. "So tell me about work. How are classes?"

"Good." The more comfortable territory relaxed Wesley somewhat. "I finally convinced the chair to let me teach a class on pirates."

"I told you they'd go for it." They'd talked about it years ago. Wesley was surprised Sam remembered.

"New chair," Wesley explained. "But you were right. I've been thinking about a summer program too."

"Taking students to some of the places the pirates used to hang out?"

Wesley nodded. "Charleston. Beaufort. Ocracoke. Maybe even diving on the wreck of the *Queen Anne's Revenge*, if I can get permission."

"You still dive?"

"Not since the Dominican Republic." Wesley had missed diving too. But diving had been part of his life with Sam, and after Sam….

"Mr. Carson?" One of the crew tapped Sam on the shoulder.

"Excuse me," Sam said. "I've got a few last-minute details to take care of. Catch you later?"

"Sure." Wesley was silently relieved as Sam followed the crewmember through the doorway to the salon.

"PROFESSOR COOLIDGE?" one of the servers asked about an hour later. The sun had begun to set, leaving the sky a riot of colors and painting the clouds deep purple with the dimming light.

"Yes?"

"Mr. Carson asked me to show you to the upper deck," the woman said. "He said there's something you need to see."

"I really don't think I should," Wesley said.

"He said you'd say that," she replied with a warm smile. "He promised he would be on his best behavior."

"He's never anything but."

"You wouldn't want me to get in trouble, would you?" she countered brightly. "Besides, there are plenty of other guests up there."

"All right."

She showed him to the stairs and waited until he climbed to the deck—the same place he'd had dinner the first time he'd sailed on the boat. He paused and looked down to the foredeck, where all the guests had been seated. Parker must have cracked a joke, because a few people laughed and Jeffrey's giggle rose over the din. Cyrus had taken a seat beside Jeffrey and was clearly enjoying the younger man's company. Who could blame him? The evening was perfect, the breeze off the water taking the edge off the heat, and the sky stunning.

"Wesley."

Wesley turned to find Sam seated on a blanket on the deck, the table where they'd eaten before gone. Sam was pulling food from a picnic basket and placing it on the edge of the blanket. No one else was around.

"I thought there would be other people joining us," Wesley pointed out.

"There are." Sam pointed downward and flashed his way-too-charming smile. "Just not up here."

"I should leave."

"Please don't." Sam wore such an earnest expression, Wesley knew he wouldn't refuse. "Have a seat?"

Wesley kicked off his shoes and sat near Sam, but not *too* near.

"Last time I had a picnic was with you," Sam said.

"Ocracoke. On the beach. I remember it well." Wesley chuckled, then added, "Fortunately, you remembered the deet."

"You drenched yourself and you still got bitten."

"Yes." Wesley took the glass of wine Sam offered and drank it slowly. He wouldn't make the same mistake twice and let his guard down again.

"Penny for your thoughts?"

"The truth? Or would you like the rose-colored-glasses version?"

"The truth."

Wesley met Sam's gaze, then said, "I want us to be friends."

"Oh."

"Seriously, Sam. You know I could never hate you," Wesley said. He didn't like the way it came out, but it *was* the truth. "We're just not good for each other."

"We could be good again."

Wesley blew a long breath from between his lips. "It doesn't work that way." He paused, trying his best to gather his thoughts. "I don't want to hurt you, Sammy. I really don't."

"I know I hurt you."

"It wasn't only your fault." Wesley swallowed hard and looked out over the water. With the wind on his face, he could almost imagine them the way they'd once been. "We let it get away from us. We *both* blew it."

"Let me make it up to you." Sam put his hand over Wesley's and leaned in toward him. It would be *so* easy just to—

"No." Wesley got to his feet, knocking over his glass of white wine in the process.

Sam followed him to the railing, and for a few minutes they said nothing. *Such a beautiful evening.* But the pain…. No, they hadn't hurt each other the way some couples might have. Neither had cheated. Neither had done anything to betray the other's trust. But the pain ran deep. Deeper than Wesley wanted to feel.

"Can I speak with Sander, please?" Wesley asked Sam's assistant.

"I'm sorry, Professor Coolidge," Diana said. "He's in a meeting right now."

"Oh. Thank you."

"Are you calling about consulting on his next movie?" she asked. "I can give you the production assistant's number, if you'd like."

Of course Diana didn't know who he was to Sam. "It's all right. Thank you. Please let him know I called?"

"Of course, Professor. I will. Merry Christmas!"

"Merry Christmas." Wesley ended the call and sat on the couch. He hadn't even bothered with the tree this year. Without Sam around to help him decorate it, he just wasn't feeling it.

When Sam finally called him back, it was New Year's Eve. "I'm so sorry, Wesley." Wesley knew Sam was. But that didn't make him feel any better. "There was this variety show, and they needed me to promote the sequel to *Tougher than Nails*. By the time I got back, it was two in the morning New York time."

It didn't explain why Sam hadn't called for nearly a week afterward, but Wesley had long since stopped questioning him. He was pretty sure Sam wasn't cheating on him—that wasn't Sam's style. But the distance between them had become a chasm Wesley was unable to bridge. Sam seemed so happy being away, and that made things so much worse.

"You could have called me late," he told Sam.

"I didn't want to wake you."

Please. Wake me up! Do something. Tell me you love me, that there's still an "us" that you can come back to. "It's okay."

"Are you doing anything for New Year's?" Sam asked.

"Going to Venka's party," he lied. There was a party at Venka's, but Wesley had already decided to skip it. He didn't feel much in the party mood.

"Good."

"Sammy?"

"Yeah?"

Wesley hesitated, unsure if he wanted to hear the answer. "Do you think you'll be coming home soon?"

"Really soon," Sam said, but he didn't elaborate. He never did. "I'll let you know when I get a free weekend, and we can go out to Fire Island."

"That sounds wonderful." Wesley figured it wouldn't happen.

"Love you, Wesley," Sam said.

"Love you too."

"I'll see you soon. Promise."

"I'm looking forward to it." The call ended and Wesley set down the phone.

That time, Sam did make it home for a weekend, and they went to the beach. But the weather was cold and rainy, and neither of them talked much. Instead they sat around and watched old movies, Wesley comfortably ensconced in Sam's strong arms. At the time, Wesley thought it felt really good. Sam was exhausted, and Wesley didn't have the heart to speak to him about the growing distance he felt between them.

"Have you thought any more about a trip to Ocracoke over Fourth of July weekend?" Sam asked.

"Sammy," Wesley chided. "You just asked me a few hours ago. I need time to think about it."

"Sorry." Sam rubbed his mouth and glanced momentarily away. "It's just that I was thinking maybe Cyrus and Jeffrey would like to come with us."

Wesley knew Sam was suggesting Cyrus and Jeffrey come so he'd be more likely to agree. "I'm probably going to spend the holiday in New York," Wesley said. He needed a weekend away from Sam. Maybe he'd call Venka and they'd go to a concert together. Anything to clear his head.

"No problem." Sam's tone was light, but Wesley knew he was disappointed. "We can do it another time."

"Sure."

The boat slowed as it came around the east side of the island. Wesley noticed a small barge anchored right outside the channel. He was just about to ask what the barge was doing when the first of the fireworks shot upward off the barge's deck. Tiny pinpoints of light showered the water, followed by a cloud of spinning silver circles that danced all around them. Wesley's heart pounded against his chest as he leaned over the railing to get a closer look.

"You always loved fireworks," Sam said when Wesley glanced back at him.

"You… you did this for *me*?"

Sam's answer was lost in another volley of explosions of sound and color as several more rockets burst over the water. The guests below them cheered and applauded. Several other boats slowed to watch the show as three large rockets soared and burst into multicolored circles that seemed to hover in the air before finally falling around them.

"*Sometimes I wish I could live inside a rainbow like that,*" came the voice in a memory—Wesley's own, as he and Sam had lain on the sand and watched the Fourth of July celebration at Jones Beach years before. Sam's hand in his had felt so good. They hadn't even considered that someone might see them. They hadn't cared.

Wesley's vision blurred and he took several deep breaths. Why did the present seem so far away?

CHAPTER FIFTEEN

"I've got an idea." Sam leaned on the doorway to Wesley's house. He wore his running gear.

"At five thirty in the morning?"

"You were up."

"What, were you staking out my place?" Wesley hadn't slept much. He'd been too wound up after the boat trip and the fireworks, and the memories had lingered like a movie geek refusing to leave before the final credits.

"You're always up by now." Sam's gaze traveled down Wesley's body. "And you're dressed for a run. So I can tell you all about it while we run."

"Has it occurred to you that I *like* running by myself sometimes?"

Sam shrugged and held the screen door open.

"Fine." Wesley took off down the road with Sam at his heels. "What's so important that you had to tell me at the asscrack of dawn?"

"I would've made you breakfast again," Sam said, "but the last few times you didn't seem too thrilled about it."

"That's because the last time you broke into my house—"

"I didn't break in," Sam said. "I borrowed the key from—"

"—and the first time you scared the crap out of me."

Sam looked just a bit sheepish. "Okay, okay! I got the message. Don't break into Wesley's house and don't freak Wesley out first thing in the morning."

"Don't freak me out *period*." Wesley headed down the nearest beach access. If Sam was going to follow along, Wesley wasn't going to take it easy on him.

"Got it."

Wesley chuckled as he climbed the wooden steps over the dune. "Thank you," he said as they made their way to the water's edge. "For last night."

"You're welcome."

"Just don't do it again." Wesley wished he sounded more adamant.

"Why not?"

Wesley didn't have to see Sam's face to imagine his grin. "Because it's not playing fair."

"I never promised to be fair. And it isn't as though I haven't been honest."

Wesley picked up the pace. "So what do you want to tell me?" he asked.

"Shit, Wesley, do you always go this fast on the beach?"

"I always go this fast, period. You're just not used to it." Wesley ran backward for a few dozen feet, biding his time until Sam caught back up with him and trying not to gloat.

"You're killing me."

"So are you going to tell me what you're so gung ho about, or am I just going to leave you in the dust?" Wesley teased. He'd slowed a bit, and Sam was now running alongside him, splashing from time to time in the waves that surged and retreated at the water's edge.

"So remember I told you I had an idea. About how to rework the script? Shake out the spiders?"

"I think that's cobwebs, not spiders."

"It's all about creativity," Sam parried. "Anyhow, you keep saying there's nothing in the historical record about why Stede Bonnet left Barbados. Well, I have an idea."

"Oh? And what would that be, Professor?"

Sam shook his head and smirked. "I think the reason Bonnet left his wife and became a pirate is that he was gay."

"There's no evidence Bonnet was gay."

"But it explains why he—"

"I've explored the theory, Sam. Believe me. I've read every document I could get my hands on. There's simply nothing to support it," Wesley said dismissively. "Nothing at all. It's more likely he craved the adventure and things with his wife weren't going particularly well. There's also some evidence he might have suffered from mental illness. There are accounts of him pacing the decks and talking to himself."

"You have to admit it's more likely than not that *some* pirates were gay," Sam said.

"Of course. There are plenty of anecdotal stories that pirates shared more than just whores and loot with their shipmates."

"My point exactly." Sam was triumphant.

"Sam...."

Sam grinned. "We don't *know* why Bonnet left the missus."

"No, we don't."

"Artistic license, Wesley. That's what this is. And think about the new territory this film would cover. What could be more avant-garde?"

"Fine." Wesley sighed and shook his head.

"Fine? So you'll go along with it?" Sam looked surprised.

"I won't fight you on it." He could live with that compromise. Given what little there was about Bonnet in the historical record, it wasn't entirely implausible. "But whatever you do, you need to make it realistic for the time period. He wouldn't have been open about it, even if he was gay."

"Deal." Sam grabbed Wesley and hugged him, nearly knocking him off his feet. "Thank you."

They were both dripping with sweat, but Wesley responded to the heat of Sam's body. Wesley closed his eyes and, for an instant, could almost imagine this was just the two of them, the way they'd always been.

No. He couldn't let himself fall back into this.

"I'll be interested to hear what Cyrus thinks," Wesley said as he disentangled himself from Sam and backed away.

"Yeah." Sam wore an unreadable expression.

"We'd better head back," Wesley said in an effort to shrug off his discomfort. "I promised Bob in props that I'd stop by this morning to approve the new weapons."

"Sure. Thanks for listening."

Wesley nodded. "No problem."

Chapter Sixteen

WESLEY MADE it to the set the next morning later than planned. His meeting with Bob Fleming to come by and approve the new swords for the fight sequence being filmed had been moved to the afternoon. He'd tried calling Carl again and, as usual, had only reached his voice mail.

Stop thinking the worst. You know he's busy. But with each day Wesley spent with Sam, his defenses crumbled a bit more.

When he reached the beach access, he slipped off his shoes and walked through the warm sand toward the area where they'd been filming the night before. It was deserted except for a few bleary-eyed assistants who stood watch over the equipment as several people—fans, Wesley guessed—looked on with curiosity.

"What's up?" he asked Claire, one of the assistants.

"Sander's giving an interview," she answered and pointed toward a crowd of people gathered a few hundred feet away. "*Night Out Hollywood* is broadcasting live from the set."

Wesley thanked her before making his way toward the pavilion, an open-air theater built on a concrete platform near a large beachfront development. The building, usually filled with a crowd of extras waiting around for their next scene, was completely surrounded with people, some standing on the fixed benches to get a better view. Although Wesley recognized some of the bystanders, most appeared to be fans who had probably made their way over from Southport on the early ferry.

Someone touched Wesley on the shoulder, and he turned to see Jeffrey. "What's going on?" Wesley whispered.

"I'm not sure. I didn't hear anything about it until this morning. *Night Out Hollywood* is interviewing Sander and Mr. Eastman." Jeffrey guided Wesley through the crowd to the side of the theater.

On the dais, a woman with perfectly coiffed blonde hair sat in a tall director's chair facing Sam and Cyrus. "Filming on an island is a challenge, of course," Sam was telling the interviewer, Tammy Blankenship, a woman Wesley recognized as someone who'd interviewed Sam before. "But the location is perfect, since Stede Bonnet used to sail these waters."

Jeffrey motioned Wesley closer, then waved at Sam, who grinned back at them.

"I'll bet you were thrilled that Sander was able to fill in at the last minute," Tammy said.

"More than thrilled," Cyrus answered with a nod in Sam's direction. "When Van Carrington left the film at the eleventh hour, I wasn't sure what we would do. But Sander graciously stepped in and saved the day. I couldn't be more pleased with the outcome."

"I hear there are some significant changes planned," Tammy said, leaning forward as if she were waiting to be let in on a huge secret. "Will you tell us what you have in store for us?"

"I think I'll let Sander answer that question. He's the one who sold me on the idea. I can say, though, that I'm very excited about the new direction for the film."

"Sander?" Tammy shifted in her seat to meet Sam's gaze. "Will you tell us about it?"

"I'd be happy to." Sam glanced out at the audience and flashed them his brilliant smile, then turned and met Wesley's gaze again. Several women squeaked their appreciation, and the crowd buzzed with excitement. "The movie will explore a little-known theory about why Stede Bonnet left his comfortable life and his wife to become a pirate."

"And what theory would that be?"

"That Stede Bonnet, the gentleman pirate, was gay." Sam sat back in his chair. The amphitheater buzzed with excited chatter.

"Now that *is* quite the announcement," Tammy said, taking the news with such grace that Wesley was sure she'd known all along. No wonder Sam had gotten the entire *Night Out Hollywood* crew to fly to North Carolina at the drop of a hat.

"We're thrilled to be on the cutting edge with this film," Cyrus put in. "It's high time we add gay pirates to the lexicon."

So Sam had convinced Cyrus. Well, kudos for that. It wasn't as if the production had been faithful to history before.

"We realize this is a departure from the traditional history of Stede Bonnet," Sam added. "We want to be sure to handle the subject in a sensitive way." At least Sam was as good as his word. Maybe they would do this right and salvage the film in the process.

"I hear you've got an expert in pirate history working on the film. What does he have to say about this new angle?" Tammy asked.

Sam looked directly at Wesley, and Wesley immediately realized he'd miscalculated. Nothing Sam did was by accident. Jeffrey had led him here because Sam had planned it. *Time to hightail it.*

"You can ask him yourself, Tammy." Sam got up from his seat and had jumped off the stage before Wesley could make it out of the crowd. Several people shouted with obvious pleasure, and the camera panned out to the audience. "This is Professor Wesley Coolidge, our resident pirate expert."

Wesley glared at Sam, who ignored him and led him onto the stage, where someone clipped a microphone onto his collar. He stared at the lights and tried to keep from blinking. What the hell was Sam doing, dragging him into this discussion? "I... well," he began haltingly, "the theory that Stede Bonnet was gay is... er... unproven." He was going to strangle Sam when he got the chance.

"Professor Coolidge is correct," Sam said, unfazed. "There's no proof Stede Bonnet was gay. But it's as good a theory as any about why he left his plantation, wife, and kids behind for a pirate's life. Why not?"

"There are some historians who believe pirates were quite accepting of homosexual relationships," Wesley heard himself say. "Some of it was situational, of course. An entirely male crew and months at sea. Other than the occasional female pirate, of course."

"That's fascinating information, Professor," Tammy said with a wink in Sam's direction.

Sam shot Wesley a sloppy grin. Oh, he was *so* going to strangle Sam!

Wesley took a deep breath, regaining his focus. "There are some who believe entire communities of pirates lived in openly gay relationships called *matelotage* and shared far more than just the spoils of their piracy."

Good God, I sound like I'm lecturing to my class! Wesley's cheeks grew hot at the realization.

"Fascinating information, Professor. Well you've all heard it first here. Gay pirates in gay marriages."

"They weren't really—" Wesley began to protest.

"Which leads perfectly into our next topic," Tammy said all too smoothly. "Gay marriage."

Thank God that's over. Wesley drew a long breath and began to walk back to his seat, but Sam blocked his path. "Great topic," Sam said. "And one we need to hear more about." He took Wesley by the elbow and led him back to the stage.

"I'm sure you don't need my help with this one," Wesley muttered under his breath.

"But I do." Sam grinned at him, and the hair on the back of Wesley's neck stood at attention. He was definitely up to something.

"Excellent choice of words," Cyrus put in.

"Sander," Tammy began, "do I hear another announcement coming?"

Sam wasn't going to…. *No, he wouldn't, would he?* Fucking hell! Wesley was *so* screwed.

"Indeed you do." Sam took Wesley by the hand and pulled him back in front of the cameras.

Oh shit.

"And it's an announcement I should have made years ago, Tammy," Sam said blithely.

"Sam—Sander," Wesley said, "I really don't think—"

"A few years ago," Sam continued, "I made a huge mistake." He smiled at Tammy, who pursed her lips and looked back at him with barely disguised glee. "It was in an interview with you, in fact."

Crap. Now Wesley remembered where he'd seen Tammy before. *The* interview. The one that had brought it all home for Wesley.

"I said something that wasn't true. Not exactly a lie," Sam added, "but the effect was worse than a lie." He turned so that he faced Wesley. "You asked me about my costar. I said something about not kissing and telling. I said no one owned my heart. That wasn't the case. I should have answered honestly." Sam squeezed Wesley's hand.

Wesley swallowed hard and braced himself. "Sander, this isn't the time to—"

"I should have told you I was a married man. And that I married the love of my life nearly ten years ago. And that man is Professor Wesley Coolidge."

It took a moment for Sam's words to sink in, but when they did, Wesley's heart took off at a gallop. For ten years they'd hidden their relationship. Ten years of worrying that Sam might be outed and his career destroyed. Ten years of wishing they didn't have to hide. Ten years that weighed heavily on their marriage. And now that it was out there—the truth they'd kept secret—Wesley didn't know what the hell to feel.

When Wesley finally came back to himself, the crowd was on its feet, screaming and applauding wildly. Tammy was motioning to the camera crew to zoom in on Wesley's face. It was all too much—the noise, the chaos, the cacophony of emotions. Wesley glanced at Sam, who now watched him with a furrowed brow, as if he'd hoped for an entirely different response.

"Where did you get married?" someone shouted.

Then another called out, "What's it like living with a superstar like Sander?"

"Is it true Sander sleeps naked?" a woman—Tammy—asked as she shoved a mic in his face.

Shit. He had to get out of here. He looked desperately for a way off the stage that wasn't already blocked. Nothing. Everything was closing in on him, and the panicked feeling in his gut made his head spin. Out of desperation, he turned toward the back of the stage and saw Jeffrey standing there.

Without looking back, Wesley took off at a near run and jumped off the stage and into the sand, nailing the landing like an Olympic gymnast. "Please," he told Jeffrey, grabbing his arm, "get me out of here."

"I… sure."

Wesley caught Jeffrey's nod in Sam's direction and Sam's wide-eyed expression of concern, then ran to the parking lot. "I don't care where you take me," Wesley said. "Just get me out of here."

Chapter Seventeen

"Have a seat," Sam told Wesley when he met him at the door.

"Thanks."

"You okay?" Sam asked.

"I… yes. I'm better now."

Sam frowned and tilted his head to one side "Sure?"

"Really." It was sort of the truth. After a few hours spent pacing at his own place, Wesley was much happier to be with someone, even if that someone happened to be Sam.

"I'll be back out in a flash. I just need to put the fish up." Sam gestured to the coffee table in the living room and added, "I poured you a glass of wine. Help yourself to more if you'd like."

"Thanks." Wesley took a deep breath and made a beeline for the living room. He sat on the couch and took a long sip of the wine. Before he realized it, he'd finished the glass. Wesley refilled his glass and stared at the empty fireplace as the realization of what Sam had just done began to sink in.

"I'm tired of the bullshit, Wesley," Sam said after being forced to attend yet another awards ceremony with one of his female costars. "Lorianna and I barely spoke all evening. Hanging out with her is about as appealing as Vladimir Putin in a Speedo."

"I'm sure the studio didn't care about the quality of the conversation." Disappointment flickered in Sam's eyes. "Sorry, Sammy." Wesley brushed Sam's cheek with his fingers. "I shouldn't have made light of it."

"It's okay. I know you don't like it any more than I do." Sam took his hand and kissed it. "I didn't marry you to hide you away."

"And you didn't marry me to tank your career," Wesley pointed out. "But you're not hiding me away."

"Someday I'm going to tell the entire world to fuck off. Tell them I don't give a shit what they think of me. Or us."

Wesley pushed the memory away and rubbed the bridge of his nose. *Why did I accept the dinner invite?*

"Penny for your thoughts?"

Wesley wouldn't go there. He felt weak and at his wits' end. If he wasn't careful, he might do something stupid. "Just thinking the wine is excellent, as always," he lied. He needed to talk to Carl, to remind himself of reality and stop getting drawn into Sam's real-life movie.

Sam refilled Wesley's glass and set the bottle on the table. "Life's too short for crap wine. I still remember the bottle of Dom Pérignon we bought that weekend at Martha's Vineyard. You told me it was too extravagant."

"It was." Wesley remembered the weekend well. They'd rented a place by the beach to celebrate Sam's first real paycheck.

"I remember thinking that I wanted to earn enough money to buy you champagne every weekend."

"Seems you got your wish."

Sam pressed his lips together and nodded, but he looked nervous. "You okay?"

"A heads-up about the announcement would have been nice."

"You're mad at me."

Wesley sighed. "Yes. No. I don't know."

"You never wanted our marriage to be a secret."

"That's true."

"But you're mad at me."

Sam got that little-boy-lost look on his face, and Wesley knew he was a goner. "I'm not mad. Not really. But why now?" Wesley knew the answer, but he wanted Sam to say it.

"Because I don't want to lose you. I don't want this divorce."

"Sam, I—"

"Please, Wesley," Sam said, "I know I didn't give you what you wanted. I want to make it up to you."

Wesley heard the sound of something sizzling on the stove and caught the faint whiff of something burning.

Sam shot to his feet. "Shit! That's the rice."

Wesley sighed as Sam ran to the kitchen. Flowers and poetry. Kisses and great sex. To begin with, there'd been far more to their relationship. Sam had needed him and his support. Sam had been shaky and unsure of himself back then, when his career was just getting off the ground. But now….

Wesley set his glass down and leaned back against the cushions. It would be so easy. *Too* easy. But what would have changed? Sam's career would always keep him on the road. They'd make the effort to see each other more regularly, but eventually it would end up the same. Wesley couldn't take that again. Sam didn't need him.

"Sorry about that." Sam refilled their glasses and sat next to Wesley. "Crisis averted."

"Good."

"So what about it, Wesley? About us?"

Wesley rubbed his mouth. He didn't want to hurt Sam—Lord knew he'd hurt him enough when he'd filed for divorce.

"Wesley," Sam said, desperation like a knife's edge cutting his voice. "I got the papers. I know you said you weren't happy. I know we haven't been seeing enough of each other, but I love you. You know that, right? Because I can't live without you, and I don't want to lose you."

"You don't have to answer now," Sam said, as if he knew Wesley's answer wouldn't be the one he wanted to hear. "Just think about it. Okay?"

"Sam, I—"

The timer buzzed and Sam once again bounded into the kitchen. "Dinner," he announced.

This wasn't going to be easy. It would hurt again. *And again, and—*

"So what plans do you have for the weekend?" Sam asked casually as he set a dish full of food down in front of Wesley.

Wesley stared at the plate. Fish, perfectly grilled with a mango pico de gallo he knew Sam had made himself, miniature zucchini and summer squash and tiny red carrots. Perfect. All of it.

Wesley still hadn't heard back from Carl, but he'd gone ahead and booked a flight anyhow. He didn't want to take the chance that there might not be any seats left. If he didn't see Carl soon....

"Have you thought any more about sailing to Ocracoke for the weekend? There's plenty of room if you'd like to come. I know you were talking about going to New York, but the weather's supposed to be beautiful. Not too hot."

Wesley knew he shouldn't have accepted Sam's dinner invitation. So why the hell was he here, doing this to himself again? *Because he's Sam, and no matter what you tell yourself, you still care about him.*

"...along for a sail tomorrow since we have a day off? ... Wesley? Everything okay?"

Fuck those deep blue eyes and that slightly crooked smile. Fuck the man for being a great cook. Fuck him for being funny. Fuck him for being so *kind*.

Wesley stood abruptly, almost knocking over his nearly finished glass of wine. "I have to go."

"But you haven't touched your food," Sam protested.

Wesley shook his head and made his way to the front door, but Sam got there first. "Wesley, please. I know I wasn't much of a husband to you. I know the last three years have been hard for y—"

"I need to leave." Wesley blinked back tears. "I thought I could handle this. I was wrong. I can't be your friend."

"Wesley… no…." Sam pulled Wesley close. "I'll do better this time. We can be friends too."

Wesley sniffled against Sam's chest. *Get it together.* He didn't want Sam to see him cry. He *wouldn't* let Sam see it. He needed to be strong.

"Give me a second chance. Please?"

It would be so easy to say yes. But what would that accomplish? They'd had three years to work things out. This was about ending things and the pain that came with it. They'd both be hurting for a while. That was normal, right?

"Wesley?" Sam lifted Wesley's chin.

Wesley knew his eyes must be red. He didn't want Sam to see that, but having Sam this close made him forget that he cared.

"I love you, Wesley. I always have. Please. Let me show you how much."

Wesley blinked back more tears. This was all going wrong. He was over Sam, or as over him as he'd ever be. Sam was the past. Carl was the present and hopefully Wesley's future. Everything had been going so well. Wesley was happy without Sam, wasn't he?

Sam slipped an arm around Wesley's waist and gazed at Wesley with *that* look. The one Wesley had fallen for years ago. The one that made Wesley's knees turn to jelly.

Sam leaned in. Just another inch and he'd be kissing Wesley. Just another inch and—

"No." Wesley pulled away. "I'm not doing this again."

"Wesley, I—"

"You'll what? You'll do things differently this time?"

"I came out," Sam said.

"The divorce wasn't about that." Anger infused Wesley's heart, displacing the grief that seemed to have taken up residence there. "I mean, I'm glad you did, and I don't mind if the world knows I was married to you—"

"*Are* married to me. We're still married, Wesley."

The bewildered look on Sam's face was all Wesley needed to know he'd made the right choice. Sam had never understood, and he still didn't.

"This was never about being out, Sammy." Wesley drew a long breath and stood straighter now. He could do this. He *would* do this. "It was about *us*. Being there for me, even if it was over the phone. Me being there for *you*. You needing me."

"I need you, Wesley."

"Then why didn't you call me? Why was I the only one who reached out?"

Sam frowned. "I was the one putting so much shit on you. I was the one on the road all the time. I didn't want to bother you."

"I *wanted* you to bother me," Wesley nearly shouted. "When things started to go wrong, I told you that."

"I know, but you were putting up with my insane schedule. The last thing I wanted to do was dump my shit at your doorstep."

"You really don't get it, do you?" Wesley fought to release the tension in his neck and shoulders. He remembered the feeling of frustration only too well. "Marriage isn't only about romance. It's not just about dinners and walks on the beach. It isn't just about sex. If it had been just about those things...."

"You thought by bringing me here, you'd get me to change my mind." Wesley shook his head. "But it's the opposite. I *know* now that we can never make it work. You do everything you think you should to get me back. You want me to love you."

"Yes. I do. I want—"

"I *do* love you, Sam. I still love you. I've loved you forever."

"Then stay with me. Please." Sam's voice caught as he spoke.

"I'm done, Sam. *We're* done. I've moved on." *You can do this. You have to tell him.* "We're not good for each other."

"We were great togeth—"

"To begin with." Wesley knew this wasn't entirely true, but he didn't want to revisit all the great times. Not now. "But we haven't really been together in years."

"But we get along so well. I like being with you, and you—"

"Getting along isn't enough," Wesley said. "We don't feel like a couple. It's like we're running in the same direction, but we're not on the same team. And I can't live like that, Sam." *That* was the truth. Wesley struggled against his tears. "I just can't. I've moved on. I've found someone who knows about my life. Someone who leans on me when he has a bad day."

"I'm trying to be that person. I'm trying to change."

"I know you're trying to change, but you're going in the wrong direction." Wesley's tears now fell in earnest. "And I feel like such a shit right now because of it, because I know how hard you're trying."

"Then tell me what to do." Sam sounded desperate now.

"I don't know. I don't know what you can do to change things. I only know I can't go through that again. The weeks without hearing from you. The way it felt like we were strangers when we saw each other. The way it felt like I was a guest in your house. You were a guest in my life." Not loneliness, but aloneness. Wesley brushed off the thought that on this point, he'd begun to feel a bit of déjà vu with Carl.

"I'll give it up for you," Sam said. "I've got enough money saved that I won't be a burden to you."

"Give it up?"

Sam nodded. "My career. Anything if you'll give us another chance."

Wesley stared at Sam. "Sammy. My sweet Sammy. You'd die without your work." He reached out and touched Sam's cheek, pressing his fingers against the warmth of Sam's skin.

"I wouldn't—"

"Or you'd come to hate me for taking it from you. And it wouldn't change anything." Wesley sighed. "I thought about giving up my job. About hopping on a plane and figuring things out when I got to LA." He'd actually purchased the plane ticket. "But then I started thinking. For the first time, I *thought* about us instead of just feeling things. And I realized we can love each other and just not work out together. Right person, wrong time.

"We had a great time. When things were good, I was happy. Please, Sammy," he said, his voice breaking, "you have to let me go."

"I can't." Sam gazed back at him with watery eyes. Sam never cried. Wesley was doing this to Sam, all because he'd been weak and hadn't cut things off. Because he still loved Sam, right or wrong.

"You have to. For both of us."

"But Wesley, I—"

"I can't see you anymore, Sammy. Can't be your friend. At least not now. Maybe someday." Wesley breathed in and out a few times, finally coming close to mastering his emotions. "Let me go. Please. It's over between us. I don't want to hurt anymore."

Sam blinked and his Adam's apple bobbed. He stood silently. Stoically. Wesley knew Sam finally understood his resolve, and the realization nearly killed him.

"Good-bye, Sam."

Wesley didn't wait for Sam to respond. He closed the door behind him and walked the few blocks back to his place. He needed to see Carl. He needed to remind himself that life wasn't over, even if his marriage to Sam was.

CHAPTER EIGHTEEN

SAM WATCHED Wesley leave, then turned around and stared at the table. The perfect dinner. *The perfect disaster.* He'd thought—he'd *known*—Wesley would come around. But instead of getting the happy ending he'd written, he'd ended up right back where he'd started. No, this was worse than where he'd started. Because when he'd made up his mind to do this, he'd had hope. Now there was nothing left.

Wesley was right. I suck at this relationship stuff. Everything Wesley had said was true. From the times when he'd been too tired to call Wesley just to check in to the times he'd figured he could deal with the problems of his runaway hit of a career without Wesley's—or anyone's—help.

Wesley had said Sam didn't need him. But it was worse than that. Sam didn't know *how* to need someone. Didn't know how to make someone *feel* needed.

Losing Wesley hurt more than he thought it could. But he'd done it to himself. He'd told himself that he'd never cheated on Wesley. But staying faithful to your husband wasn't enough to sustain a marriage. Wesley had reached out to him over and over again. What had he given Wesley? The bare minimum.

I was a selfish asshole. He'd sensed things slipping away, but he told himself things would get better and he'd make it up to Wesley. He'd never counted on Wesley having the strength to end things between them. He'd never seen Wesley as that strong.

"Sam?" Jeffrey stood in the open doorway. "Is everything okay?"

Wesley wasn't the only one who was right. Jeffrey had tried to warn him about Wesley needing something other than big romantic gestures.

"Sure. Everything's fine." The consummate actor. Mr. Perfect. *A perfect liar.*

"I thought Wesley was coming over for dinner."

"He left," Sam said.

"Oh. Things seemed to be going really well. After today…. You know, after you came out, I thought maybe the two of you might… um… start over again."

Sam shook his head. "I thought so too. I was wrong."

"You sure you're okay?" Jeffrey appeared unconvinced.

"Absolutely sure. Don't worry about me. Go enjoy your date. I gave you the night off, remember?"

Jeffrey blushed crimson. "I don't have a—"

"Cyrus talked nonstop about you," Sam said with a chuckle.

"Okay, so maybe we have a date."

"Good, because if you'd said you weren't going out with him, I'd have locked you both in one of the trailers just to get him to stop with the goo-goo eyes."

Jeffrey's face lit up. "We're having dinner in Southport. I… I might be a little late coming back."

"I spoke to Parker. We're not shooting tomorrow. She wants to rework the script over the holiday weekend. I won't need you until Monday, when we start shooting again." Sam had told Parker he'd be busy over the weekend, but seeing as Wesley had put an end to his fantasy plans, he'd be happy for something to keep his mind off things.

"Really? Great. Thanks, Sam." Jeffrey studied him for a moment, then asked again, "Are you sure you're okay?"

"Yeah, I'm sure."

"What you did today… coming out in front of the whole country? That was pretty cool."

Sam forced a smile. "Thanks."

Jeffrey nibbled his lower lip and shifted from one foot to the other. "What are you going to do next?"

"Do?" Sam shrugged. "Nothing. It was over a long time ago. I just didn't realize it."

"Oh." Jeffrey glanced down at his feet. "Is he going to stay on the island?"

"I don't know." The realization that Wesley had probably hightailed it on the ferry and wouldn't be back felt like a punch to his chest.

"I'm really sorry things didn't work out."

"Yeah," Sam said as he watched Jeffrey leave a minute later. "So am I."

CHAPTER NINETEEN

THE TAXI dropped Wesley off a block away from Carl's apartment around three in the afternoon. Carl and Wesley had found the place on a quick four-day trip to Guatemala only six weeks before, right after Carl had received news that his research grant had been funded. The last place Wesley wanted to be when his and Sam's marriage officially ended was in New York, where he and Sam had made their home, so when Carl had gone to scout Xela for a place to stay, Wesley had tagged along. Wesley had relished the idea of spending the summer with Carl and exploring the country when Carl wasn't working.

Now, as Wesley paid for two bouquets of roses from a nearby open-air market, he felt a sense of relief and of anticipation. It didn't matter that the beautifully clear skies that had greeted Wesley upon landing had given way to the typical afternoon showers. The volcanic mountains were now shrouded in clouds, but the rain couldn't dampen his spirits.

The past few weeks with Sam had pushed him to his limit. The constant reminders to himself that the island wasn't his reality—that his *real* life didn't include Sam—had frayed his nerves and weakened his resolve to look forward. Carl was his future and the promise of a life he'd dreamed of.

"Daniella," Wesley said in broken Spanish as the building's super met him out front, "thank you so much for having meeting me."

"Your Spanish is getting better, Professor Coolidge," she cooed as she ushered him quickly inside.

"Thank you. I've been doing studying." He handed her one of the bouquets. "And thank you for not telling my brain is keep empty. I mean secret. My brain is secret." He frowned. He didn't think he'd said that right, because Daniella put a hand over her mouth and was trying not to giggle.

"Señor Stephens has been working very hard. He and Señor Dalton have been traveling so much, I rarely see them."

"I know," he said. "I've had a hard talking him on the phone. I thought it will be easier that I now am here."

Daniella smiled knowingly at the remaining bouquet. "He's a lucky man." She pressed a key into his hand and added, "I hope you have a wonderful stay."

"Thank you so much for your help." He leaned in and pecked her on the cheek, then smiled back at her and headed down the hallway to the stairs. He reached the second-floor apartment and paused at the door to take a deep breath before letting himself in.

The apartment was much as he remembered it, with its handmade furniture and tile floors. Papers and books covered the small table in the middle of the room that served as both the living and dining area. The windows were open to the cool breeze, causing the thin drapes to flutter. Wesley closed the door behind him and stepped inside.

"Did you hear something?" a man said in English from the direction of the bedrooms.

"Probably the stray cat we saw in the hallway yesterday," said another voice, which Wesley recognized as Carl's. "I'll go take a look. You wait right there. And don't you move. Not when I've got you right where I want you."

The words had barely sunk in before Carl walked into the room. He was stark naked. He stared at Wesley, clearly disbelieving what he was seeing. "Wesley?" he croaked out.

Wesley stood dumbfounded. "I… I wanted to surprise you."

Carl glanced furtively at the afghan on the couch, then back toward the hallway, as if trying to decide what he should do. After another minute's delay, he snagged the throw and wrapped it around his waist. "Look, Wesley," he began, "I think maybe we should talk."

"Yeah," Wesley agreed. "That's probably a good—"

"Carl, baby, I thought you were coming right—" Robert stopped dead in his tracks. Not a stitch of clothing in sight. It took Wesley a moment to realize Robert's hands were tied behind his back with a thick red ribbon. A ribbon that matched the one tied around his cock.

Well, fuck me.

"This is where you're supposed to tell me this isn't what it seems," Wesley said when neither man spoke.

Carl glanced furtively at Robert, who looked back at Carl but appeared entirely at a loss for words.

Wesley just watched himself standing there, having some sort of crazy out-of-body experience. Then the reality of it all came crashing down and his temper blazed red-hot. "All right." He tossed the flowers onto the nearby couch. "I can see why you haven't been returning my calls," he said.

"Wesley, I…," Carl began, then apparently thought better of it and said nothing more.

"How long?" Wesley demanded. "How long have you...."

Neither man answered, but judging by the looks on their faces, they'd planned this well in advance.

"And your wife's mother?" he asked Robert. "She isn't sick at all, is she?"

More silence. Wesley gritted his teeth. "I think it's time for me to leave," Wesley said. "Sorry to interrupt your little game." He turned and quickly made his way to the door.

"My wife," Robert said as Wesley reached for the handle. "You won't... please, you can't tell her.... I'll be ruined. She'll hang me by the balls and send her lawyers to peck my eyes out."

Wesley closed his eyes and willed himself not to scream. Or strangle them both. *Calm. Stay calm.* He inhaled slowly, then turned around and faced them with his head held high. "Best of luck, Carl. You're going to fucking *need* it." He carefully closed the door and walked away.

"Señor Coolidge? Are you all right?" Daniella eyed him warily.

Did he look that bad? Probably. He forced a smile. "I am fucked," he said in perfect Spanish. Swearing, in any language, was a hell of a lot easier than small talk.

FOUR HOURS later, seated on an airplane for his return flight to North Carolina, Wesley finished a beer as he waited for takeoff. The only seat available on the flight had been first class. He didn't care that it had cost him an additional $2,000 over the cost of his original ticket—the booze was free and the male flight attendant attentive and attractive. Wesley's anger at catching Carl and Robert together began to ease, and hurt settled in like an unwelcome guest. How could he have been so naïve? Sure, he and Carl had only been together a few months, but Wesley thought he knew the man.

"We have a few more minutes before takeoff," the attendant said. "Can I get you anything else to drink?"

"Bourbon, please."

"Of course, Professor Coolidge."

Wesley leaned back against the seat and watched the baggage handlers work. Numb couldn't describe how disconnected he felt at that moment. For one quick minute, he'd actually considered booking the flight to New York and dealing with whatever legal bullshit not returning to the set might mean for him. But in spite of how shitty he felt at that moment, he knew he'd need something to focus on. Sam's new direction for the film intrigued him, and New York seemed emptier than ever with no teaching and no one to spend what was left of the summer with. Plus the money was good.

He knocked back the bourbon in two quick gulps and fell asleep as the plane left the ground.

CHAPTER TWENTY

WESLEY STEPPED off the Bald Head Island ferry at nearly six o'clock, having sent his bag ahead to be delivered to his house. The air felt heavy, and the walkway around the harbor was wet from the rain. The gray sky mirrored the numb feeling in his heart. He knew he should shrug off the gloom, but an image of Carl and Robert entwined in red ribbons lingered in his mind like the clouds over the island. *Or a bad porno.*

The flight attendant had woken him up when they'd landed in Dallas, and he'd slept through most of the flight back to Wilmington. Wesley had considered calling Marnie to arrange transportation back to the island, but the taxi driver had been happy to take him to the ferry landing in Southport, and the hundred-dollar cab fare was nothing compared to what Wesley had just wasted on the trip to Guatemala.

Rain fell in a warm drizzle as he made his way from the ferry landing to the bar overlooking the Bald Head Island Marina. He settled in at one of the tables and ordered a double shot of tequila.

While he waited for the waitress to bring his drink, he pulled out his cell to check his e-mail. He scrolled past a half-dozen e-mails until he saw it. A message from the Restus Foundation. The final word on his grant proposal. He swallowed the tequila and tapped the screen.

Thank you for your submission to the Restus Foundation. We regret to inform you that we will not be funding your proposal at this time. We receive many more applications than we can fund. You should not take our unwillingness to fund your proposal as an indication of its quality. We encourage you to resubmit at a later date.

The screen glowed brightly in his hand, imprinting dark spots on his retinas. He turned the phone off and set it facedown on the table as the server delivered his drink.

The sharp blast of the ferry's horn sounded, and he watched, only half seeing it, as it pivoted off the dock and made its way out of the marina. Water dripped onto the deck from the awning overhead and rose as fog when it touched the warm wood. He downed the tequila, ignoring the burn at the back of his throat.

Two weeks ago he'd told himself he had everything he'd ever wanted. He'd finally gotten the promotion to full professor. He had a great new apartment on the Upper West Side that he'd purchased with his own money. He had a near guarantee of a half-million-dollar grant and the possibility that it would be renewed in five years. He had a new relationship with someone who understood him and his career. He'd put the pieces of his heart back together and put Sam and their failed marriage behind him.

Now he had nothing.

Just perfect. First Carl and fucking Robert. *Or was that Carl* fucking *Robert?* Now a fucking *second*-round grant proposal totally blown off without any suggestions for how he could fix whatever the grant reviewers hadn't liked. What kind of fucking fantasy world had he been living in to think things were finally going his way?

"Another round?" the server asked.

Wesley took a deep breath, brushed his slightly damp hair from his face, and didn't bother to force a smile. "Another double. Thanks."

"Of course." The woman smiled sympathetically. "Something to eat? We got some fresh shrimp in this afternoon. I could—"

"Just the tequila, please."

"Certainly."

Wesley stared at a school of fish that began to jump into the air in the ferry's wake. A few of the passengers pointed and laughed. Wesley dry-scrubbed his face as he watched another large fish vault into the air and slap the surface of the waves.

"That's gotta hurt," someone said from a few tables away. Another woman laughed as more fish jumped out of the water, then fell back with audible splashes. Over and over again they jumped.

The server set two shots of tequila on the table. Wesley drank one, then the second. The warm buzz of the beer and bourbon was long gone, and he wanted it back. As the alcohol began to blur his thoughts, he watched the fish launch themselves up, then crash back down. He wondered vaguely if they were eating bugs or being chased by a bigger fish.

By now a small group of people had gathered at the edge of the ferry landing and were shouting and taking videos on their cell phones.

"Sir?" the waitress asked as she set the empty shot glasses on her tray. "Can I get you something else?"

"How much for the whole bottle?"

AT AROUND eight thirty, Sam walked the few miles into town. "I'll call you if I want a ride back," he told Jeffrey when he refused his offer of a ride. "Promise."

Jeffrey clearly thought he was crazy to walk in the rain. Sam didn't care. Since Wesley left the island on Saturday morning, Sam had been distracted. Lost. He'd done his job. They'd reworked the script, and Cyrus had approved the changes. He'd pretended everything was fine. But *nothing* was fine.

Jeffrey drove off in the direction of Cyrus's rental home. Sam knew he was trying not to bounce with excitement at the prospect of another date—he wouldn't begrudge Jeffrey his happiness. *At least someone's happy.*

He needed to shrug off the gloom. He'd spent the past six months working toward one goal: getting Wesley back. And he'd fucked it up as surely as he'd fucked up their relationship. He'd pushed Wesley away when he'd meant to bring him back. And in the process, he'd realized they really *were* over.

Wesley was right. It's time to move on. If Wesley couldn't see that he was trying his hardest, it wasn't fucking *worth it* to keep trying. Even he had his limits. Wesley had pushed him beyond them. *Fuck him. If he can't realize we were good together, well, just fuck him.* Only he wasn't angry with Wesley. Not really. He was pissed as hell at himself.

Somewhere along the way, trying to get Wesley back had become his focus. He'd gone into it for the best of reasons: because he loved Wesley. It had become a job like any other. He did his research. He plotted his approach, and he understood the characters. He'd played his part well, but it hadn't worked. He didn't even know what to do if he *did* get Wesley back. He had no fucking clue how to make things better.

Time to let it go.

By the time he climbed the stairs to the bar at the edge of the harbor, Sam's running shoes were pretty much soaked. He pulled off the hood of his rain jacket and the server's eyes grew wide. He plastered on a smile as she giggled and led him over to a table on the deck.

"Can I get you a drink, Mr. Carson?" she said as he hung his dripping jacket on the back of his chair.

"Scotch. Neat, please."

"Of course." She flashed him a big smile, then leaned in and handed him a menu. "Can I have your autograph? Can you make it out to me? Paula?"

"Sure." He signed the menu and she trotted off a moment later.

From his seat, he could see *Neverland* at the docks. If the weather was better, he might take her out in the morning or maybe kayak on Bald Head Creek. He wasn't in any of the shots tomorrow, and he needed something better to do with the time off than sleep in. Sleep never helped when he felt antsy. He needed to get out and do something. Anything. Even a morning run in the rain would be better than this.

Paula came back a few minutes later with his drink and a basket of hush puppies "on the house." He thanked her and sighed as he took a long sip and leaned back in his chair to watch the rain, which now fell in heavy drops that made the water dance.

"Are you enjoying your time on the island?" she asked.

Sam didn't feel much like chatting. "I am. It's a beautiful place."

"Carol…. Oh, you don't even know who she is!" Paula giggled, then added, "She's my boss. She said that big boat there is yours. Is that true?"

"Yep."

"Do you take her out a lot? Have big parties aboard?"

He shook his head. "I've been too busy to sail her recently."

"Did you see the jumping fish before?" she asked.

He wished she'd go away, but he wouldn't be rude. "No. I'm afraid I missed it."

"They were flying all over the place! I can show you a video if you'd—"

"Paula?" A fortyish woman Sam had seen behind the bar a few times gave Paula a scathing look.

"That's Carol."

Sam figured as much. "Oh."

"I'd better get back to work or she'll be really pissed at me," Paula said. "But if you want, I'll show you the video later, okay?"

"Thanks." Sam watched her leave, then took a long sip of his drink before dipping a hush puppy into a small container of ketchup and popping it into his mouth. They were quite good, and his trainer hadn't come with him from LA, so he grinned to himself and ate another one.

I'm such a rebel.

Carol waved at him as she walked by and set some food on a neighboring table. She must have told the table's occupants who he was, because Sam heard the click of a cell phone camera. He smiled at the diners, then looked around the bar. Considering the lousy weather, it was pretty crowded.

For the first time, Sam noticed a man sitting at a table at the far end of the deck. Shoulders slumped, the man supported his head with a hand to his cheek and stared blankly out at the harbor. It took him a moment, and then Sam was shocked to realize that man was Wesley. Everything about Wesley seemed wrong, from the tangle of his hair and untrimmed beard to his rumpled trousers and the plain white undershirt he wore.

Sam set his drink down, took a deep breath, and walked over to Wesley's table. "Wesley?"

"Hmm?" Wesley blinked a few times and looked at Sam with red-rimmed, glassy eyes, then sat up abruptly, teetered in his chair, and nearly fell over. He managed to right himself before Sam could offer to help him, and said in an overly casual tone, "Oh. Hi, Sammy."

"You okay?"

Wesley frowned and turned away from Sam.

"I didn't think you'd be back from Guatemala until Wednesday." Okay, so maybe he could have been a bit gentler with the delivery, but the realization that Wesley had cut his trip short had him slightly confused.

"How d'you know 'bout Guatemala? Oh, right," Wesley added before Sam could answer, "you probably talked to Viv. What'd you offer her this time? A bit part in your next movie?"

"I didn't ask—"

"Go away." Wesley struggled to his feet, pushed Sam away, then pulled his wallet from his pants. When he tried to open it, it fell from his hand. He bent down to retrieve it but teetered and grabbed the chair as he lost his balance.

"I'll take care of it." Sam picked up the wallet.

Wesley grabbed the wallet from Sam and managed to pull a few twenties out. "I can do it m'self." He wobbled again, and this time Sam steadied him with a hand to his elbow.

"Please go away. Don't need your help." Wesley pushed Sam away and tried to shove the wallet back in his jeans but missed and dropped it. He stood straighter now but walked slowly and deliberately as he headed for the stairs.

Sam retrieved the wallet. He'd give it back to Wesley later. He flagged down the waitress and pressed a hundred-dollar bill into her hand. "This should take care of it." He ignored her squeak of pleasure as he walked quickly over to Wesley.

"I told you to go away." Wesley contemplated the stairs as though they were an obstacle course.

"How are you going to get home?"

"Driving my golf cart. I left it here b'fore. I don't need help," Wesley finished with a half cough, half hiccup.

"You're in no shape to drive back to your house." Sam maneuvered in front of Wesley. At least that way, if Wesley fell, Sam could probably catch him before his head hit the sidewalk.

"It's a fucking golf cart. A two-year-old can drive it."

"Same difference. You can barely walk."

"Please move over or I'll 'unch you." Wesley furrowed his brow. "Punch you."

"Not unless you let me drive you home," Sam insisted.

Wesley glared at him. "Suit yourself."

Sam backed down the stairs, watching Wesley as he followed and breathing deeply when he made it safely down. "Keys?" he asked when Wesley stared blankly at him.

Wesley dug in his pocket, then tossed a key ring to Sam, missing by such a wide margin that Sam had to jump to catch them or they'd have ended up in the water. If Wesley noticed the NBA-worthy move, he didn't let on, instead making his way on wobbly legs over to the parking lot between the restaurant and the ferry landing.

"Which one is it?" Sam asked.

Wesley stared at him as if he'd been speaking another language. "What?"

"Which golf cart."

"Oh." Wesley looked momentarily flustered, even a bit sheepish.

"You don't remember which one is yours, do you?"

"Of course I do." Wesley blinked a few times, then made his way over to one of the golf carts and pointed. "This one."

"Okay." Sam slid into the driver's seat and put the key into the ignition. It didn't fit. "Wesley?"

Wesley frowned, dry-scrubbed his face, and looked around. "That one," he said with absolute confidence.

Sam raised his eyebrows but said nothing, instead taking a seat and inserting the key. "You're 0 and 2. Care to try another?"

"Oops!" Wesley giggled. "It's that one," he said and pointed to an eight-seater.

"You sure about that?"

Wesley looked at the cart, nearly tumbling out of the current cart as he did, then turned to look at Sam and fell into his lap. Finally righting himself with Sam's help, he met Sam's eyes and announced, "Yesh. 'M positive." Then he wobbled over to the cart and lay down on the very back row of seats. He yawned and said, "Home, Jeeves!"

Sam sighed and tried the key again. No dice. Clearly, this was going to take some time.

Ten minutes later they drove away from the docks in a bright red golf cart. The *only* bright red golf cart in the entire parking lot, Sam pointed out.

"I don't 'member it being red," Wesley said defiantly. "Maybe someone painted it while I was out of town."

"Yep."

Wesley started singing something about tying a yellow ribbon, then seemed to think better of it, because he muttered something about red ribbons and didn't sing again.

They rode in silence toward the beach. The rain had tapered once more to a light drizzle. Sam liked the mist that hung over the island. It gave the place a peaceful, almost Zen-like feeling. Zen was good.

"You going to talk about it?" he asked Wesley.

Wesley shook his head.

"Okay."

They reached the part of the island where the topography rose and fell. The cart started to slow as they reached the third hill. With each successive hill, it slowed even more, until it slipped backward so much that Sam had to use the parking brake. Finally it stopped completely.

"Fuck."

Wesley startled awake—Sam hadn't even realized he'd fallen asleep. "What?" Wesley gasped.

"Did you charge the cart before you left?"

"Charge?"

"Time to walk," Sam said with a sigh.

"Walk?" Wesley stared at Sam.

"You're full of questions tonight."

"Hmm."

"Out you come."

Wesley took Sam's offered hand. "Are we there yet?"

"We're about a mile from your house." Maybe more, but it wasn't worth trying to explain that to Wesley, who looked positively green.

"Oh." Wesley eyed Sam's outstretched arm, sidestepped his way out of the cart to avoid Sam, then teetered and landed on his ass. "Ow!"

"Need some help?"

"I can do it myself," Wesley growled.

"Have at it." Sam moved the cart onto the shoulder as Wesley tried several times to get back to his feet, with little success. Only the knowledge that Wesley must be entirely miserable kept him from laughing outright. Wesley might have trampled on his heart two days before, but Sam had no right to enjoy his misery. He knew Wesley well enough to know he didn't drink himself sick as a hobby.

Wesley covered his face with his hands.

"Hey," Sam said. "You okay?"

"No."

"Need a hand up?"

Wesley nodded. Sam pulled him gently to his feet. Wesley released his grip on Sam almost immediately, then mumbled, "Thanks."

"No problem. You good to walk?"

Wesley nodded again. He took a few steps, faltered, then recovered before Sam could grab his arm. "'M fine, Sam."

"Okay."

"Did you know it's raining?" Wesley asked.

Sam nodded and wiped his face on his sleeve.

The rain stopped as they made their way down the deserted road. Sam hoped someone might drive by and give them a lift, but apparently the rain had deterred many of the residents from getting out and about.

They had just crested the hill overlooking the development where the studio had rented houses when Wesley stopped suddenly. "I don't feel so good," he said so quietly Sam almost missed it.

"You need a hand?" Sam stepped closer to Wesley.

"Dunno." Wesley rubbed his face and shivered. "Can't see anything."

"Here, let me—" Sam's words were cut short as Wesley gasped, then collapsed into his arms. "Wesley?"

The only reply was a loud snore.

"Wesley." Sam shook his head. He had at least a half a mile to go. He considered calling Jeffrey, but he didn't want to interrupt his date. He supposed he could call someone else from the studio, but he didn't want them seeing Wesley like this. As much as he was at his wits' end dealing with Wesley, he knew Wesley would be mortified if anyone saw him this way.

He set Wesley gently down on the side of the road, pulled off the jacket he was wearing, and helped the unconscious Wesley into it. He zipped it up and pulled the hood over Wesley's head. At least he'd be a little warmer. Then he stood and hauled Wesley over his shoulder.

CHAPTER TWENTY-ONE

WESLEY ROLLED over and moaned. "Oh God. I'm gonna—" He sat up and vomited into a pot someone held out for him. After he finished retching, he looked up through hooded eyes and saw Sam at the side of the bed.

"Better?" Sam looked worried.

How totally embarrassing. Had he really managed to get drunk twice with Sam in close proximity? "I'm fine," Wesley lied. "Thank you." He was pretty sure there was nothing left in his stomach. Now if only his stomach would get the message.

"I'd offer you something to eat, but I'm thinking it may need to wait."

Wesley rolled over—more slowly this time—and pulled the covers over his head. Could he just die now and put them both out of his misery?

"HEY. SLEEPING beauty." Sam's voice. Wesley must have fallen asleep.

"Mmm."

"We need to get some water into you."

Wesley's mouth felt like the Sahara. Probably smelled like dead camel too. "Go away."

"Wesley, seriously. You've been sleeping all day. You puked your guts out. Repeatedly. And you haven't had anything to drink other than the booze."

"Please go away."

"Wesley... please."

Shit. His bladder felt like it was going to explode. "'Kay." Wesley pulled the covers off his head. Sam hadn't been kidding. It was dark outside. "Gotta pee." He tried to sit up, but the room spun.

"Let me help you."

Wesley let Sam steady him. It took a few minutes, but at last he was seated at the edge of the bed.

"I can help—"

"I'm fine." Wesley got to his feet and started to make his way across the room. Halfway there, he stopped as a wave of dizziness hit him. "Oh crap."

Sam caught Wesley as he teetered. "I gotcha. Let me help you."

This was what he'd come to? He was such a fucked-up mess that he didn't just need someone to help him pee, he needed his almost ex-husband? "Sam, please, it's bad enough."

"You need help, Wesley. I don't want you fall—"

"I hate it when you do the mother hen crap with me, you know."

Sam chuckled. "I know I'm a bit overprotective, but Wesley, you're in bad shape. I can—"

"I'm fine." Wesley pushed Sam away, lost his balance, and ended up on his ass looking up at Sam.

"Wesley, please let me help you? I was married to you for almost ten years. There's nothing I haven't seen, including you taking a piss. Look, I just want to make sure you're okay. That's all. No strings. Nothing else. I promise."

Wesley swallowed hard. The self-conscious and completely humiliated part of him warred with the near overwhelming urge to pee. "Okay."

Five minutes later, feeling humiliated but knowing there hadn't been another option, Wesley shuffled back to bed. Sam set a few pillows behind his back and pulled the covers up to his chest.

"I'm going to get you something to drink."

"I can't—"

"Just water."

"Okay. Thanks."

Sam offered him a reassuring smile and was gone a moment later. Wesley sighed and closed his eyes. He felt like shit. *Worse* than shit. And the hole in his heart…. He rubbed his eyes, which had begun to burn.

"Hey." Sam had walked back in the room.

"You don't have to do this, you know."

"I know." Sam handed him a glass. Wesley took it with a shaking hand and sipped.

"I'm sorry, Sam. I really am." Sam was being so kind to him, and what had he done in return? *I'm a schmuck.*

"For what? We all drink too much from time to time."

"You know that's not what I meant." Wesley stared at the water. "I shouldn't have snapped at you when all you wanted to do was make sure I didn't hurt myself."

"It's okay," Sam said. "I got the message. You need your space, and I was way too pushy."

"Sam, I—"

"You were right. I was a shitty husband to you. And yeah, I was angry when you told me to take a hike the other night." Sam paused for a moment, pressing his lips together and frowning. "But you were right."

Wesley exhaled a long breath. He had no words. He was tired. His body ached—no, his heart ached—and he couldn't think about anything. Not Carl, not the grant, and certainly not the ashes of their marriage. Not now.

Sam stood and took the empty glass from Wesley. "Try to rest," he said. "I'll be back later to check on you."

"Thanks." Wesley slid down in the bed, and Sam straightened the covers. Wesley closed his eyes and let his mind drift back to sleep.

"Come on, Sammy," Wesley shouted as he ran barefoot down the beach. "We're going to be late!" He caught Sam's hand and pulled him off the lounge chair.

Sam blinked up at him and yawned, then glanced at his watch. "We've got plenty of—" Sam yawned again. "—time. It's only four."

Wesley pulled harder. "It's five, Sam."

"Five?" This seemed to get Sam's attention, because he sat up and stared at Wesley. "But I—"

"Didn't change your watch. It's an hour later in the Dominican Republic than in the States."

"Fuck."

"Come on!" Wesley pulled Sam to his feet and they took off at a run down the beach, sand flying with each step.

"But I'm wearing my bathing suit."

"Your mom's bringing your clothes. Thank God her cell phone works here." Wesley hadn't paid any attention to the time either, but he'd been so nervous, he'd worn the white linen shorts and silk Hawaiian shirt they'd bought stateside to the beach.

By the time they reached the white pavilion at the edge of the pool, they were both gasping for breath and their legs were covered in sand. Sam's mother pulled him into an alcove while Venka tutted and helped Wesley brush the sand off his skin.

"Good of you two to make it," she said. "Now look at me."

Wesley did as he was told. She pulled something from her purse and proceeded to brush his wild hair into submission. "Thank you," he said meekly.

"We were beginning to wonder if you two were getting cold feet."

"We're already married, you know," he said. "This is—"

"This is the ceremony that counts. The one where you stand up in front of the people who love you and swear to stay together 'until death do you part.'" She straightened his collar. "Now take a deep breath."

"Venka—"

"Do it."

Wesley inhaled.

"Breathe out," she commanded.

He did.

"Okay." She picked up a fuchsia hibiscus. "Here."

"You're not putting that behind my ear."

She laughed. "I am not. It goes on your lapel. Or—I guess it's not a lapel—your collar. Here." She pinned the flower to the shirt, right over his heart.

"Thanks," he said.

"Well?" She glared at him, hands on her hips. "What are you waiting for, Wesley Coolidge?"

She pushed him playfully into the gazebo, and for the first time, he noticed it was covered in flowers. Inside, Lawrence Wilkins, the minister who had agreed to perform the marriage ceremony, waited for him with a knowing smile.

Wesley's mom joined them under the pergola, smiling broadly at Wesley. He kissed her on the cheek. "Thanks for coming."

"As if I'd miss my only son's wedding."

He was lucky and he knew it. Both she and Sam's parents had been nothing but supportive of their marriage. "Love you, Mom," he said.

She beamed. "I love you very much, Wesley."

Wesley turned in time to see Sam walking toward him. He looked good enough to eat—better, really—in his matching white shorts and floral shirt. The outfits had been Sam's idea. At first Wesley had resisted, but he was glad now they hadn't gone the tuxedo route as he'd wanted. This felt more real somehow. Fairy tale, yes, but that was Sam. The man who loved him even when he was still shy, epically awkward and geeky Wesley. The man with whom he was so happy to be spending the rest of his life.

Sam offered his hands, and Wesley clasped them in his own. "Wesley," he said.

"Hmmm?"

"Wesley?"

Wesley smiled back at Sam.

"Wesley, are you all right?"

Wesley opened his eyes.

"Hey." Sam gazed down at him with obvious worry. "You were talking in your sleep. I tried to wake you up, but I couldn't."

"Dreaming." *Remembering.* Shit. Why was he doing this? The little voice in his head whispered that *he* was the one who'd fucked things up with Carl because he hadn't been over Sam. Maybe if he'd given in and had sex with Carl—

"Wesley?"

"Huh?" Looking into those blue eyes just like he had all those years ago still made Wesley's chest tighten. His eyes burned. He'd thought he could deal. That he could move forward.

You also thought Carl was your future.

Everything had gone to shit.

"Wesley?" Sam's voice again, pulling him back to reality.

"I'm tired," Wesley lied. He rolled over and closed his eyes. Sam probably knew he wasn't really going to sleep, but he didn't call him on it.

"Sleep well, Wesley."

Wesley listened to Sam's bare feet on the wood floors. Only when he knew Sam had gone downstairs did he give in to his tears.

CHAPTER TWENTY-TWO

"RISE AND shine!" Sam said with as much enthusiasm as he could muster.

Wesley rolled over and pulled the pillow over his head. Not the reaction Sam had hoped for. He was worried about Wesley. Really worried. In all the years they'd been together, he'd never seen Wesley so down.

He'd left Wesley to his own devices. Wesley clearly deserved a good wallow—whatever had happened in Guatemala hadn't been good. But now Sam wondered when Wesley would pull himself out of his funk.

He'd called Wesley's assistant, Viv, and she'd confirmed at least part of why Wesley was a mess. "Since he was out of town, he had the Restus Foundation cc me on all correspondence," she told Sam. "The big grant... the one he'd been short-listed for...."

"He didn't get it."

"No." She sighed into the receiver. "He'd been hoping he would. The reviewers had such good things to say after the first round. But this time...."

Sam knew enough about the grant application process to understand this was about the worst news Wesley could have received. By asking an applicant to resubmit a grant proposal, the funder was saying the grant had some value, even if it didn't make the final cut. But a rejection letter like the one Viv read for Sam was more than just a slap in the face. It was a judgment. And as important as research was to Wesley, this was like someone had told him he was worthless.

Oh, Wesley. I'm so sorry.

Jeffrey had checked on Wesley the night before because Sam had been busy shooting a night scene. "He ate a few crackers," Jeffrey reported when Sam got back from work around two in the morning. "I couldn't get him to eat anything else."

At least Wesley hadn't locked the door. Not that Sam couldn't have gotten into the house—he'd done it before by charming one of the cleaning staff—but he'd promised Wesley he wouldn't use the master key to let himself in again, and he didn't want to break yet another promise.

"Wesley?" Sam lifted the pillow. "You can't stay in bed forever."

"Why not? I checked with Jeffrey. I'm not on the schedule for today."

Talking was better than not talking. "Because it's not good for you." Sam opened the curtains and cracked the windows to let in some fresh air. "We could go for a run," he offered when Wesley said nothing more.

"I'm fine. Really. You can go home now."

"Not going." There was no way in hell he was going to leave Wesley alone. Seeing him like this scared the crap out of Sam. How long could someone survive on a few crackers and a couple sips of water? It wasn't as though there was any extra fat on Wesley's body. "At least not until you eat something."

"Not hungry."

Sam sat on the edge of the bed. He hesitated a moment, then gently stroked Wesley's hair. To his surprise, Wesley didn't object.

"Why are you being nice to me?" Wesley asked after a few minutes passed.

"Why not?"

"Because I treated you like crap." Wesley still hadn't looked at him. "I said a lot of nasty things to you when you were trying to be nice."

"Nah. You were right. We're bad for each other. At least like that." Sam leaned against the headboard. "Took me a while to realize it." He wasn't all that sure he had realized it deep down. He wasn't willing to accept it entirely. Either way, though, he'd respect Wesley's decision to move on.

"Oh."

"Doesn't mean I don't worry about you, though." Sam withdrew his hand.

"Don't stop," Wesley whispered. "It feels... good."

"How much do you remember about the other night?" Sam asked gently.

"Enough."

"Ready to talk about it?"

Wesley seemed to consider this. "I don't think so," he said after a moment. "It's not you. It's just...." Wesley shuddered. "It hurts like hell."

"I'm sorry."

"Don't be." Wesley seemed to stare off at the wall. "My fault entirely." Sam wondered if Wesley was remembering something, but he didn't press him.

"No problem. We don't talk about it unless you want to."

"Thanks." Wesley closed his eyes as Sam continued to stroke his hair. A few minutes later, Wesley was sound asleep.

"WESLEY?" SAM set the tray of food on the bedside table and touched Wesley's back. Wesley stirred, then hid beneath the covers again. Outside, the sun had begun to rise. Another day, and Sam was about at his wits' end with worry. "Wesley. Wake up." Sam opened the curtains and miniblinds to let in the morning light.

"'M sleeping," Wesley muttered into the pillow, clearly trying to avoid the brightness.

"No, you're not. And you're going to sit up now and eat something."

"Not hungry."

"You're going to make me force-feed you, then?" Sam didn't want to do it, but he would.

"Please, Sam, just leave me alone."

"Not happening." Sam took a deep breath and reached underneath Wesley, turned him, and pulled him to a sitting position. "If this is the way it has to be, fine."

"Go away."

Sam gritted his teeth. "And let you act like a spoiled, self-destructive brat? No. You're going to eat something."

Wesley wouldn't meet his gaze.

"Wesley, look at me." When Wesley didn't respond, Sam said, "Come on, Wesley. Since when do you give up?"

Wesley shook his head. "Since I fucked up big-time."

"You fucked up?"

"I really don't want to talk—"

"I know you went to Guatemala to see Carl," Sam said.

"So you *do* know his name."

"Of course I do." Sam sighed. "I just pretended I didn't because I wanted to yank your chain."

"I figured as much."

"Things didn't go so well."

Wesley looked down again.

"Guess not," Sam said when Wesley didn't respond. "I'm really sorry about that."

Wesley looked up at him as if trying to figure out whether Sam really meant it. Sam didn't have to put on an act. He *was* sorry about it, even if he wasn't sorry the shithead was out of Wesley's life. He'd done a little research on Carl Stephens, and he hadn't been impressed by the string of men he'd worked his way through. Sam didn't like people using others, let alone people he cared about.

"Eat for me? Please?" Sam picked the tray off the table and set it on Wesley's lap.

Wesley stared at the soup and bread, then up at Sam. "You made me pumpkin soup?"

Sam smiled. "It's your favorite, isn't it?"

"But pumpkin soup… on an island… in the middle of the summer?" Wesley appeared genuinely moved. "You did that for me?"

"It's nothing." Sam had sent Jeffrey to Wilmington to find canned pumpkin when he hadn't been able to locate any on the island, but he wouldn't tell Wesley that. What mattered was that the gesture made Wesley happy.

"How can I thank you?"

"For the soup?" Sam chuckled. "You could start by eating it."

"I didn't mean that." Wesley smiled—the first smile Sam had seen from him since he'd returned to the island.

Sam knew what Wesley meant, but he said instead, "Go ahead."

Wesley complied, first tearing off a small piece of bread, then dipping it in the soup. "It's delicious," he said after he'd finished chewing.

Sam repressed a sigh, then sat in the chair near the bed and watched as Wesley ate all the soup and nearly all of the small baguette. His chest tightened, then grew warm as he allowed his emotions to take him wherever the hell they wanted. He was tired of acting the part of something he wasn't. Tired of pretending he didn't feel anything because if he *did* feel something, he might show it and frighten Wesley away.

He'd been miserable after Wesley had left. He'd finally realized what Wesley had been telling him all along: that their marriage was over and there was nothing he could do about it. The strangest part of that realization, though, was that Sam was afraid. Not afraid so much about their marriage ending, although that hurt like crap. No. Sam was afraid to lose Wesley's friendship.

TWO HOURS later Sam returned to Wesley's room. Jeffrey must have told Parker that Wesley wasn't feeling well, because she just smiled when Sam asked for another day off from shooting, then told Sam to make Wesley some matzo ball soup. "And don't you *dare* get sick too," she'd added, perhaps realizing she had sounded more motherly than she'd intended.

Wesley was sitting up in bed, reading a trashy romance novel. "These things are addictive," he said when Sam shot him a questioning look. "Charlotte just told Larimar she hates him."

Sam snorted. "Larimar? What kind of name is that?"

"A romantic one."

"How is it romantic if someone says they hate you?" Sam asked.

"No clue." Wesley waggled his eyebrows, then added, "But then she got all hot and bothered and—"

"Way too much information."

"They don't call them bodice rippers for nothing. And since when are you so squeamish about heaving bosoms? Oh, Master Bonnet," he parroted in a high voice, "you are *such* a gentleman."

"How about you accompany this gentleman outside for a bit," Sam replied in the accent he used for Stede Bonnet. "A stroll on the beach, perchance? Just to the water and back?"

Wesley appeared to consider the offer. "I stink," he said. "I look like warmed-over cow manure."

"You look a little rough around the edges," Sam agreed. "But no one's going to see you but me. Promise. And if you're feeling up to it when we get back, you can take a long shower. Or I'll draw you a bath."

"*Draw* me a bath?"

"I am a gentleman, after all," Sam replied with a wink. "Need some help getting dressed?"

"I think I can handle that myself." Wesley didn't look as sure as he sounded, but Sam let it go.

"Okay. I'll be waiting outside the room if you need me."

Wesley's jaw tightened visibly and he nodded. "Thank you," he said in an undertone. Sam fought the instinct to go to Wesley, sensing Wesley needed his space and needed to prove to himself that he could pull himself together without Sam's help.

THEY MADE their way to the beach a few minutes later, Wesley appearing pale but relatively steady on his feet. They left their shoes by the stairs and walked over the dunes and onto the sand.

"Sun feel good?" Sam asked.

"Yes." Wesley lifted his hands over his head and stretched. He made his way to the edge of the water and dipped his toes in. "I always loved the beach," he said, his tone wistful.

Sam watched as Wesley's feet sank into the wet sand with each successive wave, and he remembered the first time he and Wesley had gone to the beach together, years before. Jones Beach had been crowded, but they'd found a little patch of sand where they'd laid out the ratty blanket they'd brought along, and they'd sat there most of the day, just talking.

That was when Sam realized he was in love with Wesley. He'd never been in love before. Not like that. He'd known in that moment he didn't ever want to let Wesley go.

"Hey, Sammy! Look!" Wesley faced him, holding something in his hand. "A sand dollar!"

Wesley held the sand dollar out to him, his smile childlike, the happiness on his face momentarily brilliant. Wesley had always been the more serious one. He'd worried more about things. Sam had counted on him to be the reasonable, practical half of their relationship. But seeing Wesley like this, Sam wondered if that hadn't gotten in the way.

Wesley appeared to have similar thoughts, because he said, "Sometimes I wish I could sit with my feet in the sand all day and not worry about all the other bullshit."

Sam grinned, then sat next to where Wesley stood, where the waves ended and sand was still dry. He looked up at Wesley and said, "Join me?"

Wesley sat beside him with his knees pulled against his chest, his toes digging into the wet sand. His shoulder brushed Sam's and Sam's throat tightened. Wesley was right about them, about how they'd fucked things up and lost each other in the process. But he still worried about Wesley.

"I'll be okay," Wesley said. He'd always been able to read Sam's mind even though Sam was good at hiding things. "I've been thinking about things. About my focus. Maybe the universe is trying to tell me something."

"About?"

"About work. About the book I've been thinking of writing for years."

"The pirate book?" Sam asked.

Wesley turned and looked at Sam with obvious surprise. "I always think you aren't listening," he said. "But you really *do* listen."

Sam shrugged. "I'm not very good at letting you know, am I?"

"You do okay." Wesley leaned against Sam.

"So when do you start writing?"

"When I get home? After all this is over?" Wesley hugged his knees. "I'm thinking of submitting a grant proposal. There's some money for historical research through the North Carolina Museum of History. Your idea about Stede Bonnet… it got me wondering if there isn't more to be found about him in the historical record."

"About his being gay?"

Wesley laughed. "I'm not expecting to find that. But you never know, right?"

"Sounds like a great idea. I always wondered why you never submitted a grant proposal about your research on East Coast pirates."

"I don't know," Wesley admitted. "I think maybe I thought it didn't sound serious enough."

"I guess you can thank Hollywood and Disney for that."

"Maybe. And it might turn the funders off."

"It might."

Wesley straightened a bit. "But there's no harm in trying, right? And it's not like I couldn't afford to come down here on my own without grant money. I've got enough in my rainy-day fund."

"Can I ask you something?" Sam wasn't sure how to broach the subject, but he wanted to know.

"Sure. What?"

"Why didn't you take the settlement I offered you?" Sam asked.

"For the divorce?"

Sam nodded.

"It was very generous. But I was the one who filed for divorce, not you," Wesley replied. He didn't look at Sam as he said this.

"That isn't the reason, though, is it?"

Wesley chuckled and shook his head. "No."

"Then why?"

"I needed to know I could go it alone." Wesley ran a hand through his hair and leaned his head on his knees.

"I was overprotective of you."

"Maybe. But I kind of liked that," Wesley answered. "It was your way of showing you cared about me." He paused, then added, "I think it was just about proving to myself that I could do things on my own."

"But you'd been doing that for years anyhow. Doing things on your own." The admission hurt like hell. It hurt more that Wesley didn't argue the point. Sam took a deep breath, scooted over so he was behind Wesley, and wrapped his arms around Wesley's shoulders.

Wesley sighed and leaned against Sam's chest. "Thank you."

"For what?"

"For being my friend."

CHAPTER TWENTY-THREE

WESLEY AWOKE to the smell of something wonderful wafting in through the open windows. The sun hadn't yet shifted to the front of the house, so it must still be morning. How many days had it been since he'd made it back from Guatemala? Three? Four? He couldn't remember. He hoped Parker wouldn't fire his sorry ass. He guessed she wouldn't, not if Sam had anything to say about it. For once, he felt good that he had Sam in his corner, mother hen and all.

He slipped out of bed and stopped in the bathroom to take a piss. He caught a flash of his face in the mirror and barely recognized himself there. He'd showered after he and Sam had walked on the beach, but he hadn't felt like shaving, and he'd ended up going back to bed. Sam—true to his word—had been more than a gentleman, he'd been an angel, changing the sheets so that when Wesley got back into bed, he felt clean for the first time in days.

Wesley knew he'd done it to himself—let himself get swept away in the emotion of Carl's betrayal and the grant rejection. *And letting Sam go for good.*

"Pathetic," he said aloud as he forced himself to confront the stranger who stared back at him. *Time to buck up.* He wasn't one to wallow, and he wasn't one to feel sorry for himself. He was paid to do a job, and he'd damn well do it. He'd allowed Carl to hurt him; he wouldn't allow him to damage his career as well.

He showered, shaved and trimmed his beard, and dressed before making his way downstairs. He hoped Sam had left some food in the fridge for him, because he was starving. But when he made it to the kitchen, he was surprised to find Sam waiting for him.

"I know what you're going to say," Sam said without waiting for him to speak, "but I'm leaving. I heard you showering and decided to wait and make sure you were okay."

Wesley bit back the temptation to tell Sam he was entirely capable of showering without drowning himself, and instead he said, "Thanks."

Sam smiled, and Wesley thought he saw surprise flicker in his eyes. "I've left you some breakfast in the oven," he said as he stood and ran a hand through his hair.

"Join me for breakfast?" Wesley asked.

"I would, but I've got to get to the set."

"Lunch, maybe?"

"I don't think I'm going to get a break."

"No problem."

"I'm not trying to avoid you," Sam said, no doubt sensing Wesley's disappointment. "Maybe we can take a walk on the beach after filming."

Wesley felt relieved. He'd leaned so much on Sam the past few days, he wasn't sure what to think. "I'd like that. And thank you. For everything. I don't know what I would have—"

"Glad I could help," Sam said, clearly uncomfortable with the praise. "See you on the set?"

"Definitely."

"Great. Cyrus wants you to review the changes to the script. Make sure they're not over-the-top. Parker's anxious to get going on the new stuff. I'll have Jeffrey bring a copy by on his way."

"I'll keep an eye out for him. Thanks again, Sam."

AFTER HE reviewed the proposed changes to the script, Wesley spent the rest of the day on the set working with Parker to finalize the dialogue.

"Whatcha think?" Sam asked as he poked his head into Parker's trailer at nearly four o'clock.

"I like what you've done with it." Sam must have been at the end of his patience, waiting for word. Wesley gave him credit for waiting as long as he had before interrupting them.

"Oh?" Sam grinned. "You sound surprised."

"I guess I shouldn't be," Wesley admitted.

"I don't blame you for being skeptical." Sam nodded to Parker. "Parker and I talked about how if we didn't handle the subject tactfully, this could end up a mess."

"Wesley and I worked on a few small changes," Parker said. "We can start on the new scenes tomorrow. I think we'll only have to reshoot a few. We can probably do a little cutting and pasting on the others."

"Cutting and pasting?" Wesley asked.

Parker laughed. "Term of art. Sort of." She got to her feet. "I told Cyrus I'd fill him in on our progress. See you both tomorrow morning, then." She waved and left Sam and Wesley alone.

"I really am glad you like the changes." Sam's shoulders relaxed visibly and a hint of a smile danced on his lips.

"I do."

"I should get going, then. Tell Jeffrey—"

"Join me for dinner tonight?" Wesley asked.

"Dinner at your place?" When Wesley nodded, Sam continued, "You don't need to do that. I can make us dinner at my house."

"I want to." Wesley wanted to do something nice for Sam. "You've been taking care of me for the past few days. It's the least I can do."

Sam tilted his head to one side as if considering the offer, then shrugged and said, "Sure. What time?"

"Eight?"

"I'll be there at eight."

Left alone a moment later, Wesley leaned back in his chair and closed his eyes. This new relationship with Sam felt strange, but it didn't feel bad. Not exactly. He wondered how long it would take him to get used to it. Maybe he never would.

CHAPTER TWENTY-FOUR

"THANKS FOR inviting me," Sam said as Wesley let him inside. "You really didn't need to make dinner for me."

"I know." Wesley shrugged. "I guess you could say I really didn't, either." He pointed to the box of pizza on the stove. "I ordered it from Island Pizza."

"Looks great." Sam sat as Wesley filled their bowls with the ready-made salad he'd purchased at the grocery store and served them both a slice.

"Beer?" Wesley asked.

"Sure, thanks."

They ate in companionable silence. Wesley sipped his beer slowly. He hadn't had anything to drink since Sam dragged him home from the bar, and he didn't want to overdo it. He wanted to stay in control tonight. He'd decided he wanted to come clean about Carl, and he wanted to do it sober.

It had taken Wesley a while to realize why he'd hesitated to tell Sam about Carl. He hadn't trusted enough to tell him. Not Sam in particular, because Sam had shown himself over and over to be trustworthy. Wesley hadn't trusted *himself* to tell Sam. Had he done the exact same thing he'd told Sam he hated? Had he avoided leaning on Sam?

"Living room?" Wesley suggested after they'd washed and put away the dishes.

"Sure."

Unlike the other times when Sam had come by the house, Wesley didn't sit across from him. Instead he sat next to Sam on the couch. He kicked off his loafers and tucked a leg beneath him, trying to ignore the powerful feeling of déjà vu. How many times had he and Sam sat on the couch in their apartment, talking or watching a movie after dinner?

Sam must have read his mind, because he said, "Like old times, huh?"

Wesley nodded. "I miss those times."

"Me too. We didn't do a lot of this after I left for LA."

"No."

"I don't blame you for moving on," Sam offered. "I know you might not believe it, but I'm sorry things worked out the way they did for you and Carl. I mean, I was jealous of him. But I never wanted to see you hurt."

"I appreciate that." Wesley leaned back on the cushions. "I really thought I'd put the pieces back together. That my life was where I wanted it to be. I thought I had everything. I was convinced I would get the big grant. I thought I'd found someone I could move forward with."

"You did get the big promotion."

"Yes, I did. And I'm happy about it, don't get me wrong." Wesley rubbed his mouth and sighed. "But I realized it was a house of cards. And it didn't make me happy. Not really. I told myself it should, but…."

Sam's understanding smile made Wesley feel just a little bit better. "Do you want to tell me what happened last week? I mean, you don't have to if you don't want, but—"

"I want to tell you. But…."

"You're worried it'll hurt me to hear it," Sam finished.

"Yes."

Sam reached out and touched Wesley's arm. "I think I *need* to hear it," he said. "I know it sounds strange, but I think it'll give me a little closure too."

Wesley nodded. "Carl and I had been having such a hard time connecting," Wesley explained. "You know we were supposed to spend the summer together, right?"

"Yeah. Viv mentioned it. She's… ah… sort of been keeping me posted about what you've been up to."

"I figured as much." Wesley chuckled. "Damn good thing she's so good at her job, or she'd be out on her behind," he added.

"Carl told me that the PI on the grant—his boss for his postdoc work—had changed his mind and decided to go with him to Guatemala," Wesley continued. "I didn't think anything of it. Robert's got a good reputation at the school, he's married, and…. Anyhow, Carl gave me some excuse about there not being room for me in the apartment. It was too late for me to pick up a summer class and, well, you know the rest."

"I didn't make it easy for you, did I?" Sam asked.

"I don't know. Honestly, if I'd wanted to, I could have told the studio to go to hell once I realized this was your film. I'm not sure why I didn't." Maybe he'd *wanted* to spend time with Sam. Or maybe he'd needed to see Sam—because seeing him would give closure to their relationship. Wesley still wasn't sure. Maybe he'd never really know.

"The more time I spent with you here, the more off-balance I felt. I'd try to call Carl, and he'd almost never answer. We barely spoke at all, even when we did connect. By the time you made me dinner at your place, I was at the end of my rope. I was lonely." He didn't want to admit this next part, but Sam deserved the truth. "I didn't think I could stay away from you. I mean… you know how I mean."

Sam nodded, but to his great credit, he didn't gloat.

"So I hopped a flight to Guatemala," Wesley continued. He tried to banish the image of Robert and Carl together, naked. He wondered how long it would take to erase it from his mind. "I caught them together. I should have realized something wasn't right. And those ribbons…."

"Ribbons?" Sam raised an inquisitive eyebrow.

Wesley half sighed, half laughed. "Robert's hands were tied behind his back and… ah… let me just put it this way: the other ribbon he was wearing wasn't all that big."

Sam laughed, but his expression was sympathetic. Understanding. With Sam here, Wesley could almost forget how much it had hurt, seeing them like that.

"Don't blame yourself, Wesley," Sam said gently. "You trusted him."

Wesley closed his eyes and inhaled, trying to stem the tears that threatened. He didn't want to cry another tear over Carl, but as usual, his brain and his heart didn't seem to communicate all that well.

"I'm so sorry, Wesley," Sam said as he gathered Wesley into his arms. "I made this so much worse for you. I was a selfish bastard."

"No. You're not selfish. It felt good knowing you cared enough about me that you'd do such crazy shit on my account." Wesley snuffled against Sam's chest.

Sam pulled Wesley closer and stroked his hair, then kissed his head. In all their time together, Wesley couldn't recall when Sam had just held him while he cried.

It felt amazing. And suddenly, Wesley wanted to kiss Sam.

He didn't think about it. He followed his need. He pulled away and met Sam's intense gaze, then leaned in and just *did* it. Sam's full lips felt soft and smooth against his. Sam's body felt both familiar and strange, something from a forgotten memory that, once remembered, resonated in body and heart.

The faintest of sighs escaped Wesley's control, echoed by Sam's own moan of pleasure and obvious surprise. Sam cradled him in his firm but gentle embrace. He didn't push Wesley further, but let Wesley dictate the pace of his exploration.

Along with the rush of excitement that accompanied the kiss, relief that he wasn't fighting against his need for Sam swept through him. God, it felt good to feel so completely *wanted*, when he'd felt so bereft only moments before. Fear that nothing had changed warred with hope that this might lead where he didn't dare believe it could.

The kiss broke and they stared at each other, Sam appearing as lost as Wesley felt. But Wesley didn't want to stop. All he could think of was how he wanted Sam. Wanted him inside of him, wanted to forget the past three years. And for once, he didn't want to think. He wanted to *do* something spontaneous. Something insane. Maybe even something stupid.

He pulled Sam back to him and kissed him again, groping for Sam's shirt as he did so and releasing Sam's lips only long enough to pull Sam's T-shirt off. Sam really had bulked up over the past few years. His chest felt different, but the smooth skin under Wesley's fingers awakened memories.

"Fuck me, Sammy," he growled. "Now." *Before I change my mind.*

Sam stared at Wesley in shock.

"I'm serious. I want this," Wesley reassured him.

Sam nodded, still clearly surprised, but didn't hesitate as he began to unbutton Wesley's shirt, then gave up halfway down and slipped it over Wesley's head. Wesley made quick work of his own shorts before removing Sam's. Clothing tumbled unceremoniously, leaving a trail as Wesley led Sam to the bedroom.

"Supplies?" Sam asked with a half grin.

"Just a sec." Wesley glanced back, then headed to the bathroom, where he dug in his yet-to-be-unpacked toiletry case and grabbed his quarry. He tossed the condoms and lube on the bed. Sam was on him a second later, pressing him against the wall, pinning him loosely there. The way Sam mouthed his neck, biting and sucking, Wesley was perfectly content to be Sam's prisoner.

Sam's cock pressed against his own, and Sam took full advantage, grinding them together, using his body as delicious pressure. "Fuck, Sam!" Wesley cried out as he bucked against him. Sam got to his knees and rubbed lips and tongue over Wesley's dick. Wesley leaned his head against the wall and closed his eyes.

"Mmmm." Sam skirted the tip, mouthing the edge but not taking Wesley inside.

"Sam, please," Wesley begged. Sam licked a line over Wesley's slit. "Oh... fuck!"

Wesley felt the rumbled laugh as Sam swallowed him to the root and held him in that warm, wet heat. But before Wesley could beg him again, Sam began to suck and pull in a steady rhythm. Sam had always been amazing with his mouth—he knew everything Wesley loved, and he knew how to make Wesley shake with need. This time, though, Sam's mouth was a fucking revelation. The way he used his teeth ever so gently against Wesley's length and followed along with his soft tongue made Wesley struggle not to cry out.

Sam stopped for a moment and met Wesley's gaze. No words, but Sam knew Wesley was holding back. Wesley never could hide anything from him. Not like this. And with that thought, something inside Wesley surrendered. Nobody understood him better. Whatever this was—whatever this meant—he would let himself go and try not to think about it. This was Sam. *His* Sam. And Wesley wanted this, regardless of the consequences.

"That's it," Sam hissed, then got back to the business at hand. He took Wesley so deep that Wesley's legs shook and he struggled to stay on his feet. Sam showed no mercy at Wesley's weakness but sucked harder still.

"Oh shit. Sam, I'm gonna—" Wesley came hard into Sam's mouth.

Sam moaned with pleasure as he drank in every last drop. His eyes never left Wesley's, his gaze intense. That focus had always made Wesley feel as though there was no one in the world but him. It was part of why he'd fallen so hard for Sam.

Stop thinking. Just feel.

"Fuck me, Sammy. Like this. Now." He wanted it hard and fast. He didn't want to have to think.

Sam turned Wesley so he faced the wall. "Lean on it," he said in that silky, sexy-as-fuck voice. "That's good."

Sam studied him, watching him, taking his time so that Wesley would beg him again. Sam rubbed a hand, then two, over his ass, kneading it so it stung just a bit. Wesley strangled a groan and focused on the feeling of Sam's strong fingers.

Sam brushed a line down Wesley's spine, following it from his neck downward until he reached his waist. When he withdrew his fingers, Wesley whimpered. "Sammy, you always were a fucking tease."

Sam chuckled, and Wesley heard the snick of the cap on the lube. He closed his eyes and waited. A minute more that tried his patience, then Sam's fingers skirted his hole, slicking the surface, making Wesley clench in anticipation.

"That's it," Sam whispered against Wesley's ear. "Let it all go for me. Tell me you want it."

"You fucking well *know* I want it," Wesley growled.

Sam breached him with the tip of a finger, then paused to allow Wesley to relax. "Much better," Sam said, his breath tickling Wesley's neck. He pressed his finger fully inside.

"Yes." Wesley tilted his head back and closed his eyes as Sam found his gland.

Sam nibbled on Wesley's shoulder, causing little ripples of pleasure to make their way to Wesley's cock. Wesley relaxed a bit more as Sam inserted another finger.

"You're so tight."

Wesley wouldn't tell Sam he hadn't been with anyone like this—not even Carl—since Sam. It hadn't felt right, being married to Sam and having sex with someone else. Even the fact that they were legally separated hadn't mattered to Wesley, and Carl hadn't pressed the issue. Now Wesley wondered if Carl hadn't been cheating with Robert all along.

"Wesley." Sam's voice brought Wesley back to the moment. "Stop thinking. Just feel."

"Fuck me."

Sam pulled and stretched him a minute longer. But before Wesley could complain again, Sam pressed against his entrance. Wesley was done waiting. He wanted Sam, and he wanted him *now*. He pushed back hard just as Sam slipped past the first set of muscles.

"Fuck!" It burned like hell. "Too long," Wesley gasped. But when Sam made to withdraw, Wesley pushed back again and breathed deeply. His body released the last of its tension and he sighed as Sam tentatively thrust.

"Better?" Sam asked, concern evident in his tone.

"Perfect."

Sam thrust more forcefully now, clasping Wesley's hips as Wesley sought to steady them both against the wall. As Sam picked up the pace, Wesley's breath stuttering, his fingers struggling for purchase, the burn in his thighs was more than worth it.

"Faster, Sammy. Harder."

Sam grunted and complied, pounding into him over and over until he grew hard again. Sam must have noticed, because he grabbed

Wesley's hard cock and pumped it with his slippery hand, matching the rhythm of his thrusts.

"Come for me, Wesley," Sam coaxed. "Let me… hear you… let… go. Just. Let. Go."

Wesley didn't think it was possible, but he was on the edge again, his body responding to Sam's voice as much as his hand. His orgasm built, zinging from the base of his spine through his hips until all he could do was fall into it.

"Oh fuck!" he shouted.

A moment later Sam cried out, his skin slapping fast against Wesley's ass. "So fucking good." Sam's movements slowed, as did his breaths. He leaned on Wesley, his chest wet with sweat pressed to Wesley's sweaty back.

Sam pulled out gently. Wesley turned and leaned on the wall as Sam padded to the bathroom and tossed the condom. He came back with a damp cloth and began to clean Wesley. Something about Sam's gentle ministrations brought Wesley back to the reality of their situation.

Nothing had changed. Not really. This had happened too fast. Too soon after Carl. He wouldn't use Sam as a crutch, not when Sam had been so kind to him.

"Sammy, I…." Wesley swallowed hard as he looked into Sam's eyes. It was too fucking easy to get lost in those eyes. Or to get lost in Sam. Sex between them had never been the problem. Why was this so difficult? He found himself hesitating, as if this weren't the man he'd spent more than ten years with and called his husband.

"Say it, Wesley. Please. Whatever this was—*is*—I don't want you to feel that you can't talk to me."

Wesley nodded and took a steadying breath. "That was amazing."

"But?" Sam prompted.

"But I don't know what it means."

Sam smiled at him, his cheeks still flushed. "For what it's worth," he said, "I never meant for that to happen."

Wesley nodded. "I know." In a night full of surprises, this surprised Wesley the most. As vulnerable as Wesley felt, Sam could have easily pressed him to spend the night. And Wesley was already sorely tempted to give in. *But he understands.*

Wesley turned Sam's T-shirt right-side out and held it out to Sam, who slipped it on. Sam finished getting dressed in silence as Wesley donned the bathrobe he'd hung on the door.

"Run tomorrow?" Sam asked as he ran his fingers through his deliciously tousled hair.

Wesley didn't hesitate. "Sure. I'll meet you at your place at six."

"Good night, Wesley."

"Good night, Sam."

Wesley watched Sam leave, then closed the front door. He walked back to his bedroom and fell onto the bed, his thoughts straying to the kiss that had precipitated it all. He touched his fingers to his lips but found no answers there, only more questions.

Maybe Sam was right. Sometimes it was better not to think too much.

CHAPTER TWENTY-FIVE

SAM WALKED back to his house under a sky full of stars. A perfectly moonless night so clear the Milky Way looked like a handful of fairy dust. Yeah, call him a hopeless romantic. He'd own it. But tonight? It felt as though someone had given him a gift—one he hadn't even asked for.

Wesley.

Sam *had* given up on the idea of a second chance. But tonight, for the first time in what felt like forever, he'd found the hope he'd lost. Hope that he and Wesley might find a way back to each other. Tonight, when Wesley had let go, Sam had sensed the possibilities of something new. Different.

"Hey, Sam." Jeffrey was curled up on the sofa, reading a book, as Sam walked into the living room.

"No date with Cyrus tonight?"

"His mother's birthday's today. He'll be back tomorrow night. I figured I'd wait up for you. See if you needed me to do anything."

"Things okay with you two?" Sam asked.

"Yeah." Jeffrey looked a bit sheepish.

Sam raised an eyebrow, then sat across from him. "You going to tell me what's up?"

"My mom says I wear my heart on my sleeve."

"Maybe, but I know you pretty well. Spending nearly twenty-four hours a day with someone for months does that, you know." Sam put his feet up on the coffee table and stretched his arms over his head, then waited.

"Cyrus asked me to move in with him," Jeffrey said.

"He did? That's great news."

"Yeah. I guess so." Jeffrey set the book down and ran a hand through his hair.

"You're worried."

"I've only known him two weeks," Jeffrey blurted. "He's... well, he's so much more experienced, and...."

"And you think he'll change his mind about you?"

"Something like that."

"I've known Cyrus a long time. He doesn't make a lot of bad decisions. What do you want?"

Jeffrey shrugged. "I don't know. I mean, I like being with him. But I need time."

"Then take the time you need. Cyrus will wait."

"But what if he changes his mind?"

"He won't," Sam reassured him. "But if he did change his mind, you'd have your answer, wouldn't you?"

"Yeah. I guess you're right."

Sam winked. "I'm always right."

Jeffrey giggled. "Oh crap! I almost forgot. Your agent called."

"Corliss did?"

"Yeah. She said something about a contract she wants you to review. She says she needs an answer tomorrow." Jeffrey yawned.

"Get some sleep," Sam admonished him. "You've been up since the asscrack of dawn."

"I'm fine," Jeffrey protested. "I can—"

"Get some sleep. That's an order."

"Aye, captain!" Jeffrey saluted, then giggled again.

"Cute. Now git ye ter bed, child, or I'll have ye walkin' the plank!"

"I'm going, I'm going. Don't forget to call Corliss."

"I'll call her tomorrow. Promise."

Jeffrey grabbed his book, waved, then disappeared up the stairs. Sam hoped he would give Cyrus a chance. If Cyrus was willing to ask Jeffrey to move in with him this early on in their relationship, he must have fallen hard. And who could blame him? Jeffrey was a great kid—man—and Cyrus was as loyal as you could get.

The thought reminded Sam of Wesley and the sex. Shit, that had been amazing. And absolutely frightening. Why, though, Sam wasn't really sure. This was what he'd wanted all along. But something had changed. Wesley seemed so… fragile. What if they got back together? What if he hurt Wesley again?

Everything has its risks.

He'd given up hope that he and Wesley might get back together, but now… now there was hope again, and he didn't know what the fuck to do with that. Didn't know whether to get excited or keep his distance.

"No," he said aloud. He knew what to do. The *right* thing to do. He'd be patient for a change, and he wouldn't push. He'd wait for Wesley to decide what he wanted. What he *needed*.

CHAPTER TWENTY-SIX

WITH SOME trepidation, Wesley climbed the steps to Sam's place. He'd gone for a long run with Sam that morning. They hadn't discussed what had happened the night before. They'd gone about their business on the set. They'd been perfectly pleasant to each other. They'd talked about the new scenes. They'd chitchatted about the weather.

Wesley had avoided the topic of the sex, and that wasn't fair to Sam. He didn't want to give Sam the wrong idea, but he needed to thank Sam for being there for him. And he needed to show Sam he would survive. He hated knowing how much Sam worried about him. Even more than that, he needed to come clean about his mixed feelings. To let Sam know he needed time.

The smell of the prime rib he'd picked up at the island's grocery store made his mouth water. He might not be much of a cook himself—and certainly nothing like Sam—but he knew how to buy good food. A delicate summer-vegetable-and-couscous salad, fire-roasted asparagus, and a bottle of Portuguese vinho verde. Lemon mousse for dessert.

He was just about to ring the doorbell when he heard Sam's voice coming from one of the rooms on the side of the house. "…not going to do it, Corliss. I told you, I don't need the money…. Sure, I get that. But if it doesn't happen now, it's not going to happen. I won't sit back and do the same old tired bullshit I've been doing for the past five years. …don't have to like it. I've honored my commitments."

Wesley hesitated, unsure what to do. He didn't want to interrupt a conversation with Sam's agent, but he had no right to eavesdrop. Still, the edge in Sam's voice worried him, so he stayed put.

"No. Seriously, Corliss, let them try to do it. I'm out, and I don't give a shit what they say about it. You know that's only a bullshit excuse so I'll cave…. Yeah, I know. They can't keep me from working….

"Yeah, I know you get it. But I need to know you've got my back on this one. Contact my attorney, see what he thinks about the contract…. I know, I know. Their pockets are deeper, but…. No, I'm not going to change my mind about this…. Sure. Let me know what he says and we can talk first thing next week.

"Right. Later."

Wesley took a deep breath, counted to twenty, then pressed the doorbell.

"Wesley?" Sam grinned, his blue eyes bright with pleasure. Wesley looked for something more there, maybe a hint of frustration or anger over the conversation with Corliss, but Sam was too good at hiding his emotions.

"I hope you don't mind," Wesley began, knowing the heat in his cheeks wasn't translating into a full-on blush. What the fuck was wrong with him, anyhow? This was *Sam*, not some first date. He held up the bag with the food in one hand and the wine in the other.

"You… you brought dinner?"

"I meant dinner the other night to be a thank-you," Wesley said. "For being there when I needed you." His mouth felt suddenly dry, so he chewed on the side of his tongue and tried to collect himself. "But I got sidetracked." *That was one hell of a sidetrack.*

"Please, come on in." Sam turned quickly and gestured Wesley inside as though he felt as uncomfortable as Wesley.

"Thanks."

Sam took the food and the wine from Wesley and set them on the table.

"Honestly," Wesley continued, knowing he was babbling but unable to stop himself, "after we… well, I…."

"Wesley?"

"Yes?"

"It's me, remember?" Sam's expression was patient. Kind. "I'm going to say this once, and you're going to believe me, okay?"

"I… okay." Wesley laughed nervously.

"The sex was amazing, but it was about our past. I'm not reading more into it than that."

"Oh, thank God."

"I'm not going to hold it over your head, and I'm not angry about it either. Promise."

Wesley relaxed. This was still Sam. They'd never been uncomfortable around each other before. Why should they be now? "Thank you."

"Don't sweat it." Sam began to unwrap the food. "Grab some plates and silverware for me?"

"Sure." Wesley walked past Sam to the kitchen. Once inside, he blew air from between his lips until his heart stopped racing. *Get your shit together. This is what you wanted, isn't it? Friends. Just friends.* He snagged a few plates and silverware, then joined Sam at the table.

"Thanks again. The dinner looks wonderful."

"I should buy stock in the grocery," Wesley quipped. "It's like a mini Zabars, only a lot less expensive." Sam used to love to tease Wesley about his habit of picking up chocolate babkas at the expensive New York store.

"I'd be happy to teach you to cook, you know." Sam filled their glasses.

As if he needed more distractions! "I prefer it this way."

Sam handed him his glass, and their fingers brushed. Wesley tried to ignore the shiver the touch engendered, and quickly took a long drink of the wine to steady himself. This wasn't going well. He'd been so sure of what he wanted, and now….

"No matter what happened, I'm glad you told me about Carl," Sam said after a long silence.

"I am too. To be honest, I don't remember us talking like that before."

"I guess we didn't." Sam sipped his wine, his gaze faraway.

"I remember when your dad died," Wesley said, emboldened by the wine and the conversation. "I wish I could have helped you more back then."

"You did."

Wesley shook his head sadly. "I was there. But I didn't know what was going on in your mind. What you were thinking."

"I didn't want to dump on you."

"I *wanted* you to, Sammy. I wanted to be there for you—I wanted you to lean on me. Sometimes talking about things makes you feel better."

"I still miss him," Sam admitted, his eyes glittering. "I think about him a lot. He'd have loved this place. Sometimes when I sail the boat, I wish he could be there with me. He loved the ocean."

Wesley touched Sam's hand. "I worried he wouldn't like me. But he made me feel like I was part of the family."

"He loved you." Sam's eyes sparkled with pain, but his smile was genuine. "I know he was uncomfortable about the gay marriage thing, but he never let that get in the way. He told me I was lucky I'd found someone like he found my mother."

"Thanks."

They ate in companionable silence, the chirping of cicadas and crickets the only sound. As he had when he'd told Sam about Carl, Wesley felt warm and comfortable. The connection to Sam was different than before, but it felt good.

Wesley cut another piece of his prime rib and studied it. He hesitated, knowing what he wanted to ask but unsure of himself. *Why? Because you can't handle what it means to be his friend?* No. If things between them were going to change, he needed to step out of the box. Avoiding things had gotten them nowhere before.

"Listen, Sam?" Wesley said after he'd finished chewing.

"Hmm?" Sam glanced up at him.

"I… I overheard the end of your conversation. With Corliss." *Casual. Not too pushy.*

"Oh." Sam's face betrayed nothing, but he sat ever so slightly straighter in his chair.

"What's up?"

Sam wiped his mouth with his napkin, then picked up his wine. "Nothing really."

Okay. So you got the blow-off. Try again. "It didn't sound like nothing," Wesley gently pressed.

Sam met his gaze but remained silent.

"Sam." *You can do this.* "Do you think of me as your friend?"

"Friend? Of course I do."

"I'm not a bad listener."

"You're a great listener," Sam said without hesitation.

"Talk to me, then." Sometimes Sam was so fucking frustrating! Of course Sam knew what he was getting at. "Please? Unless you don't trust me to keep it confidential."

"Of course I trust you. It's just… I don't want to dump on you."

"I know. You've said that before. Has it occurred to you that I might feel I'm dumping on *you* if you never lean on me?" Wesley smiled and his body relaxed. "What I said before about how I wanted you to talk to me when your father died… I mean it."

Sam sipped his wine, and Wesley could almost see the internal struggle. Sam was a damn good actor, but every once in a while he let down his guard just a tiny bit.

"I... I don't like to complain," Sam began tentatively. "I've been so fucking lucky. I've got more money than I could ever spend. I've got a career that keeps me busy. Happy too."

"That doesn't mean you can't want something different. You may think you *should* be happy. But if you're not...."

Sam nodded. "I get that. Still, part of me thinks, 'who the hell am I to complain?'"

"Those things—the money, the career, even the luck—maybe those things don't always make you happy." Wesley knew all about that.

Sam seemed to understand Wesley wasn't just referring to him. "It's hard to accept it, I guess. I've never taken anything for granted. I get offers for work all the time, but it still blows me away."

"Still Sam underneath it all."

"Yeah." Sam's eyes flickered with something like self-doubt, his self-control failing him for an instant.

"So tell me. What does Sam want?" Wesley asked with a gentle smile.

"I don't know."

"I think you do know. You just don't want to say it," Wesley prodded.

"Fair enough."

"So?"

"You know I don't like to brag." Sam wore a hangdog expression. Whatever Sam was, he was modest at the core, and Wesley understood why he still hesitated to say it.

"I know. Go ahead. It's me, Sammy. No bullshit here, okay?"

Sam drew a long breath and nodded. "I... I'm a good actor. Better than good." In spite of the words, Sam appeared unconvinced.

"You're a great actor." He'd seen everything Sam had done. "I know what you can do."

"Thanks. That means a lot to me."

"But?"

Sam's jaw tensed, and he took a slow breath. "But the work I've been getting...." He rubbed his mouth and glanced briefly away. "I want more. I want to push myself, and not to do stunts. I want to *act*."

"Corliss is pushing you to take another action movie."

"She can't help it. They make a shit-ton of money. For both of us. But that's *all* I've been doing the past five years." Sam shook his head. "It's not fun anymore."

"So what happens if you turn it down?" Wesley asked.

"The studio'll make my life difficult."

"But there are other people who'd be happy to hire you," Wesley pointed out.

"Sure. For the same stuff. But if I want something else from my career, I'm going to have to rethink things."

"Rethink things like what?"

"Like what my career might look like. *If* anyone wants me for something other than action." Sam sighed. "I tell myself I'm good at what I do…."

Wesley reached across the table and touched Sam's hand. "You're a wonderful actor, Sammy. I'm not saying that just because I care about you either."

"Thanks." Sam stared at Wesley, his expression momentarily unreadable.

"What are you thinking?"

Sam shrugged. "That I'm glad you're my friend. And I…." He paused, then appeared to think better of it. "Just that I'm glad. That's all."

Hearing that made Wesley feel really good.

CHAPTER TWENTY-SEVEN

STEDE BONNET looked over the railing at something in the distance, his expression one of calm resignation. "We will fight our way to the sea," he said, his eyes never leaving the water.

"But sir," his quartermaster said, "the tide has begun to rise. We should head north, take advantage of the darkness. If the ships pursuing us should free themselves—"

"We sail to the sea, whatever the consequences," Bonnet said, turning and glaring at the man for his insubordination. "Raise the flag! Ready the cannons. We sail at sunrise."

"Aye, sir."

"Cut!" Parker shouted.

Wesley grinned at Parker. "Perfect."

"We'll use CG for the South Carolinian ships," she told Wesley. "Bob's working with special effects and our weapons master to choreograph the battle scenes."

Sam swung down on a rope and landed nimbly on the filming platform. Parker crossed her arms over her chest. "I wish you wouldn't do that. The last thing we need with a week to go is you busting your ass or falling on your head."

Sam waved his hat with a flourish. "I shall not surrender, madam. I intend to win this battle."

"Too bad history isn't on your side, Master Bonnet," Wesley joked. "If I recall, your vessel ran aground trying to escape Colonel Rhett's ships."

"Minor complication. We killed nearly thirty of those scoundrels in the end." Sam pulled his pistol from his belt and held it high.

"And you were captured. Again. After you ordered your gunner to scuttle your ship."

"Aye. My men had already surrendered. What was I to do?" Sam replaced the gun and held his hand over his heart.

"We'll shoot the surrender this afternoon," Parker announced with a snort. "Time for lunch and a beer."

"I'm liking that plan." Wesley bowed to Sam.

"Give me a few minutes to change?" Sam asked.

"Aye, sir." Wesley waved an invisible hat at Sam. "You got it."

Fifteen minutes later Sam emerged from his trailer dressed in a T-shirt and shorts and carrying a basket. "Lunch," he announced brightly.

"Picnic on the beach?" Wesley wasn't keen on the idea, since it was already pushing ninety degrees and the few clouds had begun to dissipate.

"Picnic, yes. Beach, no." Sam pointed in the direction of the trail they'd taken weeks before, the one that led to the small cabin.

"All right. Lead on, brave sir."

Sam laughed outright. "You are *so* not an actor, you know. That English accent...."

"That bad, huh?"

"Let's put it this way: you sound like Fran Drescher meets Winston Churchill with a little Les Miz thrown in," Sam said with a smirk.

"Vive la révolution."

Sam rolled his eyes, and they crossed over the dunes and made their way down the trail. "So what do you think of the new direction?" he asked as they reached the edge of the forest.

"I never thought I'd say this, but it's really good."

Sam walked backward and faced Wesley. "Come on. Admit it. You were worried this would end up Errol Flynn meets *Brokeback Mountain*."

Wesley laughed. "The thought had occurred to me. But I like what you and Parker have done with the script. It's subtle and believable."

Sam beamed and turned forward again, whistling "We Are the Champions."

"I never doubted you could pull it off," Wesley said.

"You totally doubted it!"

"Okay, so maybe I was a little skeptical." When Sam said nothing, Wesley added, "Okay, okay. *Very* skeptical."

They reached the cabin a few minutes later, and Sam opened the door. All the furniture was gone. Wesley was almost relieved not to see the bed.

"We've finished shooting all the scenes here, and with that tropical storm in Florida tracking this way, Parker told them to clean this up."

"So what do we sit on?" Wesley asked.

Sam gestured to the floor.

"Great."

"I have a blanket," Sam said as he pulled a roll of fabric from the top of the basket. Together, they laid it over the wood floor, then sat with the basket between them. "Let's see what Jeffrey put together for us."

Sam pulled out several sandwiches and unwrapped them. "This one's for you. Prosciutto with butter and cornichons on a whole wheat baguette."

Wesley took the sandwich and stared at it. "You remembered?"

"How could I forget? You were the only one who spoke enough French to read the menu."

"I'd almost forgotten that trip. Paris was pretty expensive for a grad student and an underpaid professor." They'd eaten at a three-star restaurant as a splurge, and it had taken them several months to pay off the credit card bill for that meal alone.

"Things were a lot simpler back then," Sam said as he set the other sandwich down. He retrieved two bottles of beer and opened them. He handed one to Wesley, then proceeded to unwrap his sandwich.

"Pastrami on rye with lots of mustard."

Sam smiled, mouth full of food.

"Some things don't change, do they?" Wesley mused.

Sam took a pull on his beer and nodded. "This reminds me of old times. Simple. Just the two of us."

"Everything looks better in retrospect."

"Maybe."

Wesley finished another bite of his sandwich and set it down. "Some things were always good between us."

"The sex?"

Wesley nodded.

"Yeah." Sam appeared wistful. "But that isn't what I miss the most."

"No?"

"I miss this. Hanging out. Talking. Goofing around. I miss making dinner for you. Being there when you get home from work," Sam explained.

"Me too." Wesley's chest tightened as he spoke the words.

"You think there's hope for us?"

"You mean as friends?" Wesley asked.

"Yeah."

Wesley had wanted all along for them to be friends. That way they could both look back at their marriage and smile about the good times. But instead, he felt suddenly sad. The pull that had always been there between them, making it difficult for Wesley to let go, felt more like gravity drawing him back to Sam.

That wasn't fair to Sam. After all the grief Wesley had given the man for trying to win him over, the last thing he wanted was to set them both skittering around like two big idiots again, running together, pulling apart. He'd never liked wishy-washy in other people, and he hated it in himself.

"Dollar for your thoughts?"

"Inflation, huh?" Wesley countered.

"Not high enough?" Sam took another bite of his sandwich and chewed thoughtfully.

"Plenty high." Wesley forced a smile and tried his best to appear relaxed. "I was just thinking how nice this is. You and me, like you said. Friends."

"Yeah," Sam said. "It's all good."

SAM LEFT Wesley at the props workshop while he got back into costume and makeup in his trailer.

"How are you doing?" Cynthia asked as she applied the greasepaint that would withstand the heat and humidity. It felt like someone had painted his face with olive oil, but he smiled and told her he was doing great.

Nothing could have been further from the truth. He'd said it was good that he and Wesley could be friends, and it was. He wanted Wesley to be happy, and if that was what Wesley needed, Sam would make sure he had it. But he hadn't been entirely honest with Wesley. He should have come clean when Wesley pressed him. He should have admitted he'd fallen in love with Wesley all over again and that he wanted Wesley back for good.

And then what? He watched without really paying attention as Cynthia dabbed his face and covered the tiny freckles that had made themselves known under the hot Carolina sun. *Hiding. Just like me. Because I'm afraid I'll lose him for good if I push him.* But he'd lose Wesley just as surely if he wasn't honest.

He still remembered the look on Wesley's face when he'd first proposed. And the look when he married him. He'd promised to make Wesley happy. To treasure him. Care for him. *'Til death do us part.* And he'd made the wrong choice. The *worst* choice.

He'd chosen his career over Wesley. But he needed Wesley more than his career. Funny, awkward Wesley. Wesley, whose beautiful face and body made Sam crazy horny and possessive. Wesley, whose intelligence burned so bright but who never spoke down to Sam, even when Sam said the stupidest things.

Wesley. The love of his life who was about to slip through his fingers.

I want you, Wesley. But not for the reasons you might think. Not because it's comfortable, even if it is. Not because you make me feel warm and cared for. Not because you've been there for me even when I haven't been there for you. I want you because you make me feel alive. Whole. Sam didn't care how utterly sappy it sounded. He was the romantic, right?

He had to do something. Something to let Wesley know he didn't only want Wesley's friendship.

Something big. Not just romcom romantic. Something to make clear to Wesley that he loved him and that he needed him.

"Cynthia?"

"Yes, sweetheart?"

"Can you please hand me my cell?" Sam asked.

She handed him the phone, and he tapped one of the presets. "Jeffrey?"

"Oh, hi, Sam. Do you need something?"

"A little more help in the Wesley department."

Chapter Twenty-Eight

"Good morning!" Sam grinned up at Wesley from the porch. Dressed in his Stede Bonnet costume, hat in hand, he bowed low.

Sam looked good enough to eat. Or ravish. "Sam? What are you doing here? Where's Jeffrey?"

"Helping Cyrus. It's regatta day. Didn't Jeffrey tell you?" Sam handed Wesley a large bag. "This is your costume."

"Costume? Why on earth would I wear a costume?"

Sam gesticulated with his hat. "Why, good sir, because it's not just *any* regatta. It's *my* regatta."

"Yours?"

"Master Stede Bonnet, at thy service."

Wesley sighed. The man was too damn sexy for his own good. Wesley needed to focus on something other than the smooth skin of Sam's chest where he'd untied his collar. "I'm still not following why I need to wear a costume. And you can drop the accent. That's not going to help convince me."

"They've moved the regatta up from Halloween just for us," Sam explained. "Because of the film. The press is invited, and the winners of the Pirate for a Day contest they held a few months ago to promote the movie are here. Everyone's dressing up."

"Everyone doesn't include me."

"Come on, Wesley," Sam pressed. "Some of the boats in the race even fire fake cannons at each other. The caterers are doing a huge clambake for lunch, and they're giving tours of the *Revenge* to the public. It'll be fun."

"I don't—"

"Wesley, you *need* a little fun."

Sam had a point. The summer had been stressful. And Wesley had always enjoyed costume parties. That was what this was, wasn't it? A costume party? "All right."

Sam grabbed Wesley and hugged him. In spite of himself, Wesley closed his eyes as Sam held him. Then Sam let go and both of them just stood there for a moment, Sam appearing as unsure of himself as Wesley felt.

Stop it. Hugging is perfectly acceptable between friends. Now if he could only convince himself of that.

AN HOUR later Wesley and Sam stood at the edge of the water, looking out at the Cape Fear River with several dozen other people, all dressed as pirates. The sound of cannon fire rang out from one of the boats, and a huge cloud of white smoke rose from the side of one of the vessels as it rounded one of the race markers.

"Isn't it great?" a very excited Jeffrey asked as he ran over to Wesley and Sam, nearly skipping.

Like Wesley and Sam, Jeffrey wore a three-piece suit in pale blue with a long justaucorps jacket that dipped down to his knees in the back, a long fitted vest and matching velvet knickers, and a white shirt with a frilly jabot. His curly blond hair poked out from beneath a tricorne hat. Wesley thanked his lucky stars they'd all decided to forgo the long wigs for the publicity stunt. Already the temperatures were in the high eighties, and the forecast was for nearly 95 degrees and 70 percent humidity.

Several more boats approached the marker, and shouts of "Ahoy there, mateys!" rose from the crowd. Several women dressed as wenches—Wesley was relieved to see the costumes were more historically accurate than those he'd first seen on the set—came over to them and asked Sam for his autograph.

"Enjoying yourselves, are you?" said a woman with dark hair that trailed over her shoulders. Dressed in a long gown with lace at the sleeves and bosom, she stood nearly as tall as Wesley.

"My queen," Sam said as he bowed with a flourish. "Come over from England to oversee the festivities, have we?"

"Cyrus?" Wesley asked.

"Queen Anne to you," Cyrus replied with a wink.

Wesley smiled and bowed low. "Your Majesty. It's a pleasure to make your acquaintance."

"And who might we have here?" Queen Anne turned to Jeffrey and ran a long finger under his chin.

Jeffrey blushed. "I'm but a lowly page," he said, bowing. "My name is Jeffrey."

"Jeffrey." The queen pursed her crimson lips and looked Jeffrey up and down. "You're a pretty thing, aren't you? I believe I have need of your… ah… services." She held out her hand. Jeffrey took it, and they walked away without another word to Wesley or Sam.

"Smitten," Wesley said.

"Indeed." From the look on Sam's face, Wesley had the definite impression that Sam wasn't talking about Jeffrey or Cyrus. He pushed the thought away. He was enjoying Sam's friendship. Even more, he was enjoying not having to worry about Sam wanting more from him.

"I'm getting hungry," Wesley lied. "What say thee we make our way to dine by the ship?"

Sam smiled and nodded, then extended his arm. Wesley hesitated briefly before linking arms with him. A few of the fans whispered to each other, but Wesley shrugged it off. What did he care if they thought he and Sam were still together? In a few more weeks, he'd be back home in New York, and life as he knew it would return. *With a few changes.* He wasn't exactly looking forward to seeing Carl again. But the only time they'd run into each other would likely be at the obligatory faculty parties, and those were large enough events that he could probably avoid having to speak to him.

IT WAS late afternoon by the time Sam and Wesley climbed onto the *Revenge* with the rest of the actors, some of the senior staff, including Cyrus and Parker, and the winners of the contest who'd been flown in for the event. At one end of the ship, a group of musicians played eighteenth-century jigs and other dances, and a juggler tossed swords and hats into the air while people clapped to the music.

"Thanks," Wesley said as he and Sam watched the festivities from near the ship's wheel.

"For what?" Sam asked.

"For convincing me to come along. I'm having a great time."

"I thought you might enjoy it once you relaxed a bit."

Wesley nodded. "You were right." Sam had always been fun to spend time with, and he'd always been the one who encouraged Wesley to step out of his comfort zone.

"The day isn't over yet." Sam snagged two tankards from a passing wench and handed one to Wesley. "To pirates and mayhem," he said as he tapped Wesley's drink with his own. "And to romance."

"Bottoms up!" Wesley took a long drink. The rum-laced fruit punch wasn't historically accurate—pirates generally drank their rum straight—but it was refreshing.

Wesley was on his second drink and feeling quite relaxed when the music stopped and Sam donned his hat. He walked over to the railing and shouted, "Welcome, everyone! Are you having a good time yet?"

The crowd shouted happily, and several people whistled.

"Thank you for coming to visit my ship," Sam continued. "I hope you are enjoying the entertainment and that the rum's to your liking." He lifted his drink. "Hear, hear! I wish you all happiness, fair winds, and plenty of romance!"

Shouts of "hear, hear" rose from the deck, and many of the revelers raised their glasses in reply.

"Dinner will be served on the beach shortly." Sam motioned to where some of the crew had set up tables and chairs. The smell of corn roasting over an open flame near the parking area made Wesley's stomach rumble its approval. "But before we dine, there is a bit of unfinished business to which I must attend."

Sam got down on one knee and set his sword and scabbard on the deck in front of him. Wesley stared, unsure of what to do. That was when he realized the entire set had grown quiet and everyone was watching them.

"Wesley Warren Coolidge," Sam said, his blue eyes bright with intensity, "more than ten years ago, you stole this pirate's heart. Would that I could undo the wrongs of the past and once again possess thine heart as mine own. I pray thee forgive my folly and consent to once more sail at my side. I *need* thee at my side, whether fair winds or a tempest. Will thou pledge yourself to me again? Renew thy vow to me as I thee?"

"I… I…." Wesley's throat tightened. His cheeks burned. The entire situation was ridiculous, embarrassing, and… *and wonderful.* But the answer?

Sam hesitated just a moment. Then he stood before pulling Wesley to him and kissing him. The kiss, chaste at first, deepened as Wesley opened his mouth to Sam's and their tongues tangled. Sam tasted so damn good. Familiar and more intoxicating than the rum. Wesley's body responded, and he pulled Sam closer without really thinking.

God, he'd missed Sam so much! But this—kissing Sam, having him so close, old feelings resurfacing—was too overwhelming. "Give me time?" he whispered as the kiss broke.

"As much as you want." Sam spoke the words in his own voice. Words he clearly meant just for Wesley.

"Thank you."

The entire set erupted into applause. Wesley wished there was a real-life version of fade to black, but instead he climbed down the rope ladder onto the filming platform.

Some of the fans who'd been invited to watch the shoot whispered to each other and watched him with interest, but fortunately Jeffrey intercepted them before they could approach Wesley. He led Wesley toward Sam's trailer.

"I've got your change of clothes waiting," Jeffrey said as he opened the trailer door. "I can take you back to your house if you'd like."

Wesley nodded, still too overcome to think about anything but Sam's words.

"That was the most romantic thing I've ever seen." Jeffrey had that starry-eyed look about him. Wesley was pretty sure he was thinking of Cyrus. He seemed to realize Wesley was a bit overwhelmed, because he added, "Not that I don't understand why you'd hesitate. Still...."

Yep. Still.... Wesley took a few deep breaths, then took the bundle of clothing Jeffrey handed him and went to change. He needed to think—clear his mind of the Sander swoon. He chuckled to himself as he removed his hat and ran a contemplative finger over the soft feathers that trailed down from the felt.

Avast! Best ye batten down the hatches and make headway for safe harbor, lest ye be forced to abandon ship and find yerself adrift.

CHAPTER TWENTY-NINE

SAM SAT on his front porch and watched the sun set while he sipped on a beer. He wasn't in the mood to attend the party celebrating the end of the regatta. Ever since he'd proposed to Wesley again on the boat, he'd fought the urge to knock on Wesley's door and apologize.

Judging by the look of shock on Wesley's face, he'd fucked things up again. Why did he always need to make a grand gesture? That wasn't what Wesley wanted, and it sure as hell wasn't what Wesley needed. Still, he'd hoped Wesley would understand he meant every word of what he'd said. That he needed Wesley and that he was going to do things differently this time.

Full circle. They'd come full circle. He'd given up hope when Wesley left for Guatemala. He thought he'd finally reconciled himself to the fact that he'd lost Wesley for good. He'd been ready to move on even though he hadn't really wanted to. He'd stopped trying to make things right between them. Once he'd stopped trying, he'd been able to be himself with Wesley and he'd remembered why he'd fallen for him.

Sweet, loving Wesley, who'd listened to him back when he'd been a mess of insecurities. Wesley, who'd supported him and encouraged him to audition for things he hadn't believed himself good enough to audition for. Because of Wesley, he'd found success. *And lost the man I love.* Whatever happened, Sam didn't want to go back to the status quo. He wouldn't do that to himself, and he sure as hell wouldn't do it to Wesley.

The sound of the screen door opening and closing brought Sam back to himself.

"You doing okay?" Jeffrey asked.

"Yeah. Thanks."

"That was incredible, you know."

Sam shrugged.

"That wasn't the same. I mean, I guess it was big," Jeffrey added. "But it wasn't like flowers."

"No?"

Jeffrey shook his head.

"It wasn't sappy?" Sam asked.

Jeffrey laughed. "Totally sappy. But in a good way."

"Thanks."

"I can stay if you'd like me to."

Sam shook his head. "You're off duty. You worked your ass off today and you deserve a night off. Besides, the way Cyrus was watching the weather forecast, he could use someone to calm him down."

"The hurricane people were talking about? I thought they said it was headed much farther south."

Sam shrugged. "Too early to tell. But you know Cyrus worries."

"Yeah. I think he needs someone a little more laid-back. To keep him grounded." From Jeffrey's expression, Sam knew he was speaking about himself.

"You're good for him."

Jeffrey's face lit up. "You think so?"

"Know so."

"Thanks, Sam." Jeffrey paused a moment, then added, "I think you're good for Wesley."

"Yeah?"

Jeffrey nodded. "When you told me what you had in mind, I didn't think it would work. But what you said was so… romantic. How can he not say yes?"

"The reviews are still out." Sam pressed his lips together and smiled.

"If it helps, Wesley was doing okay when I left him at his house. A little scared, I guess, but I think he was happy."

"That's good to hear." Sam wouldn't let himself get too excited about this news, but it did make him feel a bit less nervous.

"You'll call me if you need me, right?"

"I won't need you."

Jeffrey screwed up his face at Sam. "But you'll call if you do, right?"

"I will."

"'Kay."

"Have fun tonight. And tell Cyrus to chill," Sam said.

"I will. Promise." Jeffrey grinned, then bounded down the steps, skipping until he reached one of the golf carts.

Sam supposed he'd been that young once. Right now, he wasn't feeling it. Between the run-in with Corliss about turning down the action film and laying it all on the line for Wesley again, he mostly wanted to lie low and lick his wounds. Sail somewhere. Not have to face all the questions and the publicity he knew would come with his little stunt.

Never do anything without an audience, do I?

He picked up his beer and took a long pull on the bottle. He had no one but himself to blame for putting the screws to Wesley, especially after all Wesley had been through. Still, it had felt like the right thing to do at the time.

He closed his eyes and tried to focus on the feel of the cool breeze on his cheeks and the smell of salt on the air. Sometimes it was better not to think too much. What was done was done.

"Sammy?"

Startled, Sam sat up in his chair and stared. Wesley stood at the bottom of the porch stairs. "Oh, hey." He sounded anything but nonchalant.

"Mind if I join you?" Wesley asked.

"Sure. Beer?"

"I'd like that."

"Be right back." Sam motioned to the rocking chair next to the one he'd been sitting in, then slipped inside, where he pulled two bottles of beer from the fridge and popped the caps off them. When he returned, Wesley was seated with his bare feet propped on the porch railing. Sam handed him one of the beers.

"Thanks."

"Sure thing." God, was Wesley going to keep him waiting? It was better to get it over with quickly.

"I haven't made up my mind yet," Wesley offered, as if he'd guessed at Sam's fear.

"Oh."

"That's a good thing, Sammy."

"Yeah?" Sam wasn't as sure.

"Yep. What did you always say about me? That I take an eternity to make up my mind about things?"

"I seem to recall saying that when you finally agreed to marry me." Sam remembered it well. They'd been on a trip to Provincetown. He'd planned the entire thing. A cute little B and B. Dinner on the beach. Flowers. And Wesley had told him he'd think about it.

Wesley chuckled. "It was only a few months."

"Six months. It felt like an eternity. I ran more that year than I'd ever run before. By the time you finally said yes, I'd run through a brand-new pair of Brooks."

"You were never very patient." Wesley raised his beer and tapped it against Sam's.

"I have other redeeming qualities."

"I'll give you that." Wesley drank his beer and gazed off at the fading light of the sunset. "I'm not trying to be difficult, you know."

"Yeah, I know that."

Wesley hesitated a moment. "I… I thought I had it all figured out."

"What did you figure out?"

"After I got up the nerve to tell you things between us were over, I tried to put the pieces back together," Wesley explained.

"I'm sor—"

"This isn't about blame. I just want you to understand."

"Okay." Sam still blamed himself.

Wesley set his bottle down and leaned back in his chair. "I thought what I needed was someone who really understood me. And when I met Carl, I thought I'd found him."

Sam knew he needed to hear this, even if he didn't really *want* to hear it.

"Carl was a postdoc at the university," Wesley continued. "He was funny. I think he reminded me a little of you. I told myself he got what I was all about. And when I got promoted to full professor, I had someone to share the news with." Wesley sighed and shook his head.

"In the end, I've realized it was a fantasy. I created the perfect person to be with. Someone with the same interests. Same goals."

"Someone who wasn't me," Sam put in.

"Maybe. I guess I needed that fantasy. I'd convinced myself I could move on from us. This would be my perfect little life. Perfect boyfriend. Perfect career. And the big grant I'd been working toward for years…．

"So when you showed up again, I wanted to get as far from you as possible." Wesley shrugged. "Seeing you again complicated things. Made me feel things I didn't want to feel. It's funny…．"

"What is?"

Wesley turned and looked at Sam. "Sometimes complications make you see more clearly. I don't know."

"And what do you see?"

"I see someone who still means a lot to me. Someone I still love. But more than that? I just don't know. Not yet. I won't make the same mistake again, Sam. I'm not going to jump back into this without really thinking about it.

"I'm not turning you down, but I'm not saying yes either. Not yet."

"I get it." Sam *did* get it. He sighed. "I'm sorry."

"Sorry?"

"The grand proposal," he said. "It wasn't the right thing to do. It wasn't fair to you. I don't want to pressure you. I really don't."

Wesley's eyes widened, but he said nothing.

"It's like a bad habit with me," Sam continued, undaunted. "You know, the hero says all the right things and the love interest falls into his arms."

Wesley smiled and nodded. "You're perfect for that role."

"It's a fantasy."

"Yeah." Wesley offered Sam a gentle smile. "And kind of charming, in a slightly irritating way."

"I wasn't aiming for irritating."

"I know." Wesley studied Sam as if he were seeing him in a different light.

"Thing is," Sam said, "I get it. What you said about us. You needed more than I gave you. Grand gestures aren't going to make up for that." Sam ran a hand through his hair and took a long breath.

"You really *were* listening."

Sam nodded. "And you were right too."

"About what?"

"About me needing to lean on you sometimes. You listening to me about Corliss… it felt really good."

"Sam." Wesley blinked a few times, then smiled again.

"So what I'm saying," Sam finished, knowing he needed to keep talking or he might lose it, "is that I'm sorry I put you on the spot like that. Take as much time as you need. I'll be here waiting."

"Thanks, Sammy."

"I'm not going to lie and tell you I like it, though."

Wesley stood and walked over to Sam. "I know." He kissed Sam on the lips. Sweet, simple. More than friends, and not. "I promise I won't make you wait forever for an answer, Sammy," Wesley said after he pulled away.

Sam watched Wesley leave a moment later. Wesley was right. It wouldn't help either of them if Wesley wasn't ready. He'd wait as long as Wesley needed, because this time, Sam would do things differently.

CHAPTER THIRTY

WESLEY SLEPT like the dead. He'd thought the conversation with Sam would just stir things up more, but when he woke the next morning, he felt clearheaded and well-rested for the first time in weeks. He'd done the right thing by not giving Sam an answer right away. More surprisingly, Sam seemed to have understood.

He arrived at the set earlier than usual only to find barely controlled chaos. Jeffrey was nowhere in sight. Sam was on the deck of the *Revenge*, in costume, sword in hand, while half-a-dozen extras watched the fight coordinator demonstrate a battle scene.

Parker paced back and forth on the platform, clearly impatient. She spotted him and shouted, "Wesley! I need you here."

Wesley waved and made his way to the platform on the raised walkway they'd built over the surf. For the first time, water licked at the edge of the wood, spilling over from time to time. The wind, which was always a bit gustier here than in the center of the island, blew harder and cooler than usual.

"Good morning," Wesley said as he stepped onto the platform.

"Something like that." Parker began to chew one of the camera operators out for not paying attention.

"What can I do to help?" Wesley asked after she'd finished.

"Keep your eyes open," she answered. "We can't afford a hundred takes of the scene."

"Of course. Are you concerned that—"

"No concerns." She flipped some papers on a clipboard and stormed off toward edge of the platform closest to the ship.

"Cyrus had his panties in a wad this morning," Bob explained as he looked up from a table filled with swords. "Seems he bitched at Parker for not keeping to the schedule."

"I thought they'd decided to add two weeks so they could film the extra scenes." Sam had explained that the changes to the script Cyrus had agreed to would require reshooting a few of the outdoor scenes but that the majority could be filmed later on the soundstage.

"That was before they were predicting a 30 percent chance that Hurricane Drake would make landfall near Wilmington."

"Oh." Wesley hadn't checked the weather that morning. "I didn't realize they'd changed the projections."

"Apparently neither did Parker."

"Anything I can do to help?"

Bob shook his head. "Just keep your head down and ask how high when Parker tells you to jump. And don't take it personally if she bites your head off."

Wesley chuckled. He'd dealt with more than enough ornery deans—he wasn't terribly worried about Parker.

WESLEY RAN into Jeffrey on the beach a few hours later. He looked flustered and in about as good a mood as Parker. "How's Cyrus doing?"

Jeffrey's expression darkened. "Don't even ask. I mentioned that the island was under a voluntary evacuation order, and he told me there was no way anyone was leaving until they wrapped filming. Except me. I told him where he could take *that* crap."

"Sorry."

Jeffrey raised an eyebrow. "Not going to bother me," he said offhandedly, but Wesley sensed his strong resolve. "We'll make it work. Cyrus is a big baby sometimes."

Wesley repressed a grin. "What do you have planned?"

"I've already spoken to the mayor about facilities in case we need to take shelter."

"I'm impressed."

Jeffrey shrugged. "Sam suggested it. He knows Cyrus pretty well, and he figured it would take a mandatory evacuation order to get Cyrus to call off filming. I'm just making sure we have options."

"Sam trusts you. For good reason. Don't sell yourself short."

Jeffrey's cheeks reddened, as they often did when someone complimented him. But this time, rather than downplaying his role, Jeffrey said, "Thank you. I've learned a lot from Sam… and Cyrus."

"Cyrus is lucky to have you."

"Thanks. Although he might not feel lucky if I end up strangling him."

Wesley repressed a snort at the visual that conjured up. "So what can I do to help?"

"You don't need to help. I mean, you've got a job to do too."

"I want to help. Parker has things under control here. If she needs me, she'll call."

Jeffrey nodded. "I put an order in for supplies from Southport. Food and water. Necessities. Come with me to meet the ferry? I'll need to find a place to store everything until I get the okay to move the stuff to the shelter."

"No problem. I'll let Parker know and meet you by the carts later."

WESLEY RETURNED to his house at nearly 9:00 p.m., having grabbed a quick dinner on the fly. The rain had begun an hour before, sizzling on the asphalt and creating a mist that clung to the low-lying shrubs in the shadow of the dunes. He'd checked his weather app before he left Jeffrey in town. The storm track hadn't deviated as hoped. If it kept on course, it would pass about 150 miles offshore of Wilmington late the next afternoon. They were in for a rough ride if they didn't evacuate, but Wesley figured it couldn't be too bad, or they'd have issued a mandatory evacuation for the island.

The sound of a golf cart caught his attention as he headed up the front steps. "Hey, Sam," Wesley called over a gust of wind.

Sam stopped the cart and dashed up the front walkway, hair blowing about his face. In the porch light, he looked tired, as if he hadn't gotten any sleep the night before. *And whose fault is that?* Wesley pushed the guilty thoughts away as he opened the door and invited Sam inside.

"I'm glad I finally caught up with you," Sam said as he pushed a lock of hair from his eyes. "Parker kept us until nearly eight filming the fight." He rubbed distractedly at the back of his neck. "I'm going to need to soak for a few years to get rid of these sore muscles."

Wesley indicated the living room couch. "Can I get you something to drink?"

"Do you have tea?"

"Sure. Be back in a few minutes."

"Thanks."

"No problem." Wesley smiled, then went to the kitchen to heat some water. As he pulled a box of tea from the cabinet, he caught himself thinking how incredibly domestic it felt to be here, making Sam tea. He'd missed this part of their relationship too. Carl hadn't been one to have dinner at home. They'd spent nearly every night together out on the town.

Wesley handed Sam a mug of tea a few minutes later and sat facing him on one of the chairs. Sam inhaled the steam and smiled.

"I need to talk to you," Sam said after he'd taken a few sips.

"I'm not ready yet, Sammy. I promised you I'd—"

"It's not about that." Sam frowned. "I'm here to ask you to leave the island. Word is that the ferry will stop running tomorrow morning."

"Leave the island? Why?"

"The storm's coming, and it's too risky for you to stay."

Wesley set his tea on the side table and met Sam's gaze. "And it's okay for *you* to stay?"

"I can't leave. I promised Parker I'd help out."

"I told Jeffrey I'd help out too. He's got to—"

"He can get someone else to help him."

"You're serious, aren't you?" Wesley stared at Sam.

"Of course I'm serious. The path of the storm—"

"You're serious that you think I'd leave you and everyone else?" Wesley knew he shouldn't be surprised about this, but it pissed him off all the same. Sam could be so fucking intractable.

"There's no need for you to stay."

"Like hell there isn't." Wesley got to his feet.

"All the tourists are being evacuated, Wesley."

The dismissive tone of Sam's voice only served to tick Wesley off more. "Have they issued a mandatory evacuation?"

"Mandatory?"

"You know damn well what I mean, Sam." Wesley strode over to the window and watched the rain splash into a puddle at the foot of a nearby streetlamp.

"No. There's no mandatory—"

"Then I'm staying put."

Sam was on his feet now, his face flushed with anger. "You'll take the ferry."

"I'll *what*?"

"I said you'll take the ferry. You'll stay in Wilmington until the storm passes, and—"

"No fucking way!" Wesley faced down Sam. No one, let alone Sam, was going to tell him what he should and shouldn't do.

"Wesley, listen to me. Nobody knows where the storm will hit. It's too dangerous for you to stay. I've already told Jeffrey he's going with you."

"Oh, and Jeffrey was okay with it?" Wesley countered, knowing full well Jeffrey had already told Cyrus he was staying.

"Well, no, not really, but—"

"I'm not going anywhere."

"Sometimes you really piss me off," Sam snapped.

"Good. Because the feeling is fucking mutual. And if we're going to have a snowball's chance of working things out," he added, at the limit of his patience, "you're going to have to stop coddling me."

"I'm not—"

"Don't even go there, Sammy. There may be times when I *need* to lean on you, but if I tell you to back off, I damn well *expect* you to. I'm more than capable of making my own decisions. Live with it." Wesley's heart pounded so hard against his ribs, it almost hurt. But there was something exhilarating about telling Sam off.

"Wesley, I'm only asking you to leave because I care what happens to you."

"I know. But I've been doing fine on my own for nearly three years now. Whatever happens with us, I'm not going back to the way things were." Wesley clenched his jaw, then willed the tension away. "If you want me back, you're going to have to take me as I am."

Sam appeared to hesitate, as if considering what he might say to counter Wesley's surprising show of strength. "You're making a mistake," he said at last.

"Fine," Wesley said. "Then it'll be mine to make, won't it?"

Sam frowned, but something in his expression had changed. Had Sam realized he wasn't going to back down? "I worry about you."

"I know. And I appreciate that. It makes me feel—" *Loved. Cared for.* "—good."

Sam released an audible breath. "Sorry," he said.

Wesley offered Sam a reassuring smile.

"About the other thing?"

"Sammy," Wesley warned.

Sam grinned. "Okay. So I'm not as patient as I seem."

Wesley leaned in and kissed Sam on the cheek. "You never were."

CHAPTER THIRTY-ONE

"I TOLD Sam I wasn't going to leave if everyone else was staying," Jeffrey said indignantly as he and Wesley walked through the doorway of the Bald Head Island Club building. "Still, we should have packed everything up and gotten on the last ferry."

Wesley offered him what he hoped was a reassuring smile. "Even if it's a direct hit, it's only a Category 1 storm. This place is built to withstand up to a Category 3." Jeffrey appeared unconvinced.

Wesley turned back just as a truck pulled up to the entrance and Sam hopped out. Calm and confident, Sam looked very much like the hero from one of his movies with his tousled hair and just a hint of stubble on his jaw.

"Mr. Carson!" someone shouted over the howling wind. "Over here!"

Sam met Wesley's eyes and grinned, then got in the truck again and backed it up to the loading dock. A minute later, cast and crew and the few remaining islanders were hauling water and food into the building while Jeffrey shouted directions. As Wesley walked over to offer his assistance, some of the guys from the shop were putting the finishing touches on the plywood to cover the windows.

"What can I do?" Wesley asked. Someone pointed him toward a pile of boxes, and he began to help the others carry them inside.

The wind had picked up considerably in the past hour. Nothing that would cause damage yet, but the crape myrtle trees at the edge of the parking lot bent nearly parallel to the ground with the stronger gusts. The rain stung Wesley's face as he worked, but it felt good to be doing something.

From time to time, Wesley caught Sam's glance his way, but Sam didn't say anything. The realization that Sam had really listened to what he'd said the day before made him feel warm in spite of the rain.

SAM PILED up the cases of food at the far end of the room, where someone had set up a TV so they could follow the tracking of the storm. Several people watched, transfixed, as the swirling bright band made its way up the Carolina coast. From time to time, a VHF radio used to monitor emergency broadcasts crackled with chatter from fishermen and pleasure boaters making their way up the Cape Fear River to Wilmington and other safe harbors.

He'd watched Wesley from a distance as they'd finished preparations for the storm. In spite of his misgivings, he'd managed to keep his mouth shut about Wesley staying on the island. "We good?" he asked Jeffrey as he lifted the last box into place.

"Yep. That's everything." Jeffrey glanced to where Cyrus was talking to a very relieved-looking Parker.

They'd moved the reproduction ship upriver. Most of the vessels had been moved out of the marina as well, with the exception of several small fishing boats and Sam's boat. He had meant to sail her to a safe harbor upriver that morning, but he'd ended up taking charge of one of the volunteer efforts to check on islanders who might not have been able to evacuate. If the storm passed over or near to the island, the boat might take some damage, but people were less expendable.

"What do you hear?" Sam asked Parker.

"Thank God the ship made it safely to the marina near Wilmington," she replied. "They had a hard time starting the engine."

"Good deal."

Parker rubbed her face. "I could use a stiff drink. Or on second thought, maybe one of your neck massages?"

Sam stepped behind her and began to work at the tension in her shoulders. She sighed contently. "Multitalented."

A crowd had gathered around the TV, but the lights flickered and the picture disappeared. Someone turned up the weather radio, and the mechanical voice of NOAA radio replaced the Weather Channel's reporter.

"…at 6:00 p.m., winds at Wilmington, North Carolina, were gusting to forty miles per hour. Wave heights near the Frying Pan Shoals buoy measured eight to ten feet with a six-second period…."

"Good?" Sam asked Parker as he worked a particularly stubborn knot from her upper back.

Parker sighed. "Who needs alcohol with your hands around?"

Sam snorted and glanced over at Wesley. He was chatting with John, the head carpenter, who had just come inside after finishing boarding up the windows. John laughed at something Wesley said, then clapped him on the back. The niggle of jealousy took Sam by surprise, and he was just about to go over and put himself between the two men when the VHF radio crackled to life.

"…mayday. This is… sailing vessel… *Solstice*… taking on water… lost right… can't…. Mayday, mayday!"

"Excuse me," Sam told Parker as he made his way to the radio, where Leslie, a special effects assistant, played with the squelch knob to better hear the message.

"Oh, Sander," she said when she saw him approach. "You're better at this." She stepped out of the way and Sam began to adjust the receiver and tried to use the Scan buttons to monitor for more messages.

"*Summer Solstice*, this is Coast Guard Sector North Carolina," said a woman's voice from over the speaker. "What is your current position? Over."

The radio crackled with static. "We're… thirty-three… minutes north… miles west of Bald… Island. We're—" A particularly loud blast of static broke the transmission. "…engine's not…."

Shit. That was bad news. Sailboats moved incredibly slowly. Even *with* a working engine, that put the inlet onto the Cape Fear River over an hour away. Without an engine….

"*Summer Solstice*, this is Coast Guard Sector North Carolina. Please repeat your position. Over."

Sam caught Parker's eye and forced a smile, then scanned the room for Jeffrey, who was standing about ten feet away and watching with obvious concern.

"…are approximately thirty-three… forty-eight minutes north…. Seventy-eight degrees about… three minutes…. Can't get… started."

"*Summer Solstice*, can you please confirm your position as thirty-three degrees, forty-eight minutes north, seventy-eight degrees, three minutes west?" the Coast Guard radio operator said.

"…tried and engine… start. Taking… water."

"Copy that, *Summer Solstice*. We have a vessel in the area, ETA about forty-five minutes. Over."

That put the boat about five nautical miles from Bald Head Island. Five, maybe ten minutes away on the *Neverland*. Thirty-five minutes might make all the difference for the sailboat's crew.

"…wave… around fifteen feet. Not sure we—" More static, then nothing.

Sam relinquished his spot by the radio. "Jeffrey," he said, taking him by the arm, "I need your help."

Chapter Thirty-Two

"This is crazy, Sam," Jeffrey shouted as he tossed the last of the ropes onto the deck of the ship. "At least if I come with you, I can—"

"Not happening. Stay here. Monitor the radio and make sure everyone stays safe. I'll be back before you know it." Sam raced up the stairs to the bridge of the boat. He'd left the engines idling. Already the boat was banging against the dock, so he pulled out of the slip as quickly as he could, thanking his lucky stars he'd decided to back her in the last time he'd taken her out.

He half regretted having given the crew the rest of the month off. He'd considered recalling them ahead of the storm but decided against it. She wasn't easy to single-hand, although the wireless remote control made it possible, and he would have only needed to sail her up to Wilmington if the storm threatened the island. It would be fine, he'd told himself.

Sam caught Jeffrey's frightened expression as he glanced back at the docks. "Don't worry," he shouted over the caterwauling wind. "I'll be back before you know it." He wasn't sure if Jeffrey heard him.

The rain, which had been falling all day, now came down in heavy sheets, broken up only by gusts that stung Sam's face like tiny needles. "*Summer Solstice*," he said over the radio, "this is *Neverland*. Can you give me your current position, over?"

There was no response.

"*Neverland*, this is Coast Guard Sector North Carolina, do you copy? Over."

"Coast Guard Sector North Carolina, this is *Neverland*. Do you have an update on the location of the sailboat *Summer Solstice*? Over."

"Nothing new on its position. A commercial vessel reported fifteen- to twenty-foot waves in the vicinity. We'll have someone in the area in about forty minutes. Over."

No doubt the Coast Guard would already know his ship was big enough. They wouldn't encourage him to attempt a rescue, but they wouldn't discourage him—not given the perilous situation the sailboat was in. "I can handle the waves," he said into the radio. "They can't wait.

Last transmission, they were taking on water. They won't last that long out here. I can be there in five minutes. Over."

"*Neverland*, maintain an open channel on 22-alpha. We'll keep you posted on our ETA. Over."

"Roger that, 22-alpha. Over." Sam typed in the new channel and hung the radio by the wheel. "*Neverland* standing by on 22-alpha."

"Coast Guard North Carolina Sector standing by."

"You know, for a nanosecond, I really didn't think you were going to do what I thought you were going to do," a familiar voice said.

"Wesley? Holy fuck!" Sam shouted, surprised to see Wesley leaning against the copilot's chair beside him. "How the hell did you get aboard?"

"It's a big boat," Wesley said, his expression black. "I hopped onto the swim platform while you and Jeffrey were working the dock lines."

"I'll turn around and drop you off." Sam began to turn the wheel, but Wesley stopped him.

"No way in hell. If you're bound and determined to play the hero, you'll need a little help."

"It's dangerous. What if—?"

"We get ourselves killed?" Wesley furrowed his brow. "Then we do it fucking *together*. I'm sick of this shit, Sam. Sick of you taking on the entire universe by yourself and leaving me on the sidelines to wonder what the fuck happened. Besides, you'll have a hell of a lot better chance of making it back in one piece if you have someone to help you."

Wesley had a point, although it scared the shit out of Sam that Wesley was putting himself at risk. But they probably did have a better chance of rescuing the sailboat's crew and not drowning themselves if one of them could handle the helm while the other concentrated on rescuing the crew.

"All right," Sam said at last. Wes was right, as always. Besides, he'd told himself he could change for Wesley. What better time was there to prove he could do it?

"Seriously?" Wesley stared at him.

Sam laughed and tossed Wesley one of the life jackets he'd placed on the console. "Put that on and stop looking so smug or I'll take you back." He was a good actor, but Wesley probably saw through his bullshit. Wesley usually did, though he rarely called Sam out for it.

"Aye-aye, sir." Wesley slipped on the PFD, and his eyes shone bright with amusement and a hint of terror. They both knew there was no going back now.

As the ship cleared the channel from the marina onto the open water, Sam handed Wesley the paper chart of the area. "I marked the current location in red," he said. "Go ahead and enter the coordinates into the computer. The shipping channel's wide enough for tankers coming in and out of the Port of Wilmington, but the *Summer Solstice*'s engine is shot. I'm worried they may have grounded on the shoals." He tapped the spot where the shoals began. "Here."

Sam had done his research when he'd decided to bring the ship to the island—more than a hundred wrecks littered the shoals. And with waves as high as twenty feet, whoever was aboard wouldn't survive long if they fell overboard or the ship began to sink.

Wesley nodded and got quickly to work. "There should be a marker close by. You'll need to head to port to enter the shipping channel."

"I'll do my best not to run into it." Sam said this only half jokingly. He'd sailed in storms before, but nothing prepared him for the lack of visibility this time. The ship's lights barely penetrated the heavy rain, and the Oak Island Lighthouse looked dim and distant. The few lit navigational beacons still functioned, helping to guide his path as he kept one eye on the radar and GPS and turned on a course parallel to the shoals. As he turned, he saw the channel marker through the window only a few feet away. *Too damn close for comfort.*

"You got it, Sammy. Now straight ahead."

"Thanks." Sam was about to place a grateful hand on Wesley's shoulder when a wave caught them from the side. Sam struggled to maintain his grip on the wheel as the boat rocked wildly. Only Wesley's steadying arm around his waist kept Sam from ending up on the floor.

"I've got your back."

Sam's chest warmed with the words. Wesley had always been the calm in the eye of the storm, and this situation wasn't an exception. Sam felt good knowing he wasn't going it alone for a change.

The farther from the island they ventured, the higher the waves rose. Fifteen feet, nearly twenty with a stronger gust. The *Neverland*'s running lights caught the movement of the water as it rose and fell. The waves shuddered, creating ripples as the wind danced across the curved inner surfaces. And although the ship's stabilizers absorbed some of the movement that pitched and rocked the vessel, Sam still felt each wave in his bones.

"Slow down," Wesley said after a few more minutes. "We're just about at their last reported position."

"Got it." Sam slowed them down, keeping just enough forward momentum to keep them in the channel.

"Now what?"

"You ready to take over?"

Wesley nodded. In the glow of the instrument panel, the tight line of his jaw was visible.

"I've set the handheld radio on 71. That way you can keep monitoring the emergency channel and we can still talk on this." He handed one of the two small devices to Wesley.

"Got it. Thanks." Wesley set the radio on the console. "Oh, and Sammy?"

"Huh?"

"Please don't do anything stupid, okay?"

"Who, me?"

"Don't joke about this," Wesley said, his voice strong and unforgiving. "I mean it. I…. whatever happens to us after this…. What I mean is I—"

Sam kissed Wesley. A quick, sweet kiss he hoped would communicate the depth of love he had for Wesley. "I love you," he said, his voice rough to his own ears. He didn't wait to hear Wesley's answer but tightened the life vest around his chest, grabbed the second VHF radio, and stepped out into the rain.

CHAPTER THIRTY-THREE

SAM HAD always loved the view from far above the main deck, but tonight each step up the ladder felt like a mile. He slipped and slid, his shoes heavy with water. At last, tired of struggling, he held tight to the rail and abandoned the shoes for his bare feet.

Where are you?

The only answer was the howling wind, which rocked the ship so violently he lost his footing and had to cling to the step above to maintain his precarious perch. His shin slammed into one of the rungs. From the sting, he guessed the hit had broken the skin.

"Shit." The pain was a powerful reminder that he'd forgotten to tether himself to the boat. The last thing he needed was to end up falling to the deck some ten feet below, or worse, end up in the water himself.

"Sammy, you okay?" Wesley asked over the small radio attached to Sam's belt.

Sam glanced at the cockpit but couldn't see anything past the rhythmic blur of the windshield wipers. "I'm fine," he said as he rubbed his shin and winced. "Nothing broken."

Another strong gust of wind struck the boat portside and forced Sam to grab a hold of the railing with both hands. Pulled by the current and battered by the wind, the ship moved dangerously close to the outer edge of the shipping channel. Wesley managed to steer the ship to port just in time to miss hitting one of the lighted navigational beacons. They were close now, and Wesley understood that they needed to proceed slowly or they might collide with the *Summer Solstice* rather than rescue her crew. Wesley would need to find the delicate balance between using too much power and not using enough.

He can handle it. He's an excellent captain.

Sam finally made it up to the upper bridge. He unhooked the microphone from the console, dialed the radio to channel 16, then pressed the Transmit button. "*Summer Solstice, Summer Solstice*, this is *Neverland*."

No response.

"*Summer Solstice, Summer Solstice*, this is *Neverland*," Sam repeated. "Do you copy? Over."

Again, nothing. He set the radio once more on channel 22A and was just about to hail the Coast Guard when he spotted something off the starboard bow: a flicker of light bouncing up and down. A sailboat steaming light moving with the action of the waves. Located halfway up the mast, the light was a signal to approaching ships that the boat was motoring—or trying to motor, in this case.

Sam pressed the button on the handheld. "Slow her down, Wesley. I see them. About fifty yards off our bow."

"Got it."

Sam felt the ship's engines kick into reverse as Wesley worked to maintain their position.

"Coast Guard Station North Carolina, this is *Neverland*," Sam said over the ship's radio. "I've spotted the *Summer Solstice* near the last known coordinates."

"*Neverland*, this is Coast Guard Station North Carolina. Copy. Standing by on 22-alpha."

"Standing by." Sam hung up the radio, leaving the channel open. He pulled the handheld from his pocket and pressed the Transmit button.

"Wesley, do you copy?"

"Loud and clear," Wesley answered. "Please tell me you're tethered."

"I'm tethered."

"Good." The slight tremolo in Wesley's voice didn't sound like static. "I heard your transmission to the Coast Guard. What's your plan?"

"I'm going to use the crane to pull them off if I can." Sam turned on the lights to illuminate the deck. "Once we're close, bring her parallel to the sailboat and upwind. If you can keep her stable, we'll take some of the wave action. It'll make it easier for them to catch the sling."

"Got it. Just promise me you won't do anything stupid, okay?"

Sam wouldn't remind Wesley he'd said the exact same thing before. "Promise."

Sam ran to the crane atop the topmost deck, detached the dinghy, and attached the Lifesling overboard rescue system so that it swung over the foredeck. After a quick check to be sure the rescue device was properly attached, he grabbed the crane remote, took a deep breath, and clipped himself to one of the tether points. He landed safely on the main deck a moment later.

Satisfied that the crane would work, he retrieved the large spotlight he'd left just inside the main bridge, ran to the foredeck, and shone it over the water. From where he stood, he saw the outline of the sailing ship. Thirty-five, maybe forty feet long, her shredded sails flapped like streamers from the mast and jib. Sam guessed when their engine had cut out, they had tried to sail her. But with the winds gusting so high and the waves pounding the port side, the sailboat still canted dangerously close to the water. She sat low, even when she wasn't heeling over. She might only last a few more minutes before she'd completely fill with water.

"Steer us a little closer," he told Wesley as he made his way back up to the fly bridge to get a better look. A quick glance at the display there showed they were only about two hundred feet from the shoals. Plenty of room on a good day, but today was about as far from good as you might get. Wesley would need to keep an eye on their position to make sure neither boat drifted too close. One good hit to the keel of the sailboat and she might sink.

"I'm on it." The boat began to move again. "And don't worry. I've got my eye on the shoal. You just do what you need."

Sam smiled. Wesley could always read his mind. "Thanks."

As Wesley made a slow approach, Sam pulled a pair of binoculars from under the console and scanned the water to be sure not to hit the boat's occupants if they had been forced to abandon ship. Through the lenses he saw two people, both wearing life vests, clinging to the mast but being tossed about as the waves continued to ruthlessly pound the boat. They needed to protect the smaller vessel from the waves or he'd never be able to rescue them.

"Wesley?"

"Yes."

"Time to give them some cover."

Wesley maneuvered the *Neverland* into position upwind. The ship rocked side to side with each wave, but the waters between the two vessels calmed somewhat.

"Coast Guard Sector North Carolina, this is *Neverland*. I've found the *Summer Solstice*." Sam read aloud the coordinates off his navigational display, then checked their position again and headed back to the foredeck. When the Coast Guard didn't immediately respond, Sam sent the coordinates on his handheld VHF. Before he could clip the radio to his belt, a particularly large wave slammed into the side of the *Neverland*, sending him sprawling and the radio skipping over the deck. It landed in the water and sank.

CHAPTER THIRTY-FOUR

WESLEY SAW something fly into the water in front of the lights. The radio?
Shit.

He knew Sam had told him to stay inside and operate the controls because it was safer, but from where he was, he could do nothing to help. At this rate, more than just the damn radio would end up in the water, and he didn't even want to *think* about what he'd do about that.

"That's it," he snapped as the ship rocked again. He'd had enough of being mothered. Sam would fucking have to deal with it.

He double-checked that his life vest was properly secured, grabbed a baseball cap from a nearby basket, then set the autopilot. He opened the door to the cockpit and was immediately blasted with wind and water. He shut the door and traded the cap for a sun hat, then tied the string under his chin. He'd look like a dork, but he didn't care. At least this way he could shield his eyes. He stepped out into the storm and laughed at himself for thinking goggles might have been a better choice.

He slipped and slid over the metal rungs and made it to the bridge just as a particularly large wave struck the starboard side of the vessel. Wesley heard more than saw Sam hit the anchor winch on the foredeck.

"Fuck."

"You okay?" he shouted down to Sam as he took over from the autopilot and corrected the ship's position.

Sam rubbed his shoulder and glanced upward. "You were supposed to stay inside."

"Not happening. You need my help out here and without a radio"—he gestured to Sam's empty belt—"this is the only way we can communicate."

Sam gritted his teeth and wiped the rain from his eyes, but he didn't argue with Wesley. That would undoubtedly come later. Sam got back to his feet, scowled at Wesley, retrieved the light he'd lost in the fall, and walked amidships.

The deck of the sailboat illuminated, Wesley saw two people on the deck waving frantically.

"How many are you?" Sam shouted over the crashing waves. When the sailors didn't respond, he pointed at them, then held up two fingers and made a questioning gesture with his other hand. One of the sailors held up a hand with two fingers. The boat was swamping quickly, the deck now barely above the bottom of the waves. They had minutes at best before she would sink.

"Hang on!" Sam shouted. The howling wind drowned out Sam voice, but the rain slowed ever so slightly, enough that Wesley could see more clearly than before. He watched as Sam released the tension on the dinghy crane, waved the man overboard recovery device in the air so the sailors could see it, and tossed it toward the sailboat. Sam then grabbed several floating cushions from one of the forward lockers and for good measure threw them as well. If the stranded men fell into the water, at least they might be able to catch a few of them to help them stay afloat.

The Lifesling floated toward the sailboat. The sailor closest to the device reached for it and nearly fell headfirst into the water, but his companion managed to grab hold of his life vest at the last moment. Within a few seconds, one of the men had caught the line attached to the sling and had managed to slip it around his waist.

Good. At least the man wasn't going anywhere if he did fall overboard. Not even a second later, the line that tethered the sailor to the *Neverland* grew taut, and the man was yanked into the open water. As high as the waves were, even with the relative protection of the *Neverland*, he wouldn't last long.

Wesley once again struggled as the wind wailed. The shallow shoals made the waves far worse, and the ship's stabilizers did little to control the rolling. In spite of the wild rocking of the ship, Sam managed to stay on his feet. Wesley marveled at how Sam's powerful leg muscles worked like shock absorbers to control his movement so he could operate the equipment.

Sam pressed a button on the remote. Slowly, the crane raised the man out of the water. He swung back and forth with each gust of wind, and Sam was forced to slow the hoist so the man wouldn't slam into the side of the boat. Finally, when his feet were even with the top of the railing on Sam's boat, Sam turned the crane so the man dangled over the foredeck. Sam gently lowered the rope until the sailor could stand.

"Thank God," the elderly man said as he quickly disengaged himself from the Lifesling.

"You all right?" Sam asked.

The man nodded as Sam handed him a rope.

"Tie this around you," Sam told him as he took the other end and cleated it off near the bow.

"My son... Jay...." The man finished tying the rope and ran over to the railing. "He made me go first."

The sailboat was barely visible above the water. Sam glanced up at Wesley, who nodded and mouthed a silent "You can do this, Sammy."

"We'll get him." Sam took the Lifesling and swung it back over the water. A stiff wind took it skyward and blew it about twenty feet from the sinking vessel. Time seemed to slow as the device floated slowly downwind toward the sailboat. Jay slipped, managing to right himself before he ended up in the water. With one hand around the jib sheet, he leaned over and grabbed the Lifesling before it floated away. Once he had it aboard the boat, he slipped it easily around his waist.

"Almost there," Sam reassured the young man's father. He pressed the button on the crane to raise the sling, but it stopped about a foot above the waves.

Shit. The dinghy crane couldn't have picked a worse time to jam. Wesley turned and eyed the crane, which was attached to the top of the ship about fifteen feet behind where he stood.

"Don't even think about it!" Sam shouted at Wesley. "I need you to keep us off the shoals. Keep her steady, and I'll fix it."

Sam was right, even though Wesley was loath to admit it. "Okay," he said as he once again fought the current and the wind. The wheel vibrated beneath his hands with each gust, but the sensation of the connection between ship and the water was somehow comforting.

Jay swung back and forth on the rope as the wind whistled around them. From time to time, he disappeared as a particularly high wave rose on the water.

"He's going to drown!" Sam's companion shouted.

"He'll be fine," Sam said. He glanced upward and blinked away the water that ran into his eyes.

Wesley saw it now: a twist, or hockle, in the rope at the end of the crane, right near the pulley.

"What's your name?" Sam asked in the calmest voice he could muster.

"Lou. Lou Cameron."

"It's going to be all right, Lou," Sam said. "I'm going up top. I need you to take one of the spotlights and shine it on Jay."

The light wouldn't do much, but Wesley knew it would keep Lou focused on something other than the risk of his son hitting the side of the ship, or worse, drowning. In the face of such a desperate situation, Sam kept calm and focused. Wesley was terrified for both Sam and the young sailor who dangled over the water, but Sam's cool confidence reassured him as well.

The powerful sense of pride that rushed like heat through Wesley's chest took him by surprise. *My Sammy.* His Sammy. A good man who would risk his life to save a stranger. A good man who, in that moment, Wesley loved more than he imagined he could.

"I… sure." Lou swallowed visibly, his face pale in the bright lights. "I can do that."

Sam offered the man a smile and disconnected his tether. "Keep us as steady as you can," he called up to Wesley as he ran up the stairs to the top deck.

"I've got your back." Wesley fought another series of high waves as Sam looked around for a spot to reconnect his tether.

With one eye on the waves and one eye on Sam, Wesley took several deep breaths and reminded himself that Sam would be fine. And when Sam connected his line to a spot near the edge of the deck, close enough that he could reach the place where the rope had jammed the crane, Wesley blew air from between his lips to slow his racing heart.

Sam got down on his hands and knees and slowly made his way over the deck as the ship continued to pitch and roll. Several times, he slid perilously close to the edge and had to grab on to one of the cleats to keep from falling. He finally reached a spot where he could tether himself once again. Using the remote, he released a bit of tension on the rope, then stood and reached for the end of the crane.

It'll be fine, Wesley told himself, repeating the words like a mantra.

Sam leaned over the edge of the deck and reached the kink in the rope. He pulled and swore under his breath. With the rain pelting Sam, Wesley was amazed Sam could even see the knot. He yanked on the rope and twisted as one of his legs dangled over the side. Wesley held his breath now, afraid to do anything but keep the ship as stable as possible. With one last tug, however, the pulley finally cleared. Sam fell to his knees on the deck, clearly exhausted.

"I'm going to pull him in now," Sam shouted to Lou. He pressed the button on the remote and the crane once again began to wind the rope holding Jay.

"Got him!" Lou yelled from below, just as the boat pitched and listed badly to port.

"Damn," Wesley hissed.

They had recovered both sailors, but they had grounded on the shoals. The ship was now at the outermost edge of the channel, and the wind and waves had probably shifted some of the sand and rocks. Wesley prayed they weren't so deeply stuck they'd be unable to maneuver the ship to safety.

Sam locked the crane and ran to the bridge as Wesley revved the bow thrusters and steered the boat away from the shoal. Sam put a comforting hand on Wesley's shoulder. "You've got this. Take your time. You know what to do."

"Thanks," Wesley said, buoyed by Sam's touch and his words. For the first time in a long time, he felt Sam's equal.

The *Neverland* protested as Wesley turned her in the other direction, hoping the movement would free her. The engines roared. The ship seemed frozen in place. Wesley tried turning the wheel again, then alternating engines to try to free the hull from the shoal. Back and forth, nudging the ship forward a few inches, then moving in the opposite direction. Wesley prayed there was no damage to the rudder or the propellers as he continued to work forward and backward. Without propulsion or steering, they'd be as dead in the water as the sailboat had been.

Please. They needed a helping of luck or the *Neverland* would be the next boat to sink. *Something. Anything I can use.* Sam squeezed Wesley's shoulder as Wesley continued to work to free them.

Wesley was about to give up hope when there was a slight lull in the waves. Wesley knew it for the gift it was. He waited a split second, then revved the engines and thrusters. The ship slipped free and turned violently to port. He adjusted the wheel just as a huge wave hit starboard. The ship leaned dangerously, then abruptly righted itself as he increased power to the port engine. Wesley spotted the blinking buoy a few yards away as he turned into the channel.

They'd made it back to safer waters. "Thank God," Wesley said as he leaned against Sam's broad shoulder.

"I never doubted you for a second."

Wesley knew Sam meant it.

"Need any help?" Lou asked from behind them.

Wesley glanced aft to see both Lou and Jay safely tethered to the bridge's railing. Sam grinned. "I think we've got it under control." Then he turned to Wesley and said, "Lou, Jay, meet my husband, Wesley."

"I'd shake your hand," Lou said, "but you have better things to do with it right now."

"Wesley's the best first mate a captain could have," Sam said, the pride in his words obvious. "Best at a lot of things."

"Thank you both," Jay said.

Lou wrapped his arm around his son's shoulders. "We can't thank you enough."

Sam hailed the Coast Guard to let them know everyone was safe. They sailed toward the island without speaking, the only sound the caterwauling wind and the slapping of the waves against the ship's bow. Wesley nearly sighed as the lights of the channel that led to Bald Head Island came into view. It'd be a tricky entry into the small harbor with the wind and the waves, but after what they'd been through, this would be a piece of cake.

Wesley spoke into the radio as Sam turned into the channel. "Bald Head Island, this is the *Neverland*. We're on our way back. We're safe. All of us."

CHAPTER THIRTY-FIVE

SAM TOSSED the last line to the dockhand and wiped his face on his sleeve. He was soaked to the bone. Not to mention bone-tired. A friend had met the two men they'd rescued, and after thanking Sam and Wesley again, they'd left to wash up and rest. They'd take the ferry back to the mainland once it resumed service.

Now, as the first light of dawn began to illuminate the horizon, Sam got a look at the damage to the marina. Here and there, roof tiles lay scattered on the ground. Several of the smaller boats had broken loose and piled up in a corner of the marina, while bits of debris and even small tree limbs covered the decks of some of the larger vessels. The storm had missed the island by about eighty miles, so the damage was far less than it might have been.

Thank goodness.

From what the dockhand had told him, power on the island was out, but a work crew was on the way from the mainland, and they hoped to get it back online by midday. They'd been lucky as hell. Maybe next time Cyrus would listen to reason.

He headed belowdecks to shower and change into dry clothing while Wesley chatted with the dockhand. Fifteen minutes later Sam slipped into a pair of jeans and a T-shirt. He'd shave later. He turned to open the door to his cabin, only to find Wesley was standing in the doorway.

"Hey." He wrapped his arms around Wesley. "We make a great team, don't we?"

Wesley pushed him away and glared at him. "Don't you pull that bullshit with me, Sam."

Angry Wesley. Better than depressed Wesley, but not his favorite Wesley. "I'm not following."

"Like hell you're not. Leaving in the middle of a fucking storm without telling anyone. If I hadn't realized what you were doing, you might have d—"

"You were worried about me." *That*, he could work with. Not to mention it turned their argument over Wesley leaving the island on its head.

"Of course I was worried. Why shouldn't I be?"

"I don't know." This was getting more interesting by the moment.

"I care about you," Wesley said defiantly.

"And?"

Wesley shifted from one foot to the other but held Sam's gaze. "And what? That's not a good enough reason? We were married for nearly ten years."

"We'll be divorced in less than a month."

"What does that have to do with anything?"

Sam shrugged. "You tell me."

"Fuck you, fucking Sander Carson."

"I like it when you swear." Sam smiled.

"You're infuriating. Standing there trying to turn all of this around when I watched you nearly fall overboard. I thought I'd never see you again and I wouldn't be able to—" Wesley seemed to become conscious of what he was saying, his expression now a curious mix of shock and realization. "No," he continued, anger abating somewhat. "This isn't about me. This is about you taking risks. Not asking for help. Doing stupid shit and not caring about what anyone else might feel if you...."

"Yes?" Sam forced himself not to smile. Wesley was too smart not to realize that twice now he had started out talking about how badly Sam had behaved and it had ended up being all about Wesley's feelings. Sam studied Wesley for a moment. Something had changed. Something he hadn't realized before. Or maybe it was something he hadn't *let* himself realize. "You...," he began tentatively. "You're having second thoughts about the divorce."

"This has nothing to do with—"

"Tell me, then."

Wesley frowned. "You make me so fucking angry sometimes. Sometimes I wish I could just—"

Sam kissed him.

Wesley kissed Sam back with such force that Sam wondered who had stepped into Wesley's body. Not that Wesley had ever been shy, but Sam had always sensed Wesley's hesitation. He'd often wondered what Wesley might be like if he let go and stopped analyzing things.

The kiss broke.

"I.... What the hell, Sam?"

Sam shrugged. "Seemed like the right thing to do?"

"Damn you." Wesley grabbed Sam's upper arms, and his right hand met the spot where Sam had collided with the winch. Sam hissed and gritted his teeth.

"You're hurt."

"I'm fine." Sam forced a smile.

"No, you're not fine." Wesley gently lifted Sam's shirtsleeve to reveal the ugly purple bruise beneath. "Shit, Sammy. You got that when you hit the winch, didn't you?"

"Could be."

"Sit," Wesley commanded.

Sam complied, too tired to argue.

"Dammit, Sam, you could have fucking *died* out there." Wesley gently touched Sam's leg and Sam winced.

"I'm fine. Don't worry about—"

"How can I *not* worry when you take off like some fucking cowboy to save the day? By yourself!"

"Like a pirate." Sam grinned. He knew he'd pay for that, but he couldn't help himself.

Wesley sat heavily on the bed. "Fuck. Just…. Fuck."

"There's more to this than being worried or pissed at me. Not that I blame you for either," Sam added quickly, knowing full well he'd pushed Wesley to his limit.

"I don't know what you mean." Wesley sounded less confident than before.

"You're thinking about accepting my offer. About giving us another chance. Aren't you?" He'd expected Wesley would take his time the way he always did, but now he wasn't so sure.

Wesley's gaze flitted about the room, alighting everywhere but on Sam. "I… I… I don't know." He paused, then added, "Maybe I am."

"I don't want you back if the only reason you want me is that you were worried about losing me," Sam heard himself say. Why had he said that? He wanted Wesley. Who cared why Wesley was considering it? But he didn't take back the words.

"What?" Wesley seemed just as confused.

"If you take me back just because you were afraid to lose me…. That's not a good enough reason." Sam struggled to find the words.

"I'm not following."

"Why did you call it quits?" Sam asked.

Wesley stared at him and tilted his head ever so slightly to the side. "You don't want me back?"

"I want you back," Sam said. "Hell, I'm having a hard time not pushing your scrawny little ass onto the bed and...." He didn't need to go into the details. He needed to focus, and focusing on sex with Wesley was just going to confuse the issue.

Wesley's lips parted, but he said nothing.

"You didn't answer my question. Why did you call it quits?" Sam repeated.

"I.... Because we weren't good for each other."

"And now why are you considering my proposal?" When Wesley didn't answer, Sam continued, "I know you love me, Wesley. You said it yourself weeks ago—that's not a good enough reason to try again. I don't want you back if that's the only reason."

"Sammy?"

"I can't believe I just said that, but I'm pretty sure I meant it."

The corners of Wesley's mouth turned upward, and he started to laugh.

"What the hell, Wesley," Sam growled. "I just told you I don't want you, and you're *laughing* at me?"

"Not laughing *at* you. Not really. Besides, you shouldn't be complaining. A few minutes ago, I was ready to strangle you. I'm still half tempted."

"I'm doing my best here to understand." Sam rubbed his mouth. He was too tired for this.

"Don't you get it? After all the romantic bullshit, you tell me you don't want to be with me if the only reason I want to be with you is that I thought you were going to die, or that I love you," Wesley said.

"I don't see—"

"It's... well... saying you don't want me for those reasons is just another reason to *want* to stay with you."

Sam's head hurt. "I'm totally lost."

Wesley smiled. "Before I went to Guatemala, nothing between us had changed. You were trying so damn hard. *Too* hard. You doted on me. You romanced me. You tried to sweep me off my feet. I ran because I knew if I stayed, I'd fall back into it. And nothing would have changed. We'd end up right back where we started."

A glimmer of understanding started to reach Sam's dead-tired brain. "I thought you wanted to be romanced. You'd know I wanted you."

"I... yes... no." Wesley rubbed his eyes and fell back onto the bed. Sam didn't move any closer—it was too dangerous, and he knew that whatever his body wanted, he needed to work this out first. "*I'm* not even sure what I wanted," Wesley admitted. "But you made it fucking difficult, you know."

"Sorry." Sam tried to appear apologetic, but he wasn't really. *What's so wrong about letting your husband know you love him and you don't want a divorce?*

"You're not." Wesley pushed Sam playfully, then sighed and closed his eyes. "Didn't matter, though. I wasn't going to cheat on Carl." He laughed bitterly. "Not that he gave a shit about that. But it wouldn't have been fair to you either."

"Yeah." He understood that too. He loved Wesley all the more for it. In all the years they'd lived on opposite coasts, he'd never once doubted Wesley's fidelity. "But I like doing things for you."

"There's nothing wrong with romance," Wesley said. "But it's not what keeps people together. Not by itself."

"And you've figured out what does?" He meant the question in earnest.

"Yes. Or maybe I've just figured out what I wanted. Even if I had no clue before." Wesley sat up again and, to Sam's surprise, took Sam's hands in his own. "I want you. But not for the reasons you think," he added quickly.

"Okay. Then why?"

Wesley inhaled slowly, then met Sam's gaze. "After Guatemala, I felt like my entire life was falling apart. I knew I needed to see Carl— reassure myself that the perfect life I'd created for myself was real—or I'd never get over losing you. And the whole fucking thing turned out to be a mirage."

"I really am sorry, Wesley," Sam said. "I know it was my—"

Wesley put a finger to Sam's lips to silence him. "You were there for me, and you didn't ask for anything in return. You listened. Really listened to me when I needed it most. You even opened up to me. You leaned on me too.

"I was *so* pissed when you tried to order me off the island the other night. And when I realized you'd left on some cockamamie, idiotic… and that I might never be able to make up with you, I…." Wesley blew air from between tight lips. "Regardless of how ridiculously risky that was"—he glared at Sam—"I started to think about the past few weeks.

"Don't get me wrong—I'd never want anything to happen to you." He touched Sam's cheek, and the tenderness in his expression made Sam's chest tighten. "But the thought of losing you made me think about how things between us really *had* changed. And I knew that if I never saw you again, I couldn't… I wouldn't be able…." Wesley clearly struggled not to give in to his emotions. "I wouldn't be able to tell you that I still love you. That I want to be with you," he whispered. "It's why I came along for the ride."

"I'm really glad you did," Sam admitted. "I couldn't have done it without you."

"I… I like hearing that. It makes me feel like part of a team instead of like I'm running after you."

"You always beat my sorry ass when we run," Sam said with a chuckle.

Wesley frowned. "You know what I mean."

Sam nodded. "Yeah." It had felt so good, working alongside Wesley. A hell of a lot better than doing things by himself. "We work well together, don't we?"

"We do." Wesley appeared just as surprised about that as he did.

Before Sam could respond, Wesley continued, "But there's something else I need to say. Something I realized when things with— after I got back from Guatemala."

Sam pressed his lips together and waited patiently. Hearing about Carl hurt, but he could handle it. He *would* handle it.

But what Wesley said had nothing to do with Carl at all. "I was afraid…. I was afraid I wasn't good enough for you."

"But you're everything I always—"

Wesley pressed a finger to Sam's lips. "I believe you, Sammy. Mostly. I mean, I believe you up here." He tapped his temple and smiled. "The reason I let you go. Why I didn't fight harder for our marriage…. I realize now I didn't believe I was good enough for you."

"You know you are."

"I believe it more now. But back then I was just Wesley. A dork. Geek. Awkward. And you were this huge star. People loved you so much."

For a moment Sam didn't move. Couldn't move because his brain seemed to be stuck on Wesley's words. "Damn."

Wesley laughed. "That's it? Just… damn?"

"Wesley." Sam rubbed his mouth and shook his head. "There's no one else for me. The Sander stuff is great, but it's not enough. It's not what *Sam* needs." He needed Wesley to understand this.

"Those years in LA without you, I kept believing I *was* Sander. But when you filed for divorce, it was like the floor dropped out from under me. I was so lonely. Lost. I can't explain it except that knowing you were waiting in the wings kept me focused. And when I lost you, it all became clear. I wasn't just Sander. I was Sam. *Your* Sam."

He reached out and took Wesley's hands. "You're everything. Funny. Smart. Sexy. Gorgeous. Sweet. Understanding. Everything, Wesley. Without you, Sam and Sander are total fuckups. We *both* need you. And we're both going to spend our lives making sure you know how much we love you and how perfect you are." Sam pulled Wesley close and kissed him hard, waiting until Wesley's body responded, then exploring Wesley's mouth with renewed hunger.

"I love you, Sammy. I want to be with you," Wesley said as their lips parted.

God, Sam had wanted to hear those words for so long! "Do you believe me?"

Wesley nodded. "Kiss me again?"

"Hell yeah." Sam pulled Wesley so they both fell back on the bed. Before, he'd been all about the sex. Now he wanted to take his time. Feel Wesley—really *feel* him and understand *what* he felt.

"You sure you're okay?"

"I'm perfect." He didn't care about his throbbing shoulder or the ache in his leg. He'd long forgotten about them. He didn't care that his empty stomach protested. He wanted this, and he didn't intend to wait.

Wesley gazed up at him and Sam sighed. "Love you," Sam said in a half whisper, half rumble. "So much." He leaned over and kissed Wesley, slowly exploring Wesley's mouth, gliding over teeth, slipping around and tangling with Wesley's tongue until Wesley moaned.

This close, he caught Wesley's distinct scent. Sweet, with a hint of the citrus soap he preferred, Wesley smelled at once familiar and new. Before, Sam hadn't stopped to appreciate the layers of Wesley's sensuality. Over time, he'd taken them for granted. The beard was new, of course, but beneath the wiry hair, the edge of Wesley's jaw felt familiar, hard beneath Wesley's soft cheek. The way Wesley's lips molded to his, and the way Wesley feathered his fingers through Sam's hair. Sam shivered as they pulled away from each other.

"I missed this," Wesley said after a long moment.

"I did too." Sam unbuttoned Wesley's shirt, lingering on each button, not wanting to rush. Wesley watched him with an intensity that made Sam's heart beat faster. Each time he revealed a bit more of Wesley's skin, Sam kissed it and ran lazy circles over it with his tongue, tasting the slightly salty tang. When he had finally revealed all of Wesley's chest, he straddled Wesley's hips and stroked his skin, starting at his neck and working his way downward until he reached the waistband of Wesley's shorts.

"Sam."

His name on Wesley's lips, spoken in that husky whisper, was almost better than the kiss. Sam smiled, then unbuttoned Wesley's shorts, his eyes never leaving Wesley's as he unzipped them, moving so he could pull them off with Wesley's boxers until he was gloriously and completely naked. He ignored the prize of Wesley's hard cock. There would be time for that later. He wanted this to last. "Much better," he said as he found a peaked bud and rolled it between his thumb and forefinger.

Wesley hissed his approval and arched his back in a silent plea for more. Sam obliged, giving equal attention to the other nipple, then continued to lick Wesley's skin until he heard Wesley's stuttered breaths. He traced the side of Wesley's body from his chest to the top of his thigh, remembering the feel of it, learning what he hadn't noticed before. Like how Wesley's skin seemed smoother and how the feather-soft hair on his thighs and belly made Sam's fingers tingle. Or how Wesley had become even more ticklish, judging by the way he held his breath and tensed his stomach muscles when Sam's thumbs brushed his abdomen.

"I've missed this so much," Sam said as he caught Wesley's intense gaze. "Touching you. Taking the time to explore your body. Being near you."

Wesley's brilliant smile was all Sam needed to understand that Wesley felt the same. Sam claimed Wesley's lips again, this time pulling him to a seated position and exploring his mouth with the same focus as he had Wesley's body. Whereas before their kisses had been more frenzied, this time Sam met Wesley's tongue, circling it slowly, tasting the familiar mouth, drawing out the contact as Wesley moaned.

"Get undressed," Wesley said.

"Me?"

"Do it, Sammy."

Sam stood and did as he was told, taking his time not only so he wouldn't accidentally press against the bruises, but because he wanted Wesley to watch him. Wesley seemed perfectly content to do just that.

Sam slowly pulled his T-shirt over his head. He'd never been particularly vain, even though he knew his good looks had gotten him his first jobs. He'd never cared much about what other people thought about his body. Except Wesley. And watching Wesley's expression as he undressed—that was the fucking hottest thing.

"You look really good." Wesley got off the bed and traced his fingers lightly over the muscles of Sam's abdomen and chest. Sam's nipples peaked and he moaned, craving more but loving the ethereal touch. "Different than I remember. Harder." Wesley wrapped his arms around Sam and grabbed his ass, causing Sam's cock to harden. Wesley kneaded the muscles until they stung, then stepped back and sat on the edge of the bed. Waiting.

Sam grinned and unbuttoned his jeans, unzipped them, and waited until he saw Wesley's gaze flicker. They'd always loved this dance for control, even if their sex wasn't always about that.

"You're teasing me. I'm pretty sure I told you to take off your clothes." Wesley raised an eyebrow and said, "Briefs are clothing, you know."

"I love it when you lecture me."

"Some things never change." Wesley's smile was warm as Sam shimmied out of his undies. He was so hard now, he ached. "And that's a damn good thing," Wesley added.

Wesley pulled Sam onto the bed and kissed him, a sweet and tender kiss that only aroused Sam more. The playful expression in Wesley's eyes fled, replaced by a look Sam could only characterize as one of reverence. But Wesley wasn't looking at his body, he was looking directly into his eyes. Sam once might have joked about that intense a gaze, if only to shrug off his discomfort. This time he met it head-on. No bullshit. Just him and Wesley and the pounding of his heart.

"It's better like this," Sam said.

"Better?"

"The way we started."

Wesley nodded. "Captain and first mate. Friends and sex. Talking, kissing…."

"Fucking."

Wesley laughed softly.

"Make love to me, Wesley," Sam said. "Slow. Soft. The way you used to when we first met."

The edges of Wesley's mouth edged oh so slightly upward, but the love in his eyes never wavered. Sam knew what a chance Wesley was taking on him—on them.

"I can't promise you I'll get it right this time," Sam said as he held Wesley's face in his hands and lovingly caressed his cheeks. "But I'm damn well going to try."

"We're doing this together." Wesley straddled Sam and laved kisses over his jaw and neck. "Remember?"

"Yeah." Sam wouldn't blow things off this time. "But you'll probably have to kick my ass a few times."

Wesley leaned over and licked around one of Sam's nipples. "I'll be ready." He moved to the other nipple, giving it its due, then skated his hands down Sam's chest and traced his tongue on a line from his Adam's apple downward. By the time his lips met Sam's cock, it was all Sam could do not to squirm.

"Wesley."

Wesley swallowed Sam's cock, moaning and rubbing against Sam's leg as he took Sam so deep, Sam thought he'd come right then and there. As if he'd sensed this, Wesley backed off, allowing Sam time to catch his breath. Then he licked his way around Sam's crown and hummed his pleasure as he sucked.

For the past three years, Sam had dreamed about this. About Wesley on top of him, taking control, allowing him to *lose* control to his body and his heart. Wesley—*his* Wesley—beautiful and naked, loving him, reminding him how lucky he was to have found someone like this.

"Fuck!"

Wesley's rumbled appreciation shot through Sam's body like fire, and he canted his hips upward, pushing deeper into Wesley's hot mouth. *That's it, Wesley. Love me like you used to. Make me yours.*

Sam came sooner than he'd intended, but the combination of emotion and heat was too much for him to fight. He shouted Wesley's name and clung to him as he reeled with the pleasure of his release. "Wesley, God, Wesley!"

"Sammy." Wesley smiled up at him and licked his lips. *Hottest fucking thing.* "Roll over."

"Fuck yes," Sam muttered. He'd wanted Wesley inside him for so long, he was ready to beg. He rolled onto his belly and stretched, catlike, on the duvet.

"Supplies?" Wesley asked in that formal, professorial voice Sam loved to tease him about. Sam didn't, though. He wanted Wesley inside of him, and he wasn't playing around this time. Later, there'd be plenty of time for some of the games they liked to play.

"Top drawer. Left-hand side of the bed."

The bed was big enough that Wesley had to get up and walk over to the side table. Sam felt the cool smoothness of Wesley's fingers as Wesley pulled apart the globes of his ass and slid a single finger over Sam's hole. Wesley kissed his way over Sam's asscheeks as he worked Sam open. Each time Wesley pressed a little farther inside, he kissed Sam again, until Sam imagined Wesley had touched every inch of his skin. Lithe fingers worked their way up and down his back as Wesley stretched him until he opened to Wesley's touch.

Something tickled Sam's sensitive skin, causing him to shiver. Wesley's beard had grown longer. Sam guessed he hadn't had time to trim it close with all the excitement of the storm. The added stimulation only heightened Sam's pleasure, and Wesley seemed to realize this, because he took every opportunity to brush Sam's skin with that short, wiry hair.

Better than before.

Sam had long since closed his eyes. With each touch, he tried to imagine where Wesley would touch him next, sometimes guessing correctly, other times being taken by happy surprise. Tongue, teeth, and those sinful fingers caressed him until Sam felt as though he was floating.

Sam had completely lost track of how long Wesley had explored his body when Wesley pressed his cock against Sam's opening. Slicked, ready, and relaxed, Sam's body opened completely to Wesley until Wesley was seated deep inside him, abdomen pressed against Sam's ass.

Wesley moved slowly at first, leaning in to trace Sam's spine with his tongue as he withdrew almost completely, then slid in once again. Sam's groans of pleasure matched the slow, hypnotic pace of Wesley's movements as Sam's cock reawakened against the soft fabric beneath him.

Wesley shifted his position just enough that the tip of his cock brushed Sam's gland. Wesley knew that spot well. He knew how to drive Sam to the brink and pull him back before he careened over the edge of his orgasm. Out and then in once again, this time making sure Sam knew the contact had been no accident.

"Ah, shit. Wesley…."

Sam imagined Wesley's smile spreading over his face as he ghosted his hands over Sam's body and continued with low, slow thrusts. The rhythm of Wesley's body against his own had Sam moving to meet

Wesley. Before, Wesley might have increased the pace with Sam's encouragement. This time, Wesley would not be swayed. He leaned down and nipped tenderly at the soft skin at Sam's neck and maintained contact, skin to skin, as he moved in and out.

Wesley sighed, and Sam heard both desire and relief in the wordless sound. And just when Sam was about to beg, Wesley moved faster, breath stuttering, body shaking as he thrust deeper and harder. "Love… you… Sammy," he ground out.

Sam knew Wesley was close, but he waited and let Wesley keep control, riding the wave of Wesley's orgasm and only then letting himself follow as he shot all over the sheets. *Talk about a boat christening!*

Wesley held him tight until he slipped out, then tossed the condom and fell onto the bed next to Sam, who had already pulled up the covers and grabbed a blanket from a drawer underneath.

"I remember the first time I saw you," Wesley said as he held Sam afterward. "How beautiful you were. And when you kissed me at the party, I couldn't understand why you'd want someone like me."

"I remember thinking how lucky I was." Sam kissed Wesley's chest. "Why someone like you would bother with a nobody like me. A kid who cut up and dreamed about getting paid to be on stage."

"I need to tell you something," Wesley said, his eyes wide and dark with emotion.

"Did I do something wrong?" Sam asked, only half jokingly.

"No. But I want you to know that I never…. In the time we were apart, I didn't… I couldn't be with someone else." He smiled, then added, "Maybe I knew all along that you were the only one. I know it sounds corny, but—"

Sam silenced Wesley with his lips to cover his own emotional response, then thought better of it. This was starting over again, wasn't it? He would be entirely honest. Hoping Wesley might be jealous was something he might have done years before. He broke the kiss and swallowed hard.

"What's wrong?" Wesley asked with a frown.

"I…. There was no one for me, either." He brushed Wesley's cheek tenderly, tracing Wesley's mouth. "Never could be."

"You really have changed, you know."

"I don't—"

"Shhh," Wesley said with a finger to Sam's lips. "Being honest with me? That's a good thing. It makes me love you more."

Sam sighed with relief, not caring that he might appear weak. Only caring that Wesley—*his* Wesley—loved him in spite of his stupidity.

Sam held Wesley against his chest. How long had it been since they'd just held each other like this? "I like this."

"Mmm." Wesley snuggled tighter against Sam. "Love you."

"Love you too."

Wesley looked up at Sam, his expression suddenly hard. "And if you ever fucking do anything so shit stupid again, Samuel Raymond Carr, I'm going to fucking kill you. No more charging off. Unless you take me with you, that is," he added as his expression softened into a smile.

Sam did his best to appear contrite. "Got it."

"You damn well *better* have gotten it."

"We'll do the stupid shit together."

"Damn straight we will."

Sam sighed and pulled Wesley close again. "So what happens now?"

Wesley blew air from between his lips. "We figure out how to make this relationship work."

"I told you, I'll quit—"

"You're a pain in the ass, you know?" He pinched Sam's thigh.

"Ow! What was that for?"

"Stop with the self-sacrificing bullshit." Wesley spoke in his professor's voice. "This whole thing's about compromise. I give a little, you give a little."

"Okay. So what do you have in mind?"

"I'm working on that," Wesley said. When Sam shot him a skeptical look, Wesley added, "You were right. I take my time to decide things. But thinking things through and not rushing can pay off."

"Oh?"

"I did marry you, didn't I?" Wesley pointed out.

"You win." Sam couldn't keep his eyes open another minute. "I'll try to be patient."

"Good." Wesley leaned over and kissed Sam again.

It wasn't an answer, but Sam would live with it. And for now, he reasoned, that would have to be good enough.

Chapter Thirty-Six

THE CROWDS gathered around the square in Charleston, where a gallows had been erected. Stede Bonnet stood atop the platform in tattered clothes, his face unshaven and dirty, skin sallow from months of prison, dark circles around his eyes.

"You have been tried and found guilty of piracy," the stern officer presiding over the execution announced. "What say you?"

"I make no excuse for my wrongs," Bonnet said, head held high. "I alone am responsible for the choices I have made. I alone will accept my fate."

The townspeople jeered and shouted, the anticipation now reaching a fever pitch. A few people tossed rotten eggs and vegetables onto the wooden platform, several of which splashed Bonnet's face. He smiled, his eyes now focused on a point in the distance, as if he were imagining cresting a wave and the salt spray on his face.

Someone put a hood over Bonnet's head, while another wrapped a rope around his neck and tightened it.

"Kill 'im!" a woman shouted, her rough voice rising over the others. Others joined the call, until the crowd seemed to chant as one.

"May God save your soul," the minister overseeing the grim proceedings said as he pressed his hand fervently to his weathered Bible.

Someone—the governor, perhaps—gave the signal to the executioner. A moment later the sound of the trapdoor in the dais giving way rang out in the square. The crowd cheered.

The camera panned across the crowd, then settled on a dusty tricorne hat with a broken feather tucked into its brim.

"And… cut!" Parker shouted. "Excellent work everyone! Thank you for your patience. That's a wrap!"

Wesley knew they were nowhere near done filming, but they'd finished their location work, and the crew needed a reason to celebrate. But wrapping the location shoot meant soon he and Sam would be apart once again.

The extras, many of them locals who had been waiting since the crack of dawn for a chance to be part of the scene, now shouted happily and ran to where someone was helping Sam out of the noose and lifting the hood from his head. He grinned and proceeded to sign every piece of paper anyone put in front of him.

At one point, Sam glanced up and met Wesley's gaze. The pleasant expression he'd worn as he'd signed autographs lifted momentarily, and Wesley glimpsed the sweet, loving man he'd married so many years before. Still the same, but maybe now they'd have a chance at the elusive happily ever after.

Wesley chuckled to himself. Sam had always been the romantic, not him. But maybe that had changed too.

"Are you two coming to the party?" Jeffrey asked. Cyrus stood close by him. Wesley saw much of the same expression in his eyes as he had in Sam's a moment before.

"He's got a date." Sam slipped his arms around Wesley's waist and kissed his neck. Wesley shivered and relaxed against Sam's chest.

"I do?" Wesley raised an eyebrow.

Sam grinned. "Yep. Sunset cruise and dinner at my favorite restaurant."

"Sorry, gentlemen," Wesley said. "I have a date."

"So do we," Cyrus announced.

"We do?" Jeffrey frowned at him.

"Sunset cruise." Cyrus winked at Sam. "*Double* date."

Jeffrey looked to Sam, who nodded. "Double date."

"But you two probably want to be alone," Jeffrey protested weakly.

"We've got all the time in the world for that," Wesley said. "Besides, that boat's way too big for just the two of us."

THE SUN set as they finished eating dinner on the aft deck. "Feel free to sit and enjoy the view," Sam said as he stood and offered Wesley his hand. "The forward guest cabin's been made up for you. I had Kara put some bubbly on ice."

"Thank you." Cyrus leaned over and whispered something in Jeffrey's ear. Jeffrey blushed and giggled.

Sam waved, and he and Wesley walked to the foredeck to watch the last of the color disappear into the starry sky.

"They're cute together," Wesley said.

"Cyrus asked Jeffrey to move into his place."

"In LA?" When Sam nodded, Wesley pressed, "And?"

"No go. But Cyrus isn't giving up." Sam pressed his lips together and sighed. "I offered Jeffrey a two-year contract."

"Let me guess. He said he'll think about it."

"Yep." Sam shrugged.

"Not everyone makes his mind up as quickly as you." Wesley leaned in and brushed Sam's lips.

"Oh, shut up and enjoy the view." Sam's grin belied his words.

"It's a beautiful night," Wesley said as he leaned on the railing a moment later and inhaled the salty air.

"You remember, years ago," Sam began, "when we saw those big boats on Ocracoke Island?"

"You said someday you'd own one of those boats, and we'd sail all over the world." They'd been so young then, and the dream had seemed so out of reach.

"We'll do that, Wesley," Sam said earnestly. "I promise."

"That sounds lovely. But I really don't care anymore."

"You don't... why not?"

Wesley took Sam's face in his hands and kissed his nose, his chin, and finally his lips. "I dreamed about that," he said, still holding Sam close. "But if it never happens, I'm good with it. Being with you is enough."

"Oh my God," Sam laughed. "You've become more of a romantic than me."

Wesley smiled and swatted Sam on the ass. "Shut up and put up," he said, pursing his lips and tapping his foot on the deck.

Sam tapped his chest over his heart, laughed, then did as he was told, kissing Wesley until Wesley sighed and wrapped his arms around Sam. *His* Sam. His stubborn, pain-in-the-ass, wonderful, sweet, funny Sam.

This time, he was holding on tight and not letting him go.

CHAPTER THIRTY-SEVEN

New York City, eight months later

THE AUDIENCE applauded, some getting to their feet as the cast took their bows in front of the curtain. Several people whistled and shouted before receiving lethal glares from some of the other patrons. *Messy,* Wesley thought. *Just like Sam.* But in a good way.

Wesley remembered Corliss's face six months before, when she'd warned Sam he was making a huge mistake. Sam had turned down yet another sequel she'd been pushing to do an off-off-Broadway experimental production of *Shrew's Revenge*, a gender-bending retelling of Shakespeare's *The Taming of the Shrew*.

She stared at him when he told her he was ending their contract, then proceeded to lecture him about how his career was "going to fucking Hades in a butt bag."

Sam had just smiled and told her kindly but firmly, "I appreciate all you've done for me, but this isn't me. I'll honor my commitments, then we go our separate ways."

Even more surprising than Sam's choice to cut his ties with big-money Hollywood was Sam's insistence that Wesley be by his side for the meeting with Corliss. "If I've learned anything," he told Wesley before the meeting, "it's that we do this together. Talk about things. Plan for a change."

Wesley had no illusions that things would be perfect, but so far Sam was sticking to his guns. He'd moved back to New York, and they'd bought a house in Queens. Sure, Sam had enough money to afford the entire block, but that wasn't the point. "This is me, Wesley. Us."

Wesley secretly loved the house they bought on Fire Island, though, where they spent nearly every weekend and where the *Neverland* was docked. Their sanctuary and Wesley's Zen place. He might not need all the money Sam had earned making movies to be happy, but he appreciated what it paid for.

Most of his and Sam's savings, however, they stashed away. Sam had insisted they plan for a rainy day that would never come, but Wesley knew Sam worried about their future.

Wesley smiled and waited for most of the audience to clear out, then headed toward the stage and the door that led to the dressing rooms.

"Professor Coolidge," Roger, the security guy, said as he greeted him with a broad smile. "You've made every performance so far."

"No place I'd rather spend my evening." Wesley wouldn't go for drinks at the producer's Manhattan penthouse—he had a class to teach in the morning—but that was okay too. He'd wake up to Sam next to him, and when the show's run ended on Sunday, he and Sam would head to the Bahamas on the *Neverland*. That they had the week to themselves was Sam's doing: he had insisted that the end of the limited run of the experimental play coincide with Wesley's spring break.

"Best performance yet," Wesley said as Sam let him into his dressing room—not much more than a closet, and so far from the big trailers they'd had on location in North Carolina.

Sam swept him into a bear hug, smearing some of his makeup on Wesley's cheek. Wesley didn't care. When he released Wesley, Sam grabbed something from a nearby table. A folded newspaper. The *New York Times*. "Read it," he said with a self-satisfied grin.

Hollywood never understood the diamond in the rough that is Sander Carson. As Kurt, Carson adds a sweet sensibility to the role that aids this modern retelling of the Shakespeare play in striking the uneasy balance between humor and pathos. Carson is at once sharp-tongued and heartbreakingly vulnerable in this gender-bending riff on the original. And while this new production is solid, with Carson's brilliant performance, it is sure to find its way to Broadway.

"I always knew you were this good, Sammy," Wesley said.

Sam looked so incredibly *happy*. Not that he didn't deserve the rave review, but the expression on Sam's face was worth far more than the words on the paper.

"I got a call today," Sam announced.

"Oh?" From the look on Sam's face, Wesley knew Sam had struggled to keep the secret to himself.

"Another pirate movie."

"Seriously?"

Sam shrugged. "Minimal Hollywood bullshit. A historically accurate telling of Jack Ward's story."

"A Barbary pirate this time? No Errol Flynn?"

"Nope. I said I wouldn't take the gig if they went that route."

"Demanding, aren't we?"

"They're going to film it this summer," Sam continued gleefully.

"They are, are they?"

"They need an expert. Some work before filming, but they want someone on location." Sam sat in front of the mirror and began to wipe the makeup from his face.

Wesley raised an eyebrow and gazed at Sam in the mirror. "Interesting. Let's see. An English corsair. Captain Jack was one of England's greatest scoundrels. Worked as a privateer for Queen Elizabeth, but he captured a ship and converted to Islam. Made a fortune privateering. Died of the plague, I believe. Sometime in the early 1600s. What more do you need to know? I'm sure Marv Hatfield would do a great job for you."

"Wesley," Sam prodded. "Come on. You know you want to do this."

"I need to think about it."

"Cyrus is backing the film." Sam chuckled and added, "Jeffrey's been pestering me all day to give the studio an answer. He's starting to act more like my agent than my assistant."

"You kept this a secret all *day*?"

"More like five hours," Sam admitted sheepishly. "So you'll do it?"

"I said I'll think about it."

Sam frowned at him. "Sometimes I think you do that just to piss me off."

Wesley grinned.

"You're enjoying this too fucking much."

"You know I'm going to say yes eventually."

Sam stood and faced Wesley down. "Say yes now, or ye'll be walking the plank."

"All right." Wesley kissed Sam. "Yes."

Sam hugged Wesley tight. "You're a cute pain in the ass, you know."

"Back at you."

"So, matey," Sam said with a devilish grin, "what say ye we sail at dawn?"

Wesley rolled his eyes. "We're going to need to work on your dialogue," he said, then kissed a line up Sam's neck to his ear.

Sam shivered and sighed contentedly. "That's what you're here for, right?"

"Always, Sammy," Wesley said. "Always."

SHIRA ANTHONY was a professional opera singer in her last incarnation, performing roles in such operas as *Tosca*, *Pagliacci*, and *La Traviata*, among others. She's given up TV for evenings spent with her laptop, and she never goes anywhere without a pile of unread M/M romance on her Kindle.

Shira is married with two children and two insane dogs, and when she's not writing, she is usually in a courtroom trying to make the world safer for children. When she's not working, she can be found at the Carolina coast aboard *Land's Zen*, a 35' catamaran sailboat, with her favorite sexy captain at the wheel.

Shira writes what she loves, be it contemporary musicians, shifter mermen, or time-traveling vampires. Her Mermen of Ea trilogy book, *Into the Wind*, was named one of the best books of 2014 by both Scattered Thoughts and Rogue Words and Hearts on Fire Reviews, and was a finalist in the 2014 Goodreads M/M Romance Member's Choice Awards. Her Blue Notes series of classical-music-themed gay romances was named one of Scattered Thoughts and Rogue Word's "Best Series of 2012," and the most recent book in the series, *Dissonance*, was named one of the best books of 2014 by Hearts on Fire Reviews.

Shira can be found on:
Facebook: www.facebook.com/shira.anthony
Goodreads: www.goodreads.com/author/show/4641776.Shira_Anthony
Twitter: @WriterShira
Website: www.shiraanthony.com
E-mail: shiraanthony@hotmail.com

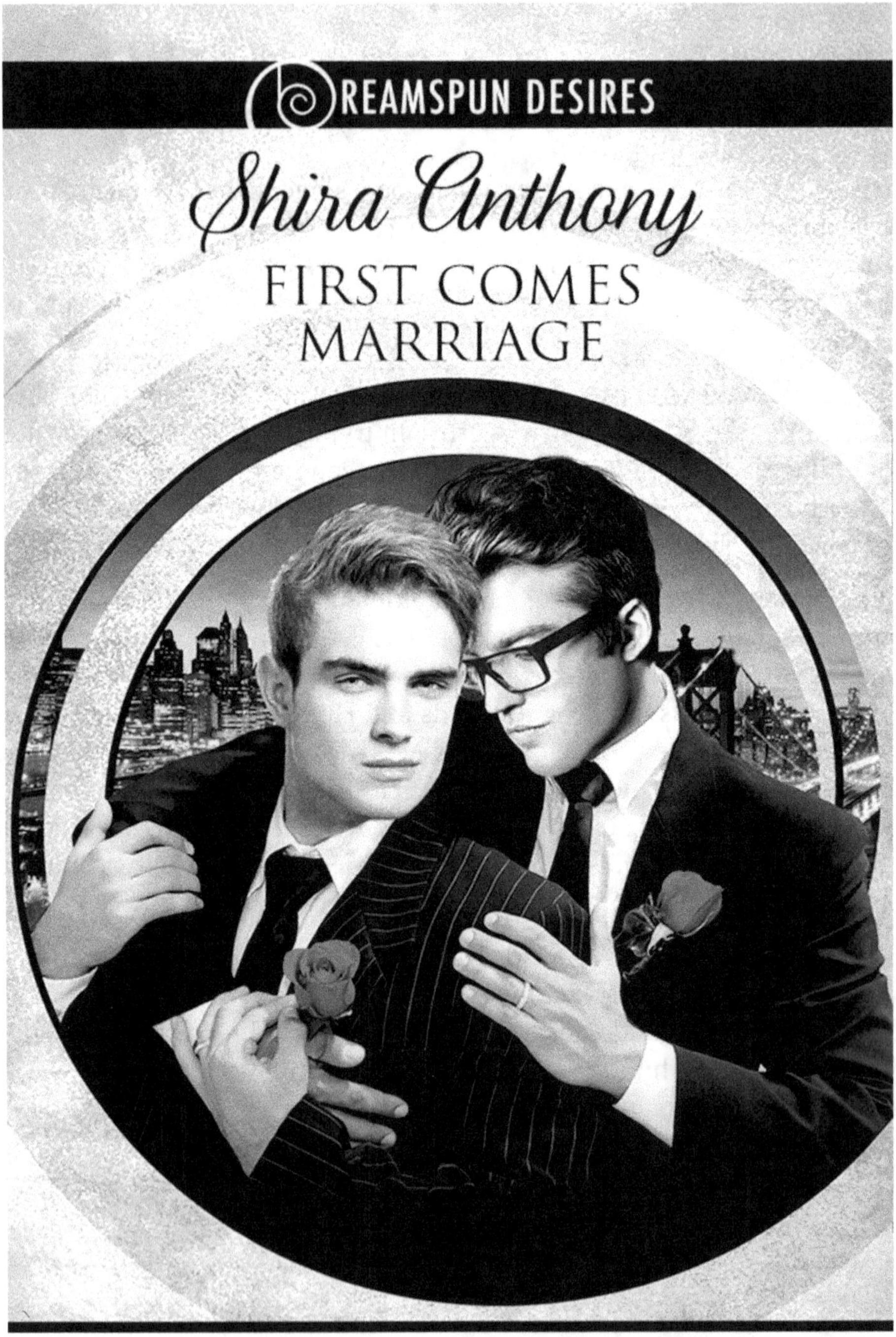

DREAMSPUN DESIRES

Shira Anthony

FIRST COMES MARRIAGE

Their marriage was supposed to be all business….

When struggling novelist Chris Valentine meets Jesse Donovan, he's interested in a book contract, or possibly a date. The last thing Chris expects is a marriage proposal from New York City's most eligible bachelor!

Jesse's in a pinch. To keep control of his company, he has to marry. So he has valid reasons for offering Chris this business deal: in exchange for living in a gorgeous mansion for a year, playing the doting husband, Chris gets all the writing time he wants and walks away with a million-dollar payoff. Surely Chris can handle that. He can handle living with the most handsome and endearing man he's ever met, a man he immediately knows he wants in the worst way and can't have. Or can he?

www.dreamspinnerpress.com

A Solitary Man

SHIRA ANTHONY
And
AISLING MANCY

Sparks fly when Chance meets tall, sexy Xav at a Wilmington bar and they have the hottest one-nighter of their lives. But Chance doesn't do repeats, Xav seems detached, and they go their separate ways without a word. Later, when closeted Assistant District Attorney C. Evan "Chance" Fairchild meets Dare's Landing's newest deputy sheriff, Xavier "Xav" Constantine, Evan isn't only wary. He's irritated as hell.

Xavier is a former FBI agent turned deputy sheriff who is hot on the trail of a South American child prostitution ring. Evan is fighting to put an end to rampant cocaine trafficking and chafing under the thumb of an election-hungry boss. When someone tries to kill the eleven-year-old witness who holds the key to both their investigations, they're forced to work together as they put their lives on the line to protect him. As Chance and Xav collide in the heat of a sweltering North Carolina summer, dodging bullets and chasing bad guys isn't the only action going on.

www.dreamspinnerpress.com

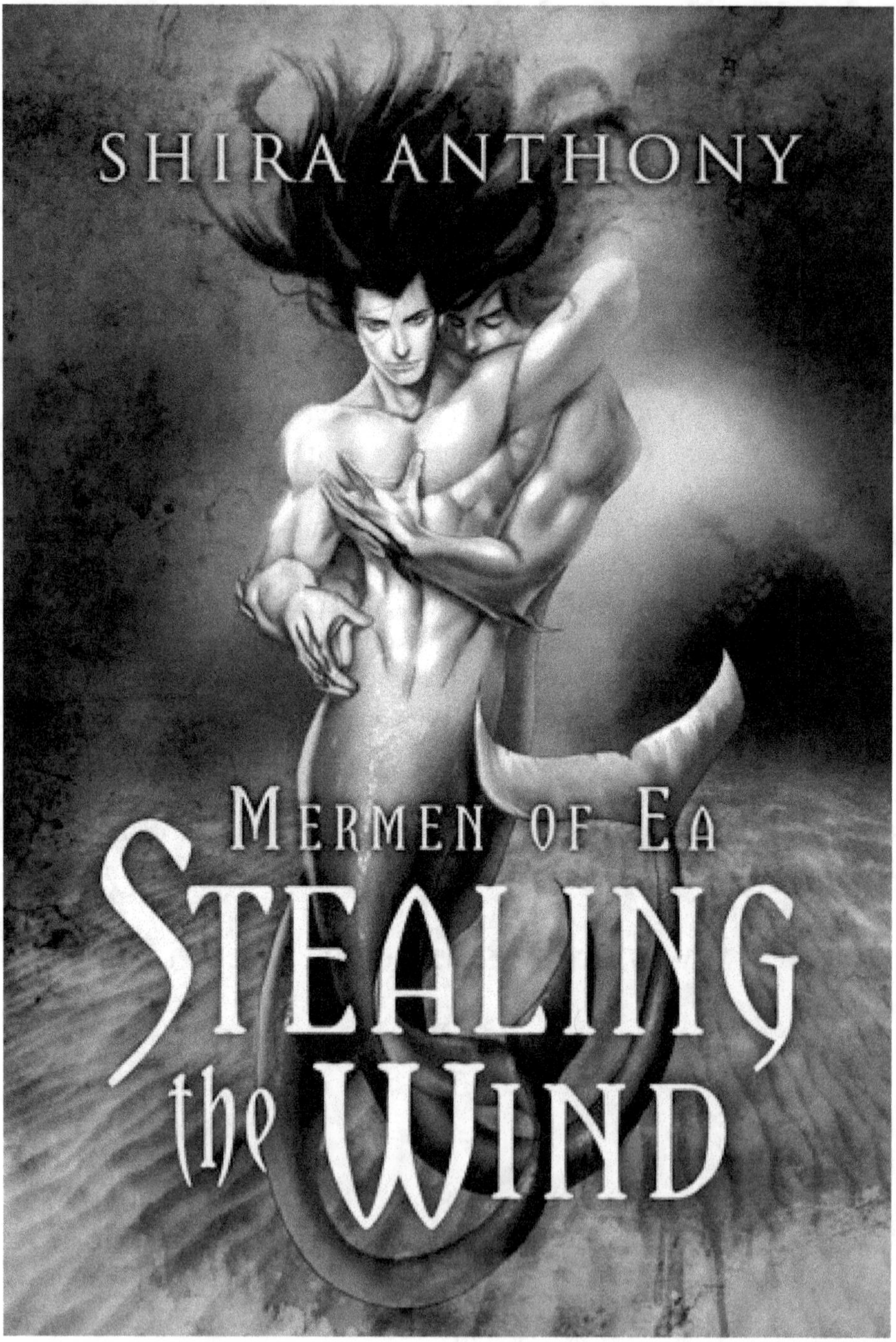
SHIRA ANTHONY
MERMEN OF EA
STEALING the WIND

Mermen of Ea Trilogy: Book One

Taren Laxley has never known anything but life as a slave. When a lusty pirate kidnaps him and holds him prisoner on his ship, Taren embraces the chance to realize his dream of a seagoing life. Not only does the pirate captain offer him freedom in exchange for three years of labor and sexual servitude, but the pleasures Taren finds when he joins the captain and first mate in bed far surpass his greatest fantasies.

Then, during a storm, Taren dives overboard to save another sailor and is lost at sea. He's rescued by Ian Dunaidh, the enigmatic and seemingly ageless captain of a rival ship, the Phantom, and Taren feels an overwhelming attraction to Ian that Ian appears to share. Soon Taren learns a secret that will change his life forever: Ian and his people are Ea, shape-shifting merfolk… and Taren is one of them too. Bound to each other by a fierce passion neither can explain or deny, Taren and Ian are soon embroiled in a war and forced to fight for a future—not only for themselves but for all their kind.

www.dreamspinnerpress.com

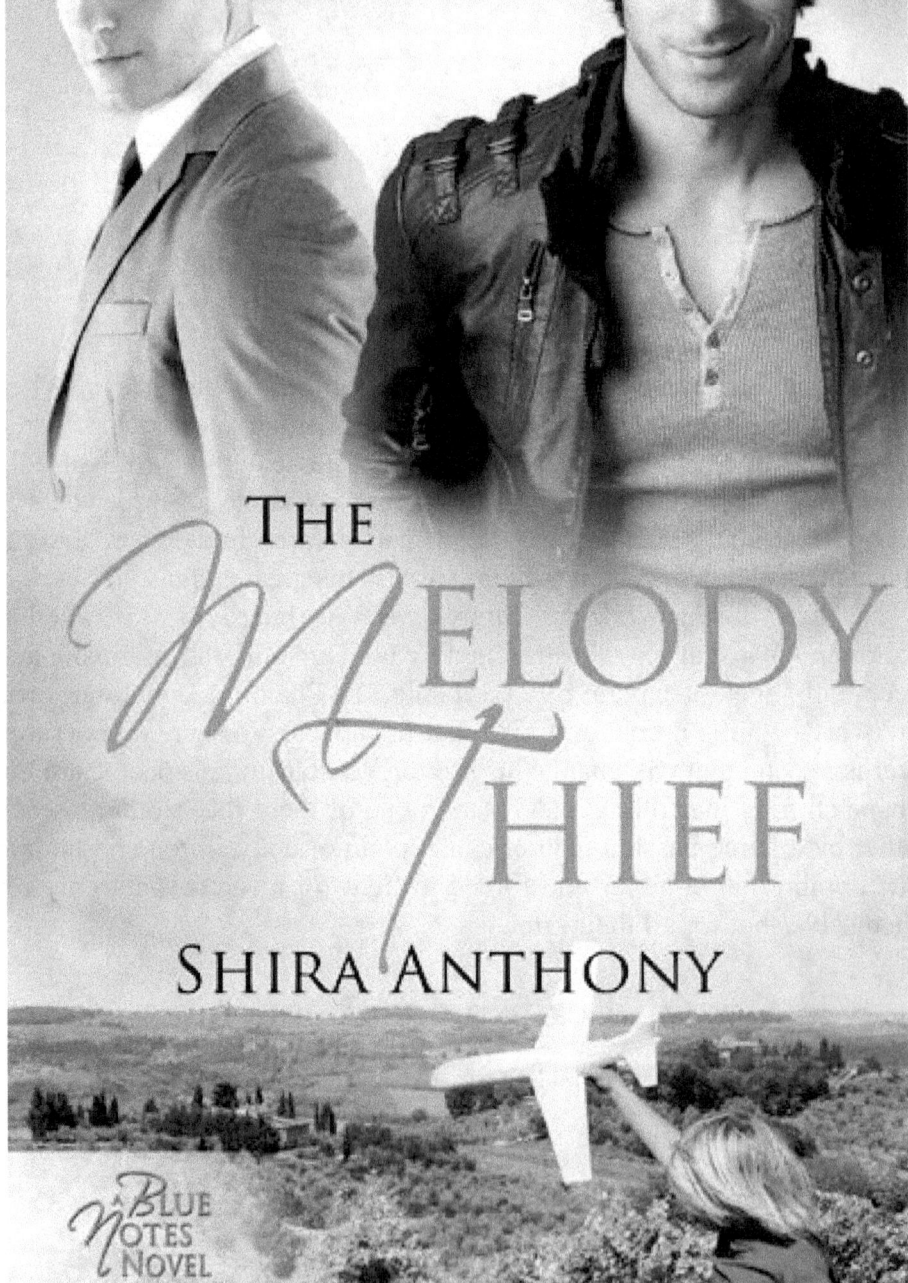

THE MELODY THIEF

SHIRA ANTHONY

A BLUE NOTES NOVEL

A Blue Notes novel

Cary Redding is a walking contradiction. On the surface he's a renowned cellist, sought after by conductors the world over. Underneath, he's a troubled man flirting with addictions to alcohol and anonymous sex. The reason for the discord? Cary knows he's a liar, a cheat. He's the melody thief.

Cary manages his double life just fine until he gets mugged on a deserted Milan street. Things look grim until handsome lawyer Antonio Bianchi steps in and saves his life. When Antonio offers something foreign to Cary—romance—Cary doesn't know what to do. But then things get even more complicated. For one thing, Antonio has a six-year-old son. For another, Cary has to confess about his alter ego and hope Antonio forgives him.

Just when Cary thinks he's figured it all out, past and present collide and he is forced to choose between the family he wanted as a boy and the one he has come to love as a man.

www.dreamspinnerpress.com